***"I want to go into that barn and make love to you,"***

Joe said honestly. "I want it more than I ever wanted anything. But I need to know how much it matters to you first."

"Don't do this to me, Joe," [illegible] eaded.

"If it's all [illegible] st something [illegible] 're probably b[illegible] g in any deeper. [illegible]

"Last night y[illegible] we were already in deep."

"*I* am," he admitted quietly.

"What is it you want me to say?" she demanded.

He just needed something to hold on to. He needed her to say that she didn't roll on hay bales as a matter of course.

What he really needed, he realized, was for her to say she'd changed her mind and was going to stay with him. He needed her to say she loved him.

Dear Reader,

Any month with a new Nora Roberts book *has* to be special, and this month is *extra* special, because this book is the first of a wonderful new trilogy. *Hidden Star* begins THE STARS OF MITHRA, three stories about strong heroines, wonderful heroes—and three gems destined to bring them together. The adventure begins for Bailey James with the loss of her memory—and the entrance of coolheaded (well, until he sees *her*) private eye Cade Parris into her life. He wants to believe in her—not to mention love her—but what is she doing with a sackful of cash and a diamond the size of a baby's fist?

It's a month for miniseries, with Marilyn Pappano revisiting her popular SOUTHERN KNIGHTS with *Convincing Jamey*, and Alicia Scott continuing MAXIMILLIAN'S CHILDREN with *MacNamara's Woman.* Not to mention the final installment of Beverly Bird's THE WEDDING RING, *Saving Susannah,* and the second book of Marilyn Tracy's ALMOST, TEXAS miniseries, *Almost a Family.*

Finally, welcome Intimate Moments' newest author, Maggie Price. She's part of our WOMEN TO WATCH cross-line promotion, with each line introducing a brand-new author to you. In *Prime Suspect,* Maggie spins an irresistible tale about a by-the-book detective falling for a suspect, a beautiful criminal profiler who just may be in over her head. As an aside, you might like to know that Maggie herself once worked as a crime analyst for the Oklahoma City police department.

So enjoy all these novels—and then be sure to come back next month for more of the best romance reading around, right here in Silhouette Intimate Moments.

Yours,

Senior Editor and Editorial Coordinator

Please address questions and book requests to:
Silhouette Reader Service
U.S.: 3010 Walden Ave., P.O. Box 1325, Buffalo, NY 14269
Canadian: P.O. Box 609, Fort Erie, Ont. L2A 5X3

# SAVING SUSANNAH

## BEVERLY BIRD

Published by Silhouette Books
America's Publisher of Contemporary Romance

SILHOUETTE BOOKS

ISBN 0-373-07814-5

SAVING SUSANNAH



This edition published by arrangement with Harlequin Books S.A.



**Printed in U.S.A.**

**Books by Beverly Bird**

Silhouette Intimate Moments

*Emeralds in the Dark* #3
*The Fires of Winter* #23
*Ride the Wind* #139
*A Solitary Man* #172
**A Man Without Love* #630
**A Man Without a Haven* #641
**A Man Without a Wife* #652
*Undercover Cowboy* #711
*The Marrying Kind* #732
*Compromising Positions* #777
†*Loving Mariah* #790
†*Marrying Jake* #802
†*Saving Susannah* #814

Silhouette Desire

*The Best Reasons* #190
*Fool's Gold* #209
*All the Marbles* #227
*To Love a Stranger* #411

*Wounded Warriors
†The Wedding Ring

---

## *BEVERLY BIRD*

has lived in several places in the United States, but she is currently back where her roots began on an island in New Jersey. Her time is devoted to her family and her writing. She is the author of numerous romance novels, both contemporary and historical. Beverly loves to hear from readers. You can write to her at P.O. Box 350, Brigantine, NJ 08203.

# *Prologue*

"I'm sorry."

They were the only words Kimberley Mancuso heard. A whole stream of them had come before—medical technology that had gone over her head, inadequate assurances, vague explanations. All ending with those two words: *I'm sorry.*

Why do they always say that? she wondered giddily. What kind of doctor, what kind of human being, would be delighted to impart this news? Her daughter was gravely ill. Her daughter was dying. Kim didn't expect Dr. Manuel Parra to dance on his desktop.

"Leukemia," she repeated very carefully. Actually, she realized, she had heard *three* words clearly. That had been the other. A four-syllable explanation for Susannah's uncharacteristic lethargy, her dwindling appetite, the sudden profusion of bruises that neither Kim nor Susannah could ever quite figure out the source of. And the fevers! Every little germ Susannah had come in contact with this past summer had taken grip with a vengeance, leaving her a little weaker, a little more depleted, than the one before.

Leukemia.

She was only ten.

"Fix it," Kim said, her voice finally cracking.

"I've already taken measures," Dr. Parra assured her. "The best course of action, that which we've had the most success with, is bone marrow transplantation. Let me try to explain. Stem cells are located in one's bone marrow. Susannah's stem cells are producing an excessive number of white blood cells. Therefore, what we must do is kill those stem cells via chemotherapy and radiation. We'll follow this therapy by replacing her damaged stem cells with a graft of healthy cells. They in turn should produce healthy marrow and blood. I've put Susannah's needs into the marrow registries, but I must tell you that an anonymous donor is something of a long shot."

What Kim heard was hope, an answer, a solution. "Then take mine. Take my stem cells or whatever."

He grimaced. "You're not compatible. Your blood was tested when we ruled out inherited anemia."

"I'm her *mother.*"

"I'm sorry," he said again.

Kim's knuckles were going bone white where she gripped the arms of her chair. She stared at them, collecting herself again after that short rush of hope. Only her hands revealed her panic, her terror, she thought.

She had learned a long, long time ago not to reveal agitation. It was alternately a blessing and a curse. It had probably cost her a fiancé, but no one ever saw her sweat. She was proud of that, and had perfected a haughty, even cold, demeanor over the years to show people that she could not be hurt.

But she was hurting now. The doctor's words clamored in her head, nausea swelled in her stomach and her eyes stung as she refused to cry. She was unaware of the fact that she had all but gnawed a hole in her bottom lip. *Not my daughter, not my baby.* It required an almost superhuman effort to push the emotion away this time.

"This isn't as simple as matching a blood type, Ms. Mancuso," Dr. Parra continued. "What we need here are HLA matches. Human leukocyte-associated antigens. These rest on the surface of the blood cells to differentiate our own from that of another person. We look at six HLA antigens when we do a transplant of this nature, and most physicians require a match on five. The higher the number of matches, the greater the chance that the patient's body will accept the graft."

"Then what?" Kim asked thinly.

"There's still a minor risk of rejection. However, unlike solid organ transplants, the body learns to tolerate transplanted marrow after some time. Antirejection therapy needs to be continued for only six months in these cases, as opposed to the rest of Susannah's life. There's also the matter of GVHD—that is to say, graft-versus-host disease. That's sort of a reverse rejection. In the case of GVHD, the *donor* cells recognize the recipients's organs as foreign and attack them."

Kim blanched.

"Again, therapy is continued against this eventuality for approximately six months. The good news is that children are far less susceptible to GVHD than adults. We don't know why. Ms. Mancuso, I want to assure you that this conjunction of therapy produces roughly ninety percent remissions for three years or more. The absolute cure rate is over fifty percent. Susannah's condition does not necessarily need to be fatal. Not today, not with our current knowledge and technology."

Kim nodded and looked at the wall clock. It was eleven in the morning. Susannah was in school. She wouldn't be at lunch yet, still in class, Kim found herself thinking absurdly. She had picked her daughter up for doctors' appointments so often lately that she knew Susannah's daily schedule by heart. Susannah was currently learning history or some such thing without a clue in the world that her life hung by a thread.

"Since we've already taken a blood sample from you," Dr. Parra was saying, "there's no need for further HLA testing. You don't even have the same blood *type*. You're AB with a negative Rh factor. Your daughter is B positive."

"How can that be?" she managed to ask.

"No doubt her father is B positive."

Kim stared at him, then slowly closed her eyes in despair. She didn't even know where Susannah's father was anymore, she thought helplessly. She hadn't laid eyes on Bobby Guenther in eleven years. He didn't know he had a daughter. That hadn't been a conscious decision on Kim's part. It had simply been the way things worked out.

"I'll find him," she vowed, and when she heard her words,

the shock waves reverberated through her entire body. *No, I can't go back there.*

"That would be an excellent place to start," the doctor agreed. "Our best hope is family—yours, Susannah's father's. Contact your kin. Susannah's siblings would generally provide the best matches, but since she has none her parents, grandparents, aunts and uncles might also work. If we're forced to look to the donor registries for marrow, we've only a ten percent chance of finding a match. Actually, that's high, because donor registries have gotten a lot of press and attention these past few years. With more available donors there are more matches. Up until recently, the success rate among strangers was little more than five percent."

He was trying to reassure her, Kim thought. But it wasn't working. The mere mention of family made her tremble even more.

"There's been some recent evidence that matching ethnic and racial backgrounds sometimes works, as well," Dr. Parra continued. "I'd like to enter that with the registries." He looked at Susannah's chart again. "Mancuso. Susannah is of Italian descent?"

The lie was on Kim's lips. Habit, she realized. But the truth was important now. "No." She choked out the word.

Mancuso was simply the name of the restaurant across the street from her first apartment in L.A. She had so desperately needed to wipe the slate clean, to erase her past and start over, when she had fled from Texas and her family eleven years ago. She had started using a different name. For a while, she had even bleached her long, dark hair blond, as though that could turn her into a different person, someone without haunted memories, someone who slept without having nightmares, a girl who was wholesome and normal.

She had finally been forced to accept that a few superficial changes weren't going to make that happen. But by then she had grown so accustomed to using the name Mancuso it seemed simplest just to keep doing so.

"Actually, I'm...Irish," she told the doctor. "Susannah's father was—" She broke off. She didn't know that for certain, either. She had never asked Bobby. It hadn't mattered when they were seventeen and in love for all time.

Her throat tightened almost painfully. *In love.* What a crock, she thought bitterly. Bobby hadn't followed her when she'd run from Dallas. No matter that they had planned to be married as soon as she graduated. No matter that they'd had so many glorious plans. He'd let her go. She had run only as far as L.A. Bobby could have found her if he had tried hard enough.

What had his ethnic background been?

"Guenther?" she whispered.

"German, I would guess," Dr. Parra answered. "But you should find out for certain and let me know."

"I'll do that."

Then she was on her feet again, not quite sure how she had gotten that way. She wanted desperately to believe that this was all a very bad dream, that she would wake up and be weak with relief that it wasn't really happening. Not now, when life was finally reasonably good. She had worked so hard to put horror and heartache behind her.

But it wasn't a dream. It was a nightmare that had slowly and inexorably been settling over her and Susannah for six months now. It was real, and she did not know how to escape it. This time she had encountered something they could not run from.

She did not remember thanking the doctor. She had no memory of leaving his office, of sliding behind the wheel of her old car, with its rusted tailpipe. She did not know how she got onto the Ventura Freeway, and only realized she was there when traffic slowed to a crawl and she blinked and looked around. She got off at the first available exit and drove the streets in circles, until she somehow ended up north of Encino, parked beside the chain-link fence that protected the playground of her daughter's school.

It was lunchtime. Susannah was leaning one shoulder against the jungle gym. She was talking to another girl, and she looked so normal—a beautiful child with long, shaggy, blond hair and her father's brown eyes. Kim's heart broke. There was still a hint of the tomboy in her, but it was fading as she got older and under the stress of her illness. Susannah rarely had the energy to climb trees anymore.

She looked ethereal, frail and fairylike, in the sunlight. Kim searched her face for the telltale pink splotches that always appeared high on her cheekbones with a fever. They weren't there this time, though her eyes seemed unnaturally bright.

Kim reached for the door handle. She meant to get out of the car, to go over to the fence. She wanted to tell Susannah that she was going to the principal's office to take her out of school yet again. Then, when they were alone, she would tell her what the doctor had said, and tell her they were going to Texas.

Kim's stomach heaved. She had vowed never to return to Dallas. There was only one thing on God's green earth that could convince her to go back on that promise to herself. She would do it for her daughter.

*Mom, Dad, Jake, Adam.* Dr. Parra had suggested family, and they were the only relatives she had, dubious as their relationship was. If none of them matched, then she would go to Bobby and his family. She would do it with pride and dignity, and she would not mention the painful fact that he had never come looking for her.

Kim really did mean to get out of the car. Instead, with that thought, she slid down in the seat as far as she could go. Then she covered her face with her hands and sobbed as she had not done since she was a teenager.

# Chapter 1

Kim took her eyes off the highway long enough to dart yet another glance at her daughter. Susannah hadn't spoken since Albuquerque, and they were now crossing the state line into Texas. She was staring out the window, her face averted.

"Scared?" Kim finally asked. *Of course she's scared. Don't be an imbecile.*

"No." It was more a mumble than a word. "Well, a little."

"Me, too," Kim admitted. That brought her daughter's eyes around to her at last.

"It's okay, Mom," Susannah assured her. "It's not like I need a heart or anything like that. That would be *really* bad."

Not for the first time, Kim was overcome with wonder that she had produced this optimistic child—she, who had learned long ago to believe in nothing. "I'll keep that in mind," she managed to say, her throat tightening.

"I mean, I might be a little sick for a while as my body readjusts, but it's not like they have to cut me open or anything," Susannah continued.

She had repeated Dr. Parra's words verbatim, Kim realized. They had gone to see him one last time before they'd left L.A.

At least she knew her daughter had been listening, not tuning out in that prepubescent habit she had recently picked up.

"I'm not freaked out about that," Susannah added.

Kim stiffened. "What then?" But she knew what was coming.

Susannah's eyes went stubbornly back to the window. "Mom, you *lied.*"

Kim felt her heart beating strangely and distantly, as though it had dropped way, way down below the pit of her stomach. "Yes," she admitted, because it seemed pointless to deny it.

"I mean, you said we had no family in the whole world. That it was just you and me."

"Well, it is, baby. For all intents and purposes, it is."

"But you've got parents. And brothers."

And they were on their way into Texas to find them, Kim thought, her stomach rolling.

She wondered, even if they were successful in locating her family, would any of the Wallaces help her? A wave of dizziness hit her, strong enough to make her consider pulling off the highway for a moment, but she shook her head and kept doggedly on. Her brothers would probably help, she decided. She held nothing against either Jake or Adam. They had done nothing to her that she had not also done to them. They had hidden, they had cowered, they had not come to her rescue—but neither had she ever gone to theirs. In the Wallace household, it had been each man for himself.

As for her mother, Kim had to wonder if Emma Wallace even had any bone marrow left. She'd been drinking heavily even before Kim had run from Texas, using the bottle to hide from her abusive husband.

That left Edward, her father. And he was just as likely to decline to have his blood tested out of pure meanness as he was to help out because he figured something might be in it for him.

"Tell me about them," Susannah said. "*Please.*"

"I...I don't know much," Kim answered. "Not anymore."

"Then what did you *used* to know?"

She had lied to Susannah about them enough, Kim thought. And there was something else, another strong reason to tell her the truth now. She did not want her daughter to be shocked or disillusioned once they found them.

"Adam is...uh, my oldest brother."

"How old?"

What did it matter? Kim thought helplessly, but she did some quick math in her head. She was twenty-eight now.

"He'd be thirty-eight," she answered. "No. He just had a birthday. He's thirty-nine."

"That *old?*"

Kim grimaced. "He used to play baseball," she continued, grasping for what little she had allowed herself to remember over the years.

She remembered in sterling detail the moment she had become aware of the fact that Adam was playing ball. She had been waitressing at a sports bar back then. There had been televisions all over the walls. And even above the raucous crowd, she had heard the announcer speak his name. Adam Wallace. The Astros' catcher.

Kim had frozen in midstride, looking at each of the screens to catch a glimpse of the player. The catcher wore all sorts of protective paraphernalia, including a cagelike thing over his face. The name wasn't unusual. It could have belonged to any Adam Wallace. Still, her brother had always loved baseball. He'd been a high school all-star and had been playing in the minor leagues when she had left home.

She had kept one corner of her attention on the game until the guy came up to bat. And then they had shown a close-up of his face. It had been him. Her brother. The same shaggy blond hair. The same blue-gray eyes. The same face roughened by too many years of care. *He had escaped, too.* Adrenaline and euphoria had rushed through Kim so fiercely she had dropped a tray of beer bottles.

At least two of them had gotten out, she'd thought. It hadn't mattered that Adam was still obviously in Texas—the Astros were Houston's team. He had escaped Decataur Avenue and the big white house at the end of it that was always in need of paint or repair. He had escaped Edward Wallace's clutches.

Impossibly, she heard her father's voice crystal clearly in that moment, as though he were sitting between her and Susannah, as though it had not been eleven long years since she'd been forced to listen to him: *"You're no better than that pile of dog dirt over there. You're a Wallace. And the world never gave a Wallace a fair break. That's why we're on welfare."*

Sometimes it had been unemployment, Kim reflected. Sometimes Edward Wallace had actually worked. But always he had neglected to mention that the Wallace before him, Kim's grandfather, had gotten a few fair breaks, had worked his way up in the oil business with barely a high-school education, and had built the big white house on the end of Decataur Avenue. Edward Wallace had mortgaged the house to the hilt because he'd long since run through his modest inheritance and he couldn't hold down a job. He was always too lazy or drunk to repair the holes in the walls.

"Mom?"

"What?" Kim looked over at Susannah quickly.

"*Baseball?* Real baseball? The big leagues?"

Kim nodded. "He did good."

"Is he still playing?"

"Uh, no. He just retired all of a sudden. The newspapers said it was because of personal problems." She had never heard what they were, and had always wondered if Edward had had something to do with them.

"Who else?" Susannah asked. "Who else is there?"

"Jake. My other brother. He'd be...thirty-seven now. He was always, well, the funny one." Cocky, she remembered, almost smiling. Brazen and arrogant and charming. A real Irish scoundrel.

"What does he do?"

"I don't know. I lost track of him." She hadn't actually tried to *keep* track of him.

"What about your mom and dad?"

Kim's stomach clenched at that one. She took a deep, deliberate breath and told Susannah the harsh part. It was better that she find out now, she thought again, before they got there.

"They're not nice people, Suze," she said carefully. She softened the judgment with her pet name for her daughter. "That's why I never told you about them. That's why you've never met them."

In fact, she had left Texas so her father wouldn't hurt Susannah. When he'd found out Kim was pregnant, he'd beaten the living daylights out of her. She'd taken her mother's grocery money to pay to see a doctor, but Edward had wanted it for beer and found it missing. She'd always thought his fury was more because of the missing beer money than because of any real anger at her morals, but it didn't matter. The bottom line was that she'd known she couldn't allow it to happen again. Susannah hadn't been hurt—Kim had kept doubling over so Edward couldn't punch her in the stomach. But he'd broken her arm. Then she'd run out of the house and she'd just kept going.

She had never been able to tell Bobby what had happened. She couldn't find him in time. He'd worked for a pizza restaurant that year, and had been out delivering when she went to look for him. Edward had been driving all over the city searching for her at the same time. She'd caught sight of him once or twice, but had always somehow managed to duck into a phone booth or a store to avoid him.

She'd had twelve dollars of her mother's money left. When Bobby's boss had told her that he was out on the road, she'd caught the first bus out of Dallas. There hadn't been time to do anything else. She couldn't risk having Edward catch up with her. The bus had taken her into Fort Worth. She'd waited tables for a week and slept in a park, wishing for a miracle, hoping either Adam or Jake would tell Bobby what had taken place so he would come looking for her. It hadn't happened.

She'd never been able to have her arm set properly, either. She'd gone to a free clinic in Fort Worth and they'd put it in a sling when she'd refused a cast. But she hadn't been able to wait tables in either one. Before the end of the week, she'd tossed the sling aside, and just lived with the pain by favoring it.

By then she'd collected enough in tips to move on to Abilene. She did the same thing there, working a bit, then moving on. She'd kept going west until she got to the Pacific Ocean and there was nowhere left to go. But that had turned out to be far enough. The miles, the emotional distance, the fresh start by the sea had slowly enabled her to put everything behind her.

What she remembered most of those first months, of her time traveling, was feeling dirty, she thought now. It had been almost three weeks before she had accumulated enough money to splurge on a motel room and get a real shower. She'd spent the interim washing up in service station rest rooms. All in all, it had been an ugly time, a terrifying one. She could have died, she thought, as she had a thousand times since then. She could have trusted the wrong person, someone pointing her to a doorway or to a park where it was reasonably safe to sleep. Then again, that was unlikely. Even then she'd known not to trust or depend on anyone other than herself.

Kim glanced at her daughter. She could tell none of this to Susannah, she realized. Though Suze had aged far beyond her years in these past months, there were just some things she didn't need to know. She prayed Susannah wouldn't ask any more questions, and she didn't.

While Kim had been woolgathering, her daughter had fallen fast asleep.

At six o'clock the following evening, Kim halted the Mazda on Decataur Avenue at the edge of Dallas. She'd stopped a whole block away from the house, before the street dead-ended. Susannah was asleep again, her head resting against the window. Kim winced for her. The position had to be uncomfortable, she thought. But Susannah took sleep where she could find it, and she generally found it more than twelve hours a day now.

The ache in Kim's stomach grew, and she pressed a hand to it. "Okay, baby," she whispered, needing to speak aloud but not wanting to wake her. "We're here. Now I can do something about all this. I hope."

But she would do it carefully. She would do it alone.

She got out of the car, locking the door and easing it shut. She paused and looked down the street in the direction of the humble Wallace abode. She was shaking like a leaf. The tremors seemed to come all the way up from her soul.

They'd finally paved the street, she noticed dispassionately. In her memories, it was dusty, furrowed where cars had passed through the mud after a good rain, before the relentless Texas sun came back and baked everything hard again.

Kim began walking. Susannah would not wake up. Kim was

ninety percent sure of that. And if she did, she would probably have the good sense just to wait for her mother to return. Kim was ninety-five percent sure of *that,* if only because it would take too much energy for Suze to get out of the car and look for her. Good odds, she thought. And there was no sense in subjecting her daughter to Edward Wallace unless she had to. For all she knew, the bastard would still hold that beer money against her.

The house looked even worse than it had when she had lived there. A gutter hung loosely from one eves. She doubted if the place had been painted since the day she'd run. Sheaves of decaying white bubbled and buckled from the sides, revealing something gray and ugly underneath.

The house was dark—not even a single light on within. A torn shade hung lopsided in one of the front windows. Kim stepped up onto the porch, and there was a squeaking sound as one of the boards protested even her relatively insignificant weight.

The aluminum screen door was hanging ajar, connected only at the bottom, the top leaning precariously toward her. She stepped quickly toward it and rammed a hand against the inner door. Nothing. She knocked again.

"Kimmie? *Kimmie?* Why, as I live and breathe!"

Kim jumped at the voice that came suddenly from behind her. She turned around and searched through the gathering dusk. A round woman in her early sixties rushed toward her. She wore a tattered yellow housecoat, and a pair of glasses dangled from a gaudy metallic chain around her neck. She grabbed the spectacles and pushed them onto her face, but as she came up the walk, Kim saw that she was still squinting anyway.

Mrs. Madigan. Their neighbor.

"It *is* you!" the woman squealed. "I thought so. I said to Ralph, that's got to be little Kimmie. Nobody has hair like that. So pretty!"

Kim touched it self-consciously. Given Mrs. Madigan's eyesight, the woman had probably been pressed to the window with a pair of binoculars trying to see what was happening over at the Wallace house, Kim thought. No surprise there.

"How are you?" Kim answered carefully.

"How am I? How am *I?*"

Kim remembered too late that the woman had a bad habit of repeating everything.

"How are *you?*" Mrs. Madigan asked.

"Well, I'm...uh, good," she lied. "Are my folks around?"

"Oh, dear. Well, of course you don't know. You've been gone so long."

Kim's heart started that deep-down, painful kind of accelerating beat again. "Don't know what?" she asked carefully.

"Well, dear, they're dead," Mrs. Madigan said. "They've all quite passed on."

Kim's heart slammed this time. "*All* of them?"

"Oh, no. Not your brothers. Just your ma and your daddy."

*Amen.* In some part of Kim's psyche, she wanted to feel shame for her reaction. Yet she couldn't manage anything but relief, almost a sense of justice. Edward Wallace was dead, and Emma Wallace was probably better off not being alive. Kim did not think her father would be able to follow her mother to heaven. Surely someone up there would slam the door in Edward Wallace's face.

"What happened?" she managed to ask.

"Well, your daddy died shortly after you left. He drove right off the I-30 beltway into the Trinity River, he did."

"Was he drunk?" Kim asked flatly. He must have been, she thought.

Mrs. Madigan flushed. "Well, dear, I wouldn't know about that."

No, of course not, Kim was certain. She would have looked the other way, just as she had when Kim had screamed for help at the top of her lungs.

"What about Mom?" she asked.

"Her liver got her, it did. Not too long after your daddy went."

"Ah." Kim cleared her throat. "And Jake and Adam?"

"Well, now, let's see. Adam was quite famous, you know. But I heard he sold all his Texas property. Oh, what a grand house he had down in Houston when he was playing ball! I saw pictures in a magazine."

"Where is he now?" Kim demanded. She didn't have time to exchange niceties and gossip with this woman. She wanted facts. She needed them quickly. Her gaze went back up the street to the Mazda. Kim didn't want to leave Susannah alone too much longer.

"Oh, well, he left," Mrs. Madigan said. "He was married, you see, to a beautiful girl, but I heard she had, well...one of those *drug* problems." Her voice dropped to a conspiratorial whisper. "She took Adam's little boy and disappeared. It was horrible, it was. It took him years to find that boy again. And would you believe Bo turned up in one of those religious cults in Pennsylvania? Then Adam married a *good* girl from up there, and he's living there now."

Kim's brain spun. A religious cult? *Adam?* The woman had always been a gossipmonger, though inclined to be right. "What about Jake?"

"He's still here."

Relief swept her. Between that and her amazement over Adam, she had to grip the porch rail for support. Then she grew angry.

"Is he living here?" she demanded, looking back at the house in disbelief. How could he let the place go like this? She remembered Jake's being meticulous with his appearance, his car, everything he could call his own.

"Oh, no!" Mrs. Madigan burst out. "No, dear, no one ever bought this place. It's been sitting empty since your ma died. I believe your brothers listed it for sale—there was a sign here on the lawn forever—but neither of them ever put any money into fixing it up. They just let it rot." Disapproval crept into Mrs. Madigan's voice.

Good for them, Kim thought. "So where is Jake living now?"

"Well, last I heard he had an apartment in the city somewhere, one of those garden things. But, of course, he's married now—and all those kids—so I don't know if he's still there or not. And he was with the police department for the longest time, but he left them just this past year and took over Adam's detective company. Now, what *is* the name of that place? Wait, dear, I'll look it up in the phone book. I'll know it as soon as I see it."

She waddled off, back to her own home next door. Kim stared after her, her jaw literally hanging open.

What in the name of God had happened to her brothers?

Mrs. Madigan's words kept buzzing in her head in disjointed sequence: *a religious cult...all those kids...married...detective company...the police department.* The *Wallaces?* she thought disbelievingly.

As far as she could remember, the law had never treated any of them fairly. It had never defended or protected them. She couldn't see any of them going into law enforcement. As for family and children, well, they were the last things Kim would ever imagine either of her brothers getting involved with. She hadn't been able to hold *her* engagement to Mark together. Four months into it, Mark had fled. He'd finally given up on her. She'd never been able to entirely trust him. He'd said she just couldn't learn to give. He'd said she was cold, wouldn't open up. He was right.

"ChildSearch!" Mrs. Madigan bleated from across the fence several minutes later.

"ChildSearch," Kim repeated dazedly.

"That's the name of Adam's company. Well, it's Jake's now. It's over on Story Road. And I remember now, about his new wife. Tiny wisp of a thing, and *pretty?* My, is she pretty! She was from that cult, too. He brought her by here once to show her the old house. Now, see, she had four little ones from her previous husband, except it turned out that he was never really her *husband.* And they were all here with them that day, with Jake and his missus—the kiddies, that is. I took the liberty of calling there for you, dear."

"Where? The cult?" Anything felt possible now, Kim realized. This was preposterous.

"Well, now, I was wrong. It's not a cult. It's those Pennsylvania Dutch people. I remember now—once the girl at ChildSearch said it. I wanted to let Jake know his baby sister was back, and of course they have people on the phones there twenty-four hours a day. The girl said that Jake and his wife are visiting up there in Pennsylvania in that settlement. So..."

She finally seemed to run out of steam.

"Jake's in Pennsylvania, too?" Kim asked. This was not good, she thought. It wasn't good at all. She was doing this on limited savings.

"Yes, well, for now, that's true," Mrs. Madigan answered.

"The girl on the phone said Jake isn't expected back for several weeks."

"Does she have a number where he can be reached?"

"Oh, no, dear. They don't have phones up there. That's what she said."

Pennsylvania. A considerable drive. "Do you know what might have become of Bobby Guenther?" she asked, shifting her focus, because the possibility of going on to Pennsylvania was daunting. "You remember, I was dating him before I left."

"Bobby! Oh, of course I remember him, God rest his soul."

The dusk went abruptly to black, or maybe it was only her own vision. "He's dead, *too?*"

"A hunting accident, not long after you left him. Never even got the chance to marry, poor boy."

Kim sat down hard on the top step. It explained a lot. It explained too much. Such as why he had never come looking for her. "His parents?" she inquired.

"Well, now, they were old even then, weren't they? I believe his ma's still alive, in a nursing home somewhere. She's senile. But his daddy's gone, and of course Bobby never had any brothers or sisters."

She couldn't ask a frail old woman in a nursing home for bone marrow, Kim thought helplessly. But she would. Of course she would. That woman was Susannah's paternal grandmother. But she would try Jake and Adam first. It was the only thing that made sense. Presumably, *they* were still young and healthy.

In a religious community in Pennsylvania. She laughed shrilly.

She'd had seven strong possibilities when she'd left L.A.—Bobby, his parents and the four members of her own family. She'd even hoped that maybe Bobby had eventually had other kids, as well. Now she was down to only two feasible possibilities—her brothers—and they were thousands of miles away.

Three, she corrected herself. She was down to *three* potential donors. Mrs. Madigan had said that Adam had a son—Susannah's cousin. A little genetically removed, perhaps, but kin all the same.

She would find them. Her only other choice was to stay and wait for Jake to come back to Texas. Given the little money she had left, that wasn't an option. She couldn't afford to hang around in a motel for several weeks, and she couldn't bring herself to seek shelter in this battered old house, with all its painful memories.

She got to her feet again, her head pounding. "I guess I'm going to Pennsylvania."

"Divinity," Mrs. Madigan said.

"Pardon me?"

"Divinity. That's the name of the village where they are. The girl on the phone said so."

Divinity, Kim thought disbelievingly. As though there were a true and loving God somewhere who would save her daughter. She was reasonably sure He would dwell in a place called "Divinity." The problem was, she had stopped asking Him for help a long time ago. If she lived to be ninety, she would always remember praying, praying...before succumbing to yet another of her father's blows.

Kim left Mrs. Madigan standing at the fence and started back toward the street. To the best of her calculations, without actually digging into her wallet to be sure, she had roughly two hundred dollars left. She had maybe three hundred dollars' unused credit on her one and only credit card. She had gotten to L.A. all those years ago on a lot less, she reasoned.

Susannah woke up this time when Kim tried to slide soundlessly behind the wheel.

"Mom?" she asked groggily. "Where did you go?"

"To find out everyone's gone," Kim answered tensely.

"What?"

"My brothers are in Pennsylvania. My parents have passed away. So has your father, baby. I'm sorry."

Susannah said nothing. Kim hoped she wouldn't feel much in the way of grief, for any of them. Up until a week ago, she had never even known she had grandparents. As for Bobby, Kim had told her daughter long ago that her relationship with him just hadn't worked out. That much was true, and Susannah had seemed to accept it.

"I didn't know we were looking for him, too," Susannah said in a small voice.

"Suze, I'm looking for anybody at all who can help us."

"So what do we do now?"

"Now we've got a long drive ahead of us, I guess." She started the car. It coughed, sputtered, then the engine caught. "Assuming our transportation holds out."

"We're going to drive there? To Pennsylvania? Now?"

"You got it."

"Cool."

Kim looked at her and wished desperately that she could bottle some of Susannah's optimism. At the moment, she had none of her own whatsoever.

## *Chapter 2*

Joe Lapp closed the barn door behind him and stared across the road in the direction of his home. Lanterns glowed in every window as dusk settled over the farm. At least five women were in there right now, he thought, tending to his children, cooking their supper, cleaning some corner that had already been exorcised of the dust bunnies that had gathered since Sarah had died.

*Sarah had died.* It came again immediately—that kick-punch in his chest that made it impossible for him to breathe for a long moment. Then the pain splintered and shattered and left him feeling almost normal again, or at least numb.

Joe generally tried not to think about his wife. Sarah had been gone since the verdant peak of summer, four months now, or it would be on Friday. He could almost escape her ghost during the day. His dairy farm demanded backbreaking toil, especially the way the Amish worked, without benefit of electricity or tractors. During the days, Joe sweated and strained, and he was almost okay. Then evening would come. He would go back to the house—Sarah's house—and there would be the women, her sisters and well-intentioned neighbors, hovering over him and the children Sarah had left behind. They would not allow him to forget. By their mere presence, they reminded him of how horribly wrong things had gone. Still, Joe needed them. He simply wasn't capable of taking care of his children and running the farm besides.

His eldest son, Nathaniel, would be nineteen next month, old enough that he contained his own pain and dealt with it on his own terms. But Dinah was trapped between adolescence and maturity, he thought. Barely fourteen, she had just finished with school last June. Joe knew that half of her wanted to sob like a baby, and let all the women comfort and take care of her, as well. But the other half was determined to oversee the house in her mother's stead, no matter that these were the years she should be running around, mildly abusing her freedom before she was baptized and married and settled down.

Grace and Matthew were still young enough to...well, to bounce back from tragedy, Joe thought. They had crumbled beneath the weight of their mother's loss for a month or so, then they had straightened up, dried their tears and gotten on with their lives. Gracie was eleven, and Matt had just turned nine.

Then there was Hannah.

Joe squeezed his eyes shut and leaned back against the barn with a groan. Hannah had lived. He wrestled every day with the unconscionable, heinous need to blame the baby for her mother's death. Guilt, Joe thought, was a very unruly animal. It was quite untrainable. There was no predicting the directions in which it was likely to lash out.

His guilt wanted to make him snarl at Hannah. He thanked God that he was a reasonable man. That he understood his reaction. That he was able to recognize and control it somewhat. But rational or not, it would not be overruled entirely.

He and Sarah had known since she had nearly died giving birth to Matt that she dared not have more children. In fact, they had guessed that it would not be easy for them to have a large family long before that, when five whole years had passed between the births of Nathaniel and Dinah. Sarah had suffered innumerable miscarriages in between. They had guessed early on that their own family would be forever small by Amish standards, where most kitchen tables seated families of nine or ten or even more. Birth control was against the *ordnung,* the rules of their Amish faith.

Nonetheless, Sarah and Joe had broken that rule in good conscience. The doctor in Lancaster who had saved her life after Matthew's birth had given her some birth control pills, and Sarah had taken them religiously. They already had four children who needed their mother. Joe could not fathom a God who would want Sarah to leave them. He had lived every day of their nineteen years together depending upon Sarah's warm presence at his side. He could not believe that God meant him to go on alone, without her.

He'd been wrong.

Or had he? Joe gave a bitter laugh. God gave choices. He had always believed that, though it didn't completely mesh with what his Amish bishop taught. The bishop—Sarah's own father—spoke of God's will, of bending oneself to it. But Joe didn't believe that God ordained events in a man's life. He just built forks in the road. Going left or right was a man's own choice.

Joe had had choices. He could have left his beloved wife alone, to absolutely ensure that she did not conceive again. He could have refrained from touching her. Everything in their marriage had been about him, he'd come to realize. What he wanted. What he needed. And Sarah, sweet, loving, docile Sarah, had gone along with that without a murmur of complaint.

Then the pills had failed. Sarah had refused to go so far as to abort the pregnancy. It was one thing to buck her religion enough to swallow those little tablets in the morning, but getting rid of her child, even to save her own life, was simply beyond her.

Seven months into her pregnancy, Sarah's placenta had ripped free from her uterine wall, just as it had done when she had been pregnant with Matt. But Matt had been full term and she had been in labor when it had happened. The settlement midwife had already called in a doctor when the profuse bleeding had started. He'd had an automobile, and they had managed to get Sarah to the hospital in Lancaster quickly enough to save her life and Matthew's, as well.

This time Sarah had been alone in the kitchen while Joe

was in the fields. This time she had lain down on their kitchen floor, and had nearly bled to death before anyone could help her. Joe had found her that way when he had come in to wash up before dinner, and there had only been time to say goodbye. She had died on the way to the hospital.

Somehow, incredibly, the technicians in the ambulance had saved Hannah. Born two months prematurely, she had barely survived after being robbed of oxygen, and she had come home from the hospital only two months ago. And that was when all the women from the settlement had really started coming to his home, to help him care for her. They were painful, physical, nearly overwhelming reminders of Joe's loss and all the shattering changes in his life. Joe couldn't live with their presence, and he couldn't live without their help.

"Pa? You okay?"

Joe opened his eyes from his own harsh thoughts. Nathaniel was watching him. His son had just come in from the fields. He was wearing a worried frown. Joe knew that this particular frown had little to do with his mother's death, and everything to do with his father's mental and emotional well-being.

Joe pushed away from the barn wall. "Sure."

"We ought to be getting in for supper," Nathaniel said, as though speaking to a child who might be inclined to throw a tantrum. "Don't you think?"

"Are *you* looking forward to it?" Joe countered honestly. Suppers had become a time of overly bright chatter, what with all the women around lately.

Nathaniel winced. "I never knew so much talkin', Pa. And lately Dinah just falls right in with it, babbling with the rest of them. You notice that?"

"She's trying to be one of them," Joe said. "Grown up."

Nathaniel nodded sadly.

"This can't go on," Joe said suddenly.

Nathaniel looked at him, surprised. "What are you going to do? How are you going to stop it?"

"I'm going to send them all home. Well, most of them." He'd need one to stay, he allowed reluctantly. Dinah needed help. The baby and the house were too much for one young girl, nor was it right that she should have to give up everything else to handle them. "And you're going back to Berks County to get on with your life," Joe decided.

Nathaniel immediately began shaking his head. He had been all but packed for the move, when Sarah had died. Now he had postponed his departure indefinitely. Joe knew it was time for new pain, fresh loss. He was going to have to force his son to leave. Otherwise, Nathaniel would never go.

"You're not happy here," Joe said. This Lancaster County *gemeide,* their church district, was Old Order Amish. It was a smidgen more liberal than most Old Order sects, but it was Old Order just the same. The people adhered to the strictest rules. No telephones, no electricity. The men wore long beards, longer hair—except Joe, who had obstinately bucked that rule from the start. His dark beard and his hair were short and trimmed, a tiny tribute to his own New Order, Berks County upbringing.

But those were not the things that grated on his elder son. Nathaniel strained most against the confines of the Amish staunch nonresistance to trouble. Nathaniel disapproved of the *meidung,* the horrible punishment that made a person "disappear" when he or she committed some sin against the *ordnung.* Then the remainder of the congregation could no longer "see" that person. The sinner was shunned, shut out, ignored. It had happened to too many of their close friends in recent years for Nathaniel's comfort. Sarah and Joe had decided that Nathaniel should go to Joe's family's New Order settlement to receive his baptism. But then Sarah had died.

"I've sent word to my father," Joe continued. "He'll be expecting you."

"But—" Nathaniel began.

"I'll have the same amount of work to do without you now as I would have had before your mother died. You were going to go away then anyway. The farm chores are not a factor, Nathaniel."

"I—"

"There really is no excuse any longer—except, perhaps, that you fear for my sanity."

Nathaniel flushed.

"I will survive," Joe said, though sometimes he doubted it. "It's time."

"I'll think about it," Nathaniel hedged, sounding as though he just wanted to change the subject.

"You must go."

"We'll talk later."

They would have to, Joe realized, finally looking across the road at the house again. A small, very loud, dark blue car had just parked in front of his walkway. Owning automobiles was against the *ordnung*, too.

"What is this?" Joe wondered aloud. They both moved away from the barn, through the front paddock, to lean against the fence nearest the road and watch. Joe hooked one muddy boot on the lower rung. He reached a hand up to pull down the brim of his black, broad-brimmed hat. The hat came in handy, Joe had realized of late. Properly positioned, no one could see his eyes. No one would know if they were reddened by loss. And no one could tell if he was watching, like the woman who was just now getting out of the small blue car.

She definitely wasn't Amish.

"She's a beauty," Joe said, without realizing he'd spoken. He became aware of it when Nathaniel whipped his head around to look at him.

"Guess so," Nathaniel agreed finally, as though reserving judgment on the startling fact that his father could actually consider a woman attractive.

"I've got to say I like the jeans those women wear," Joe continued.

"Uh...yeah," Nathaniel said slowly, nodding.

This woman's were quite possibly painted on. Joe had not had much occasion in his thirty-nine years to observe women walking around in painted-on jeans. Not even in Berks, in the New Order *gemeide* he had been born to, did women wear anything but plain dresses and aprons. But while the Lancaster settlements prohibited education past the eighth grade and insisted that their children be taught in their own one-room schoolhouses, the Berks people sent their kids to public schools. College was prohibited, but going to high school was just fine.

Joe had seen his share of jeans back then, on those days that he'd gone off to school. That had been back in the seventies. He fondly remembered hip-huggers. He'd considered it a sad day when they had gone out of style, even if he had since graduated, married and moved to Lancaster with little if any excuse to go into the city to see such bounty again.

"Now what do you reckon she's doing?" Nathaniel asked as the woman paused and looked up at their house.

She was hugging herself, Joe saw, and the jeans hugged her, conforming tightly to her bottom and what seemed to him miles of legs. They were tucked into boots that were more fashionable than serviceable. She wore a short, navy blue jacket that warmed her only as far down as her waist.

The settlement—especially the villages, Divinity included—saw its share of tourists. The *anner Satt Leit* people who comprised mainstream America were fascinated with the Amish culture. They came to gawk, to marvel at their horse-drawn carriages and their simple dress. The "Plain People"—that was what they called the Amish. But the tourists visited mostly in the summer. This was November.

If this was a tourist, then she was probably lost, Joe figured. But she had to know by now that she would not find a telephone here to borrow. There were no phone lines, no electrical wires, anywhere in evidence.

"Reckon I ought to go point her in the right direction," he said, pushing away from the fence, still watching the woman. "If she knocks on the door and encounters all those women talking at once, she'll never make out a word they're saying."

"Yeah," Nathaniel agreed. "And truth to tell, I'd kind of like to see those jeans up close."

"I wouldn't be averse to it." It was a deliberate statement to make Nathaniel believe he was fine, healing, getting over the loss of Sarah. It worked. His son gave him that sharp look again, then he grinned slightly.

They climbed over the fence and started across the road. Then they stopped cold again. The front door opened. A tall man with nearly black hair passed across the screened-in porch. He stopped on the steps there, and he stared at the woman, as well. The man was Jacob Wallace.

The settlement's infusion of Wallaces had begun ten months previously, when Adam had come looking for his son, Bo. Bo had been dropped on Joe Lapp's doorstep nearly five years ago, and Joe and Sarah had raised the boy as their own. They had not notified the authorities. The woman who had left the boy had said she'd be back for him. She never came, and calling the authorities was against the *ordnung*. It was considered God's will that the boy had been left with them.

They thought they would lose Bo entirely when his father finally found him this past January. But then Adam had married an Amish woman, Mariah Fisher, and rather than take the boy back to his native Texas, the Wallaces had stayed on.

Jacob, Adam's brother, had descended upon them the following month. One of the same people who had been responsible for Adam's son ending up in Divinity had seen the ripe pickings the settlement's children provided to the *anner Satt Leit* world. That man had begun kidnapping them, selling them to childless *anner Satt Leit* couples who had given up on the idea of legitimate adoption. After all, the Amish way was one of nonresistance. The Amish steadfastly refused to have anything to do with American law. There was no one to stop the man from stealing their children. The old deacons considered it God's will that the little ones had vanished—so Joe himself had led an uprising and had formed this new *gemeide* with more lenient rules. Then Adam had called his brother to come look for the kids, and Detective Jake Wallace had swaggered into town with his figurative guns drawn. Both the kidnapper and Katya Essler, a young Amish woman, had succumbed to him.

Jake and Katya had not remained in the settlement. Since she was already considered married in the Amish faith and divorce was against the *ordnung,* Katya could not divorce and marry Jake. They settled in Texas, but they came back fairly frequently.

Joe watched Jake stop short of the woman from the car. He rubbed a hand over his short beard and considered the situation.

"You know what I reckon?" he said to his son.

"What's that?"

"I think we might have ourselves another Wallace to contend with."

Nathaniel looked startled. "There's *another* one?"

Joe nodded. "Seems to me I remember Jake and Adam mentioning something about a sister. Now look at this."

The woman in the jeans hurled herself at Jake. He caught her and they stood for a moment in an emotional embrace. There was just enough light left in the day for Joe to tell that Jake's hair was exactly the same shade as the woman's. Both were caught somewhere between rich chocolate brown and pure black. Their noses were identical—long and straight. On the woman, it looked haughty. Her hair fell in utter disarray to a point past her shoulders.

Interesting, Joe thought. Not only was he unaccustomed to women in blue jeans, he had not seen a woman with her hair down since Sarah had died. Amish women always wore theirs bound up in public. And even though Katya had left the Amish faith, she had respectfully taken to wearing dresses and tucking her hair up again when she and Jake came back to offer him their help in his bereavement.

Joe thought briefly of touching this woman's hair, because it looked so incredibly thick and rich and he wondered if it would feel that way, too. He was appalled when he realized what he was considering. Something thorny rolled over in his gut. He shoved his hands deep into the pockets of his black, broadfall trousers and cleared his throat.

Jake and the woman came apart. She looked Joe's way. He had been right. She was a beauty. And there was something else. He saw a hunted-animal kind of pain in her eyes, the kind there was no escaping from, the kind he recognized intimately.

He'd had every intention of introducing himself. It was, after all, his home she had come to. Joe Lapp opened his mouth. Something guttural came out.

"You okay, Joe?" Jake asked. "What's wrong?"

Joe wrestled one hand free of his pocket. He held it out to the woman. He wondered if it was shaking, or worse, sweating. "Hello," he managed to say finally. "I'm Loe Japp."

## *Chapter 3*

Kim stared at the man, too rattled to respond. Jake was still staring at her, and though she wouldn't look at him again, she felt it. Waves of emotion seemed to be rolling off him. True, she had thrown herself at him first, out of relief and her own indescribable emotion at coming to the end of this trail. But she had quickly collected herself, as she always did. Jake, on the other hand, had hugged her hard enough to hurt her ribs.

At last her brain assimilated what this other man had said. Loe Japp? She wondered with not a little panic if these Amish people spoke English.

She finally took his outstretched hand. It was callused and it dwarfed her own. And something happened when she touched him, something that rattled her even more than she already was. She had the most startling, instinctive, unwarranted thought: *Everything is going to be okay now.*

She found her voice with difficulty. "Hi. I'm Kimberley Mancuso."

"You changed your name," Jake said sharply.

Kim looked at her brother again quickly. Odd, she thought. One minute she had been excruciatingly aware of his extreme emotion, then she had somehow forgotten about him. ''Uh...yes,'' she answered. ''Sort of.''

Jake seemed to think about that, then he nodded. ''That's why I couldn't find you.''

Her heart skipped a beat. ''You were looking for me?''

Once more, a million emotions played across Jake's face. ''We...I...have this company called ChildSearch. We look for missing persons, children mostly.'' His voice changed, going suddenly hoarse. ''Did someone tell you we were looking for you? Is that why you came?''

Kim shook her head. ''I...no. I didn't know. I came on my own. I found out in Dallas that you'd come here, so I followed you.''

Jake looked troubled by that, she thought, then just confused.

''We should go in,'' Joe interrupted.

Jake's expression became alarmed. ''Uh, not a good idea,'' he said. ''They're all in the kitchen. There are eight of them now.''

*''Eight?''* Joe echoed, then he groaned. ''Dear Lord.''

''They've been arriving through the back door.''

''Pa, you got to make them go,'' Nathaniel pleaded.

Joe latched on to the excuse. It was something logical he could do to gain a few more moments in which to collect himself. He hurried inside.

Kim cleared her throat. ''Who's in there?'' she asked.

''A whole lot of women,'' Nathaniel answered. He thrust his hand at her. ''I'm Nathaniel Lapp, Joe's son.''

''Joe? Lapp?'' She was so shaken up she wasn't even hearing straight! She groaned and shook the young man's hand.

The car door opened with a rusty squeak. Susannah stuck her head out from the passenger side. She'd been sleeping when they'd arrived.

''Mom?''

''Right here, baby,'' Kim called back. ''Come and join us.''

*''Mom?''* Jake said, then he looked at Susannah more closely. ''Were you *pregnant?* Is that why you left? Did Dad beat you up when you were pregnant?''

''No harm done,'' she said flatly, but her heart did an odd jump.

"I didn't do a damned thing about it."

Kim looked at him, startled. "There was nothing you could do." Still, she gripped Susannah's hand a little too hard when the girl reached them, because the memories would always hurt.

A whole flock of women burst from the house then. Kim stepped back quickly, pulling Susannah with her so the women could pass without trampling them.

"That ought to do it," Joe Lapp announced, coming back to stand on the porch. "Of course, they probably won't speak to me until the next Church Sunday. If I'm lucky."

Both Nathaniel and Jake laughed at that, surprising Kim. Oh, she thought, there was a lot about these people she didn't understand. She was astounded to find that she was even curious. She didn't intend to hang around long enough for all these little undercurrents to matter.

"Come in," Joe said. "Please. There's coffee on. And there are easily twelve casseroles in the refrigerator. Another two in the woodstove."

"I need to find Adam," Jake said suddenly.

"I'll do it," said a soft voice from the porch.

A woman had come outside to stand beside Joe. Kim looked her way. She was extremely pregnant, and no less beautiful for it. Not even her strange clothing detracted from that. She wore an azure blue dress beneath a black apron, plus sensible shoes and dark stockings, and her hair was severely pulled back beneath a small white bonnet. The strings dangled down to her shoulders. From what Kim could see of her hair, it was a rich, deep black. Her hands were clasped together demurely over the swell of her unborn child.

The woman stepped down off the porch. "I'm Mariah," she said. "I married your brother. Adam," she explained.

Kim felt her heart slam. She stared at the woman's misshapen waistline again. *Four possibilities. Four now.* Adam had another son or daughter on the way.

Shame heightened Kim's color and she looked away from the woman quickly. She felt almost mercenary for thinking only of what might be in all this for Susannah. Then she got angry. She had not seen her family in eleven years. Susannah was what mattered. Susannah was her family, her everything.

And Susannah was dying. Remembering that, Kim felt her knees go weak. The pregnant woman's image seemed to swim out of focus for a moment.

*Oh, my God,* Kim thought, *I'm actually going to cry.* No, she wasn't. Damned if she was. She sniffed hard.

"I'll go get your brother," Mariah said. "He'll want to be here."

Joe backed off suddenly. Kim watched him return to the house, frowning.

"He lost his wife last July," Mariah explained quietly. "Of childbirth complications. I don't usually come over here these days because...well, I know my condition must surely remind him." Then she smiled. "What a happy coincidence that I did so today."

She headed off toward a buggy waiting on the other side of the road. Jake went inside, waving back at Kim and Susannah to come in, also. The boy—Nathaniel, Kim remembered—headed for the house, as well.

Joe was waiting at the inner door. Kim started that way, her eyes determinedly on her toes. She recalled the odd feeling she'd had when she shook his hand. She didn't want a repeat of *that* silliness. But when she reached the porch, there seemed nothing else she could do but look up as he held the door for them.

"I'm...uh, sorry for intruding this way," she murmured.

"It must be necessary."

She was startled. She met his eyes. They were a very dark brown, depthless somehow. She had the absurd impression that all the wisdom of the universe was in them for the taking. Yet they were haunted.

Of course they were haunted, she chided herself. His wife had died recently.

"Yes," she answered. "It is."

She left him and went inside, into a square central hall. Susannah was hanging back a little, dragging on her hand.

"Mom, they seem okay," she whispered.

"Well, only one of them is actually family so far," she said. "Hedge your bets for a while."

"But—"

"Let's just get through this, Susannah. Please. Just let me do this."

Susannah stopped walking. "You're not just going to ask them to give me their insides and go again, are you?" she accused.

Put that way, it did sound horrible, Kim realized. Cold and ungiving, just as Mark had so often accused her of being. But she supposed it was no more horrible than seeing Adam's unborn child as a potential donor.

Suddenly, it was all too much. Her emotions had been running raw and wild for weeks now. The events of the past few days had just piled on. She'd driven thousands of miles inside of less than a week. Before she knew it was going to happen, the room tilted. Kim heard Susannah cry out, more in surprise than alarm. Then she hit the floor of Joe Lapp's foyer.

Joe watched her come around. He'd carried her to the sofa in the living room, and now he hunkered down beside it. Her daughter was roaming the keeping room, where church services were held when it was Joe's turn to host them. Every once in a while the girl would call out a question about the German Bible or the woodstove in there. Mariah was with her, telling Susannah everything she wanted to know.

Joe just watched Kimberley. Her skin was far too pale, he thought. Now he realized that she had the Wallace high cheekbones, as well. She really was beautiful, and he felt embarrassment rush hotly inside him all over again. There'd be no easy way to tell her what his name really was without mortifying himself, he realized. Historically, he had not had much savoir faire when women poleaxed him. Frighteningly, he'd been poleaxed only once before. He had made a fool of himself when he'd met Sarah for the first time, too, but at least then he had been barely nineteen years old. This time he was a grown man in the throes of loss.

He knew somehow before this woman even opened her eyes that she was going to be embarrassed because she had fainted. He had watched her outside, and she seemed to have her own share of stiff pride. It made him feel somewhat better about getting so flummoxed he hadn't even known his own name.

He was still thinking about that when Kimberley's eyelids flickered once. That was all the warning he got. Then she gasped and came up off the sofa like a shot.

"Where's Suze?"

She asked clearly, as though she had not been unconscious a moment before. Then she looked around the room like a cornered animal judging its obstacles, he thought.

"Sit," he said soothingly, catching her hand, trying to pull her back to the sofa again. "She's fine."

She snatched her hand away. "Where's my daughter?"

"With Mariah."

"The pregnant one?"

Joe winced. Kim remembered a moment too late what Mariah had said about his recent loss.

"Your daughter is very curious about us," he noted in an emotionless tone. "Mariah is showing her about."

Kim finally sat again. She did it fast and hard. She covered her face with her hands. "Oh, God. I can't believe I did that."

"I imagine stress might have something to do with it."

She cracked her fingers to look at him. She was a little amazed by this man. A strange woman had just collapsed on his floor, and he was watching her as though he had known her from the day she was born and he wouldn't have expected anything else under the circumstances.

*Everything is going to be okay now.* She shivered and actually shook her head this time, as though to drive the crazy, irrational impression away.

She dropped her hands. "I'm not the swooning type," she said tightly. "The only other time I've even come close was when I was pregnant and worked two eight-hour shifts without a break." Too late she realized she had just committed the same faux pas all over. She wasn't good at tiptoeing around people's feelings, she thought helplessly. "I'm sorry," she said awkwardly.

Joe shrugged, and to Kim the gesture seemed too deliberate. "Someone has told you about my Sarah."

Even the way he said it—*my Sarah*—made Kim feel his pain. It made her uncomfortable. It felt too...intimate. "Mariah," she explained. "Mariah told me."

"She would," Joe answered.

He had taken his hat off, she realized. His hair was the same rich brown as his eyes, brushed back from his forehead. It stopped just shy of his collar in the back. He wore a short, neat beard that just coasted around his jawline. Above it, his face was a little too craggy and hard and weathered to be arresting, she reflected, but it came close. It was inarguably appealing. There was strength there, she realized, and a great deal of pride.

"Pardon me?" She realized he had been speaking to her, and flushed.

"I asked what it is that you need from them," he said. "From your brothers."

"I need one of them to save my daughter's life."

Kim had said it without thinking. She'd opened her mouth and the words had simply found their way out. Panic instantly built in her at how easily it had happened. Maybe it was the pain that haunted his eyes, she thought. Maybe she sensed that he would understand hers better than most.

But that was pure foolishness, craziness. Worse, it was dangerous. She didn't even know him. She needed to keep her reasons for this reunion under her control, so she could plead her case well, so nothing could go wrong. She shot to her feet again and began pacing.

"Then they'll do it," Joe said.

"You don't even know us or what we need!"

"It wouldn't matter," he answered, and pushed to his feet, as well.

Kim gazed at him disbelievingly. Then a shadow darkened the door to the foyer. She looked that way slowly, feeling her heart hitch just a little.

Adam was shorter than Jake, but somehow, he had always seemed bigger. Jake was almost lanky. Adam was strong, broad in the shoulders, just a bit heavier. He was blond to the darkness that Kim shared with her other brother. Adam stepped into the room, his arms held out to her as though it had never occurred to him that she might not go into them.

And she did, though she felt awkward about it.

"Ah, Kimmie," Adam said, his voice raw as he hugged her. "You don't know how happy this makes me."

# Chapter 4

An hour later, they were all gathered around a kitchen table, more people than Kim had ever seen at a table before in her life. In fact, an additional picnic-bench-type thing had been pulled in from what they called the "keeping room" to help accommodate everyone. Kim looked around at all their faces.

No one seemed to think this incredible sum of humanity was odd. In fact, Susannah seemed enthralled by it all, she realized. Outside of those few months they had spent with Mark, there had never been more than the two of them at any given meal.

Now there was Adam and Mariah and his son, Bo. There was Jake and his new wife, Katya, and her four children. There was Joe Lapp's brood—five of them, counting the infant napping against Katya's shoulder. Kim had gathered from what Mariah had said that the baby had died with her mother, but apparently that wasn't so.

There was Joe, keeping to himself in one corner of the kitchen, and enough food to feed an army.

Most of it appeared bland and unappetizing, to Kim's way of thinking. She eyed it as Mariah brought it to the table. She'd always had a strong preference for Tex-Mex herself. Voices rose to the ceiling, and there were bursts of laughter. Bedlam, Kim thought. Pure, happy bedlam. It made her feel confused. She would never have pictured her brothers in an environment such as this.

She knew she should get up and help serve, but the truth was that she felt too much like an outsider. She decided to remain very quiet, with the vague hope that they all might forget about her. But when Joe finally took his seat at the head of the table, Kim felt him looking at her.

Her eyes went warily to his. Brown met blue. There were questions in his, she realized. Her heart gave an odd thump.

She wondered if he was going to tell Jake and Adam why she had come here to find them. Why had she trusted this man with that? she despaired again. Then she assured herself it didn't matter. She certainly intended to ask for their help at this meal. There was no sense in dragging things out.

Jake raised his glass of milk in a toast, laughing. "Here's to the passing of Sugar Joe. Long live Loe Japp."

Joe reached up quickly to tug down his hat. He looked abashed when he found it wasn't on his head, Kim thought.

"It's going to stick, Pa." One of his sons hooted—Matt, Kim thought his name was. "You know it."

"Who's Sugar Joe?" Kim asked tentatively.

"It's a long story," Adam said. "First you've got to understand that everyone in the settlements has maybe one of only ten different last names." He glanced at his wife, as though to make sure he had things right. "They're all descended from the same group of immigrants. And all their first names are usually German or biblical, so..."

Kim heard nothing more. *German?* She'd thought these people were Dutch. Yes, the Amish were called "Pennsylvania Dutch."

Adam was rambling on. "There are a lot of Rachel Fishers, for instance, and a lot of Joe Lapps."

"So folks have nicknames," Nathaniel explained. "That way we can differentiate between one another. Call out 'Joe Lapp' at a Church Sunday, and twelve guys will answer. So we've got a Chicken Joe and a Boundary Joe, and so on. Dad's always been called 'Sugar Joe.'"

"Uh...why?" Kim asked, though she could have sworn she

didn't care. Her mind was still circling around that single word—*German.* Which Bobby had been.

"When he met my ma, it was at a Church Sunday," Nathaniel continued. "He saw her across a paddock and went silly before he ever spoke a word to her. He even forgot to get his own ma a cup of coffee. Grandma had to remind him. So then he went and got it, and he poured the whole sugar canister into it because he was staring at Ma. It spilled all over—coffee, sugar, everything."

"He's been 'Sugar Joe' ever since," Mariah said, laughing.

"Not quite," Joe said shortly.

At that, they all grew more subdued. Even Nathaniel seemed to realize some obscure implication in what he had just said. His face went crimson and hard.

"Well, that's true," Mariah said quietly after a moment. "People have stopped these past few months out of respect for Sarah's passing."

Kim's heart thudded strangely. In that moment, it dawned on her why they were teasing Joe. He'd "gone silly" when he had met his Sarah. And his tongue had apparently fumbled over his name when he had met Kim. It hadn't been her hearing at all. She shot to her feet. Panic, embarrassment and a crowded, threatened feeling tightened her muscles. Then she inadvertently met Joe's eyes. And once again she saw comfort there, commiseration and understanding.

His eyes said, *I'm not comfortable with what I did, either.*

Kim sat down again slowly, still staring at him. She pressed a hand to her stomach. She was on an emotional roller coaster.

She realized everyone was talking about a wedding now. "Who's getting married?" Kim heard herself ask, because it seemed easier than dwelling on the man at the head of the table.

"Adam and I," Mariah said happily.

Kim's eyes fell to the woman's pregnancy and widened a little. Mariah laughed.

"We were married in your world ten months ago, by a justice of the peace in the city. But we couldn't have an Amish wedding until Adam converted. He did that. He was baptized last week."

Kim's gaze moved uncomprehendingly to her brother.

"You converted to...to all this?" She looked around at the quaint, old-fashioned kitchen. Full dark had fallen outside. The light hanging over the table wasn't electric, she realized. It had a flame in it. Three other lanterns were hanging on the walls. They gave off a warm golden light, too, rather than the harsh white of electric bulbs.

Suddenly, her heart began beating hard. Not at the idea of Adam getting married—she'd thought he already had, and legally, technically, that was true. It was at the idea that he had joined this religion. That he had reached out to a God she had always believed abandoned them.

"Why?" she asked, her voice cracking. "Why would you do that?"

"Because I believe in it."

She shook her head helplessly.

"It didn't happen overnight," Adam conceded.

"Hey, I'm still a little blasted by it myself," Jake offered.

Kim's head finally cleared as she thought she understood. "You're doing it because of the baby."

"I'm doing it because this place has given me everything I never had."

Kim felt something as solid as rock cram into her throat.

"A lot of it was Katya's doing," Adam continued. "What she went through brought a lot of things into perspective for me."

Kim looked at Jake's wife. They hadn't spoken much yet. Katya seemed vaguely shy, definitely quiet. She was sitting apart from the table, her food on her lap, and Kim thought that odd.

"I think what he's trying to say is that I left this place," Katya explained. "The settlement. It didn't turn out to be exactly right for me. I was raised here. I lived twenty-nine years here. But I was married to a man who hurt me, and the *ordnung,* our...well, our rules, wouldn't allow me to leave him and start over. It wouldn't give me or my children a second chance at life. So I took my babies and I left."

Kim felt herself nodding.

"I had a problem with any society that treated women as second-class citizens," Adam admitted. "With an *ordnung* that controlled their lives and left them no choices. It reminded me of Mom and the rules of the Catholic Church, the way they wouldn't let her divorce Dad."

Kim felt something spear deeply into her heart. It made her whole body jump. She never even allowed herself to *think* about her parents anymore. Now they were creeping up naturally in conversation.

"I always blamed the church for the fact that she couldn't leave Dad," Adam said. "Then I realized that adhering to that Catholic doctrine was her own decision. Just as *not* adhering to Amish doctrine any longer became Katya's decision. I came to realize that the people here really *are* here of their own free will."

"People have the right to leave," Joe said.

It seemed to Kim that his voice was pointed now. He was looking at his elder son.

"In fact, Nathaniel will be leaving for a New Order settlement shortly, the one where I was born and raised."

"Unfortunately, it's written that when one breaks the *ordnung,* we're shunned," Katya explained. "And leaving the faith, as I did, is most definitely against the *ordnung.* So no one can see me here anymore. No one can speak to me. I can't eat at the same table or from the same bowls as everyone else."

Kim finally understood why Katya was sitting back from the table. "It doesn't seem like that big a deal," she muttered, unsure herself if she was talking about this shunning business or what Katya had done.

"The *meidung,* this business of shunning, can be horrible," Joe said. "It pushes some people beyond endurance. I don't necessarily approve, which is why I refuse to follow the *meidung* to the letter in my own home."

Kim looked at him sharply. "Yet you're willing to see your own son shunned if he leaves?"

"Nathaniel hasn't been baptized here yet. People are only bound by the *ordnung* once they're baptized and have vowed to live by Amish rules," Joe answered. "And we don't allow baptism until a child is old enough to understand what he's getting into." Abruptly, he changed the subject. "Half an hour," he said suddenly, looking down the table at the kids. "Nathaniel, would you mind haying the horses? The rest of you can burn off the last of your energy for a little while. Then it's off to bed for the lot of you."

Matthew and Gracie shot to their feet. Adam's boy, Bo, stood more slowly, looking at his father as though for confirmation.

"You, too," Adam said. "We'll leave in about half an hour."

Jake glanced at Katya's kids. "You share the rules of the house while we're here," he said. "Be back in half an hour." That throng bolted for the foyer, too.

Susannah stared longingly after Katya's eldest girl, Rachel. Then she looked back at Kim.

Kim stifled a moan. She wanted to keep Susannah nearby so they could leave as soon as possible, as soon as she had either gotten or been denied the help of her brothers. But so many of these kids were close to Susannah in age and perfect playmates, Kim noted.

*What if she really does die?* The pain and protest that reared up merely at the thought of that were unbearable. The possibility tightened Kim's skin. It made her want to scream. But she had to force herself to acknowledge it. And if it happened, then she wanted every remaining day Susannah knew to be one of pure, unadulterated happiness.

"Sure," Kim said, her voice strangled. "You go play, too."

Susannah ran out into the foyer. The steady banging of a door somewhere distant echoed in the room as the kids spilled outside.

Mariah got up to begin taking their plates. Dinah, Joe's eldest daughter, was still standing beside the table uncertainly, holding the baby.

"Pa?" she asked tentatively.

Joe shot to his feet. "Excuse me," he said shortly, and left the kitchen.

Dinah looked down at the baby and her eyes seemed to fill with tears. Kim saw Mariah and Katya exchange helpless looks.

"I'll take her," Mariah said. She collected the baby and Dinah went outside with the others.

Kim stood, as well, to clear the table. She felt eyes on her, boring a hole in her back between her shoulder blades as she turned toward the sink.

"Why did you come here?" Jake asked suddenly now that the adults were alone.

Kim's fingers tightened around the casserole dish she was holding. Oddly, she wished that Joe were still here. For moral support? Because he knew the basics of why she had come and he hadn't seemed to judge her for it? She'd always stood on her own two feet. She had never needed anyone. She placed the casserole dish carefully on the counter, then turned and leaned against it, meeting Jake's eyes.

"Katie wants me to believe that God waved a magic wand and brought you," he added. "But I don't think I buy that."

Kim managed a tight smile. She looked at Katya. "Well, God waved something," she answered.

Jake shot to his feet. "You didn't even know we were looking for you," he said again.

"No," she agreed.

"But here you are."

"I need your help." There. It was out. Her heart began thumping.

"Of course," Adam said evenly. "With anything. Whatever you need."

She gazed at him. "What's happened to you?" she demanded. "Eleven years ago we never paid any attention to one another! It was each of us for ourselves! I didn't help you—you didn't help me. We just...survived. We're not normal! We were never normal! We didn't care about each other! Now you don't even know what I need, but you're acting as though you're willing to jump through hoops to give it!" Just as Joe had said, she remembered.

"You're wrong," Adam argued.

Jake's face appeared white.

Kim shook her head. "I was *there.* I know how we always were."

"You were a toddler when we were in our teens." Adam looked at Jake, too. "There's a lot you probably don't remember."

"She remembers what counts," Jake said harshly. "Like

the day Dad bounced her off the walls in her room and I didn't help her."

Suddenly Kim did remember. She remembered looking over her father's shoulder when he lifted her to throw her. She had been about eight. Jake would have been seventeen or so. She had opened her mouth, had started to cry out—and then her father had dropped her and Jake was flat on the floor.

"I was trying to tell you to go away," she whispered wretchedly. "I'm sorry."

Jake was thunderstruck. "*You're* sorry?"

"I never had a chance to get the words out before he hit you."

"*I* should be sorry," he said angrily.

That was when Kim recalled that both her brothers had always been extraordinarily stubborn, as well. It was a Wallace family trait.

"I started searching for you this last time late last summer, to tell you that," he admitted. "That I was...am...sorry."

Kim blinked at him in confusion.

"I should have stopped him that day."

"He would have killed you! He nearly did!"

"I was bigger than he was, at least toward the end."

"No. Not really. You were taller, maybe. But you were skinny back then, Jake. He was like a bull."

"I always said I would!" Jake yelled.

"And none of us believed you could!" she hollered right back.

"So much for family reunions," Adam said dryly.

Silence fell, and it seemed to have weight. Indeed, it seemed to Kim that none of them was even breathing.

She took a deep breath. "I knew you wanted to," she stated. "I knew you wanted to stop the nightmare with all your heart. But there was nothing any one of us could do, Jake. Except survive. We only survived. And one by one, we got out."

Everything appeared to go out of Jake—the air and his strength. He sat down hard. "What do you need?" he asked finally, hoarsely. "Tell me what you need, what brought you here. Let me give it to you. I need to give it to you. I need to...make amends."

Kim stared at him. Even moments ago, she had been here

purely for her own selfish reasons, to save Susannah, nothing more. She could have sworn she didn't give a damn about any of them beyond that. She believed that for as long as it took her to look into Jake's eyes. She swerved her gaze to glance at Adam.

They would help. They wanted to help. It was almost overwhelming.

"Susannah's dying," she whispered. And that was the exact moment she saw Joe Lapp reappear in the kitchen door. Adam made a startled, strangled sound and Jake only continued to stare at her.

"It's leukemia." She rushed on. "She needs a bone marrow transplant. Even then, there's only a fifty percent chance that it will cure her." The words were tumbling over each other now; she felt helpless yet desperately hopeful. "But there's a ninety percent chance the transplant will let her live at least three more years. She'd be able to wear lipstick for the first time. She could go to a school dance—" She broke off briefly as her throat constricted. "The doctor says the closest marrow matches are...family."

She expected either Jake or Adam to answer. But they continued to stare at her mutely, apparently still in shock. It was Joe who came to her, Joe who spoke, simply and without all the poignant emotion she'd always avoided.

"Well," he said slowly, "that's one thing you've got, Kimberley. It's lucky you were able to find them."

"Is it?" she murmured, looking at Adam's and Jake's faces again. Then her legs gave out and she sat down at the table hard.

# Chapter 5

The half hour they'd given the kids stretched into an hour. None of the children came inside to question their good fortune.

Kim told the adults everything she knew of Susannah's condition. And Jake contributed some solid facts of his own. "They have these donor lists now," he said. "It's all computerized. They're trying to get more minorities involved. When an African-American kid needs marrow and no one in his family matches, he needs an African-American donor. Same goes for any and all other ethnic backgrounds."

Kim stared at him. "That's true. But how did you know?"

"Jake's a walking encyclopedia," Adam said. "His mind has more files than the Library of Congress."

Jake ignored that. "What doctor did you speak to?" he demanded.

Kim blinked. "His name is Manuel Parra."

"Never heard of him."

"Why should you?"

"Because just last month ChildSearch was looking for a kid who'd been diagnosed with an immunity problem. Not HIV, something else. Something rare and congenital. He needed a marrow transplant, too. His father took off with him—the guy was the noncustodial parent—and the mother called in every law enforcement agency and every child welfare system in the country. Anyway, I figured he'd need to get the kid help, so, on a hunch, we checked with all the best transplant doctors and facilities in the country. This Parra wasn't on that list.''

Kim wasn't sure that she had even *heard* of a marrow transplant before last week. Now it would seem that the brother she hadn't seen in eleven years had had cause to learn all about it, a month before even she knew she needed his help. Her head spun.

''Did you find the boy?'' she asked, her voice thin.

Jake nodded. ''Sure.''

''Is he...okay?'' She had this irrational feeling that if he had survived, then Susannah would, also.

''Don't know yet,'' Jake answered. ''But his dad took him to Children's Hospital in Philadelphia. Turned out that he only snatched the kid to get him help. He wasn't satisfied with the treatment he was receiving in Albany. The parents are together again, by the way, at least until the issue of the kid's health is resolved. Anyway, we need to get Susannah to Children's Hospital,'' he continued. ''That's probably the best pediatric place in the country insofar as this sort of thing is concerned. Let's see what they have to say.''

Kim stiffened. *We.* Old, instinctive panic pressed in. ''This is my problem,'' she said irrationally.

''You came to us for help,'' Adam stated.

''Seems to me we can't give you marrow until we're tested to see if we're compatible,'' Jake countered. ''And I'd kind of prefer the best doctor I can find for that.''

She couldn't argue with his logic.

''So tomorrow we'll drive over to Philly,'' he added. ''We'll see what the story is.''

Kim swallowed carefully and gave a small nod. Then something else occurred to her. ''There's no way I'm going to take a horse-and-buggy ride through the streets of Philadelphia,'' she blurted.

Jake let out a bark of laughter. ''You've got company on that one. I don't do the nineteenth-century routine, either. We'll all squeeze into your car.''

Kim was relieved. Adam may have converted to the Amish religion, but at least Jake seemed as irreverent as ever.

"How have you been getting around while you're here?" she asked curiously.

"Clip-clop," he answered dryly. "But Goliath and I have come to an understanding."

"Who?"

"Adam's horse."

Kim got to her feet. "Well," she said lamely. "We ought to be going, then."

"Going?" Mariah looked at her blankly. Adam and Jake did, too.

"I saw a lot of motels on the main road coming in. I need to collect Susannah. I'm sorry to cut this short, but I'm..." She looked at all of them. "Exhausted."

It bothered her to admit it. She hated to show weakness. But the fact of the matter was that seeing them again had done what even these past several weeks of worry and heartache hadn't achieved. It had enervated her. It had sapped the last of her emotions. She had nothing left to give anyone right now. Unfortunately, they were going to argue with her, she realized. They were going to make her dredge up a little more energy to stand her ground.

"You can't go to a motel," Adam said. "That's ridiculous."

"I'll come back here first thing in the morning," she promised.

"Why bother?" Jake countered.

"Because I can't take any more!" she burst out. "I need to be alone."

"That can be arranged," Joe said, speaking for the first time.

Kim looked at him gratefully. "Please."

"Your old house hasn't sold yet, has it?" he asked Mariah.

Mariah looked stunned. "Why didn't I think of that?"

"I don't understand," Kim said.

"Mariah has a one-bedroom *grossdawdy* house in the village," Joe explained.

"A what?" Kim asked blankly.

"A grandfather's house," Mariah elaborated. "When our

elders get too old to run their own farms, we build them small cottages of their own on the property and take over the spread ourselves. My house used to be part of the Miller farm. But then Ethan, their grandfather, became a deacon of their *gemeide,* their church district. They built him a somewhat bigger place next door so he could hold services there, and I bought the little one when I came back from college. It was perfect for me at the time. Small, cozy and cheap.''

''College?'' Sometime during the course of this evening, Kim was sure someone had mentioned that these Old Order Amish weren't educated past the eighth grade.

Mariah smiled a little crookedly. ''Oh, I was punished for it. They put me under the *meidung.* They shunned me, shut me out, refused to see me, just as we must technically do to Katya now.''

''But that's archaic!'' Kim exclaimed. ''For going to *school?*'' She could scarcely believe that Adam had bought into all this.

Mariah looked down at her clasped hands. ''It was difficult, but it all worked out. I changed *gemeide*s. It's a long story, but Joe arranged to lift my *meidung* when I came here.''

Kim's gaze moved to Joe again. ''*You* did? How?''

''I'm a deacon here. I voted for it.''

''A deacon,'' she repeated.

''I've devoted my life to my church. I serve the people here.''

Yet he loosened the rules of the *meidung* in his own home. She was getting a headache trying to figure this man out. He was proving to be a lot to think about.

''We took all the furniture out of your old house,'' Adam was saying as he glanced at his wife.

Joe's chair creaked a little as he pushed it back. ''I haven't slept in my own bed for four months. Take mine.''

Kim looked at them disbelievingly.

''Good idea,'' Adam said. ''We can load it into that old open wagon I have.''

''Yeah, let's make Goliath work for his hay,'' Jake agreed with almost malicious pleasure.

''You're going to move a whole bed to a different house just so I can sleep there for a night or two?'' Kim said. She looked at Joe. ''Doesn't anyone but me see how absurd this is?''

Joe opened his mouth but never had a chance to respond.

''You'll be here longer than that,'' Jake decided. ''If one of us is a match for Susannah, you'll have to hang around long enough for the transplant.''

''Thank goodness that place never sold,'' Mariah said.

''There's a reason for everything,'' Katya insisted quietly. ''God provides.''

''The house has no lights or heat,'' Mariah added, ''but we'll send some lanterns, as well, and I never took the woodstove out of the kitchen—''

''Stop it!'' Kim cried.

This time they really looked at her.

''I can't do this. This is crazy! Moving furniture and... and...'' She trailed off helplessly.

''What choice do you have?'' Joe asked in that steady tone he had. ''How long can you afford a motel?''

She flinched at that, then she rallied. ''I won't let you do this,'' she said. ''I don't need to be alone. Not if it means going through all this hullabaloo. I'll just...Susannah and I can sleep on the floor.'' She looked at Joe. ''If you'll have us. Or your floor, Adam.''

''I've got ample floor space,'' Adam agreed. ''But not much in the way of extra beds. Still, there's always the sofa. You're welcome to it.''

''That's not necessary,'' Joe said, getting to his feet. ''As I said, I haven't slept in my own bed for months now. Jake and Katya have been too stubborn to use it in the event I might suddenly change my mind come some midnight hour. But that's not going to happen. I'll remain on my sofa, they'll stay in Nathaniel's room with the children and you and your daughter can take my room.''

''But what about Nathaniel?''

''He's been staying in the barn loft, and he's happier for it.''

Kim opened her mouth to argue, and knew it was the best she could hope for. If she protested, there was very little doubt in her mind that she'd blink and find them loading that bed into a buggy, with some poor horse named Goliath struggling and sweating to take it to some other house.

"That would be fine," she said stiffly.

"We're staying?"

Kim looked up sharply to find Susannah in the door. How much had she heard? It didn't matter. Her eyes were bright, and not with fever this time. "We're staying," Kim said with difficulty. "For a little while."

"Cool! I gotta go tell Rachel." And with that Susannah was gone to tell her newfound friend the exciting news.

Kim sat down again, as though her breath had gone out of her. She looked at Jake. She looked at Adam. "Bullies," she said finally. Then she paled.

That was exactly what she had said to them a hundred years ago, when they had all lived in that house on Decataur Avenue, on the rare occasions when life had seemed reasonably normal and they were just two average teenage boys driving their little sister crazy.

# Chapter 6

Joe shifted restlessly on the sofa as the grandfather clock in the living room chimed once. When it announced the quarter hour, he sat up. He had not slept well since Sarah had died, but tonight was worse than usual. His mind was full, his thoughts racing. Most of them concerned the woman upstairs in his bed.

Some of them were as sour as milk left in the sun, and those had more to do with the bed than the woman. He knew everyone figured he could not sleep there because he was reminded of the nineteen years he had shared it with Sarah. That wasn't necessarily true. He was reminded of what he had done with Sarah there that had resulted in her death and the baby currently asleep in a cradle in the girls' room upstairs.

That cradle should have been in his room. He should have been there in the bed beside it. He couldn't manage it, and his guilt over that was almost intolerable. He could not stand the sight of Hannah. His daughter. His own child. The child who had killed his wife. The child he had created out of his own needs and determination.

Joe groaned. *There's nothing I can do about feeling this way,* he prayed. *I'm only human.* But that was a cop-out. His weakness and his guilt were now poisoning the rest of his family.

Was that why God had sent Kimberley Wallace?

Kimberley. Her name suited her, he decided, prowling the downstairs rooms. It made him think of the tree in his front yard, sturdy and strong and magnificent, yet somehow feminine as its limbs dipped and swayed. It had withstood the tornado that had roared through Lancaster County many years ago, and it had done it by bending.

Kimberley Wallace "Mancuso" bent when she had to. He liked that. She hated doing it. He respected that, too.

He couldn't get her out of his mind.

Joe stopped at the foot of the stairs and looked up. He thought he heard the baby stirring, and he moved quickly for the back door. He went outside into the night, just in case she woke up.

One particular idea wouldn't go away. It had been haunting him all night, from the moment he'd understood the full magnitude of Kimberley's dilemma and that she would probably be staying in the settlement for a while. And it was dangerous and selfish, because it would allow him to continue to hide from the infant who had hopefully gone right back to sleep upstairs.

He had to get rid of all these well-meaning women, Joe acknowledged for the thousandth time. Neither he nor his children could tolerate their chirping, chaotic cheerfulness much longer. Then there was Nathaniel, who didn't want to go to Berks because he considered his father too fragile emotionally for him to leave. Dinah had missed two church socials in the past month alone. Matt and Gracie were so far reasonably unblemished by it all—except that Mariah, who still taught at the closest school in spite of her pregnancy, had said that Gracie was slipping in her studies. And Joe knew that that was because she was up late most nights helping Dinah with the baby. The aunts—in fact, all the women except Katya—went home at night. And Katya and Jake couldn't stay here indefinitely.

Joe needed help. He needed it desperately. He needed those women to go, but he could not bear to care for Hannah himself. He knew that he and Kim could help each other. She could get him over this hump, and he thought she might do it if he asked. She didn't *want* to be touched by anyone else's problems, but she was. It was there in her eyes. Joe had watched them all night.

He had simply been trying to judge her character. Clearly, she was beautiful. But he was a man who had just lost his wife. He certainly wasn't thinking about her in any romantic, sexual way, although he did wonder if she would be wearing those jeans again tomorrow.

Joe tore his eyes from the sky and went back to the house. He stood in the foyer, listening for a moment, and heard nothing but soft snores drifting down the stairs. He was immeasurably relieved that Hannah had indeed gone back to sleep. He would not have to wrestle with himself about taking a bottle to her so neither of his elder daughters would have to get up to do it.

He returned to the sofa and lay down, staring at the ceiling. And he prayed, a prayer that was no more reverent or worshipful than anything else he had been feeling lately.

"What do You want me to do here?" he whispered. "You gave me this fork in the road, you dropped her at my doorstep, so now give me a hint. Which way I am supposed to go?"

He received no answer. He never did when there were forks in the road.

Kim slept so well and so deeply it surprised her. For as long as she could remember, she'd been prone to insomnia. Yet here in this strange house, with people she'd only just met and others she'd lost years before, she'd let down her guard enough to actually dream. She could not remember what the dream was about, but it had left a lingering feeling of goodness that made her want to crawl back into it because the day ahead was not welcoming.

She opened her eyes, instead, and looked around the room. A bright, cold sun poured through the windows to her left. They were bracketed by white cotton curtains with small, yellow, embroidered flowers. Sarah's work, no doubt. Kim frowned.

Her eyes skimmed the rest of the room. She hadn't really

looked at it last night, partly because she'd been truly tired, partly because she couldn't have seen much anyway in the glow of the single lantern she'd carried upstairs. It sat beside her on the bedside table now, next to a thumb-worn Bible and a ceramic vase full of dried flowers. She craned her neck to look up over her head. The framed sampler quilt above the bed made her heart squeeze. It was the Lapp family tree. The baby's name had not been added to it. The woman had never been able to finish it.

There was no closet in the room. How could a man and wife live without a closet? Kim answered herself immediately. Because these people didn't have the extensive wardrobes of everyone else in the world.

A row of pegs ran high along the top of the wall opposite the bed. Those on the right were bare. On the left side hung several pairs of black trousers, some shirts—white and blue and lavender, all starched—a straw hat and a pair of suspenders.

Her heart squirmed uncomfortably, partly at the intimacy of using Joe's bedroom, of even being here to see all this, and partly at the idea that a man who lived this way could intrigue her so.

Is that what he did? Yes, she admitted, taking a moment to sort through her chaotic thoughts and impressions from the day before. He was so steady, so calm—in contrast to his troubled eyes. He was devout—a *deacon,* for God's sake!—but he had loosened the rules of that *meidung* thing in his own home. And he was sending his son away to a less strict settlement.

There was a strong and stalwart masculinity about him, and a pull to him that always let her know when he was looking at her. He had looked at her a lot last night. Remembering the business of "Sugar Joe" and "Loe Japp," she had decided that it was safest to ignore it. But he had been searching for something, she thought now. She couldn't imagine what it might be and wondered if he had found it. The thought that he probably hadn't—at least, not if he was expecting joy at this family reunion—left her feeling a little sad.

Kim finally tossed the quilt aside and sat up. Then she gasped. Oh, it was cold! She hadn't done anything with the wood-burning stove last night, the one that sat in the corner of the room. Never in her life had she had to arrange for her own heat. It had never even occurred to her.

She wondered where Susannah was. Her daughter had pleaded and begged to be allowed to spend the night in Dinah's room with all the other girls, and Kim had seen no harm in it. But it made her feel guilty. Everyone else was piled up four or five to a room, and she'd ended up with this one all to herself. Still, she wanted Susannah to enjoy all that she could, while she could.

Her heart squeezed again, hard enough to take her breath away.

She needed to find her daughter now, needed to assure herself that she was healthy today, so far as that went. She put her feet to the cold floor, shivered, and went to her suitcase to dig for a clean pair of jeans and a warm sweater. She found her toothbrush and her cosmetics case, and carried them out into the hall. Then she stopped dead. She hadn't thought to ask where the bathroom was, either.

"Downstairs," a deep male voice said.

Kim whipped around. Joe watched the way her tangled dark hair swirled. In the clear light of the new day, she looked young and achingly vulnerable, though he knew from Jake and Adam that she was in her late twenties.

"Thank you," Kim managed to reply. And she wondered again what it was about him that rattled her with his mere proximity.

"And yes, we have running water," he added.

Her jaw dropped. He laughed. It was a rich, dark, rusty sound—and he looked as startled as she was when he heard it.

"I never thought about that," she admitted. "No electricity, no plumbing. No heat." She shivered again.

"I thought of it for you. It's true that we have no electricity—the *ordnung* prohibits hooking up to *anner Satt Leit* power sources and becoming dependent upon your world. But we have generators and hydraulic motors to supply what energy we need. And we have wells and septic tanks and all that good stuff."

"Thank God," she said fervently.

His mouth crooked into a smile again. "Come on. I'll show you the way."

He went down the stairs, and Kim followed. The bathroom was beyond a door next to the one that led outside into the backyard. It was tucked behind the kitchen like an afterthought. It probably had been, she mused. In the daylight she realized that the house could easily be a hundred years old, though it showed signs of having been lovingly tended.

"Thank you," she said yet again, but he'd gone. Kim frowned and looked up the hallway to the foyer. It was empty. For a large man, he moved like smoke.

Probably because of the time right after she had run away, Kim had never stopped appreciating showers. They were the highlight of her day. They not only cleansed her, they soothed and relaxed her. But Joe Lapp did not have a shower. She filled the tub, instead, and sank into it. She couldn't remember the last time she had taken a bath. At first it beat all the blessings of a shower hands down. Then she began worrying about Susannah again.

She got out and dried off quickly, dressing anew, brushing her teeth with one hand while she worked the snarls out of her long hair with the other. She pulled on jeans and a sweater and anchored her hair into a braid, then hurried into the kitchen.

Joe was at the woodstove, and didn't hear her come in. She heard him swear mildly and was startled. Another contradiction, she thought.

"I can help," she heard herself offer.

He turned toward her. His face was such a study in torment that it took her breath away.

"Do you know," he said slowly, "that I never once touched this contraption until the day after Sarah died."

Kim couldn't think of anything to do except nod. She eyed the "contraption" and tried to gauge what he was attempting to make on it.

"I'm not much of a cook, but I can scramble eggs," she volunteered. "Although I'm not sure I can do it on that thing."

He shook his head and threw the whole frying pan into the sink. When he turned on the faucet steam hissed up angrily.

"I'm going to give up the challenge and throw some cereal into a bowl," he decided.

"Where are all those women who were here yesterday? Can't they help?"

His dark eyes flicked to her. "They're gone, thank heaven. Most of them were Sarah's sisters. They won't speak to me for a while now after I chased them away. And Katya seems to be suffering a spell of morning sickness. She came down earlier to feed the children, then she went back to her room."

"*Morning* sickness?"

"She hasn't said as much, but I can't think what else it might be."

Kim put a hand to the back of one of the chairs to steady herself. The Wallace clan was certainly blooming. She had never believed any of them would ever allow themselves the chance to procreate—just in case Edward's genes lingered and kept sprouting like a bad seed. Susannah, of course, had been an accident, though she was a beloved one. And Suze seemed to have gotten a good dose of Bobby Guenther's genes, instead, thank God.

"Are you German?" she asked bluntly, then she flushed. "I mean, not you particularly." She waved a lame hand. "Your people in general."

He watched her levelly. "Yes."

"So where does the Dutch come from? You know, Pennsylvania Dutch?"

"Ah. Well, it's kinder than some of the things they call us. It's not Dutch, actually. It's *Deutsch.* It's German, our dialect."

"But you speak English."

"Not always."

Her heart started pounding hard. They were German. "That's wonderful," she murmured.

"Is it?" He raised a brow at her curiously.

Kim decided not to pursue the subject. Not yet, not now. She looked around the kitchen. "Where are Jake and Adam?"

"Adam has a small woodworking shop in the village. He's gone over there for the morning."

"A *what?*" she asked, startled.

"He carves things, little gewgaws in Amish motifs."

"*Adam* does?"

"Turns out he has quite a flair for it." Joe went to a cupboard and brought out a box of cereal that looked somehow incongruous in this kitchen—a piece of mainstream America caught in a nineteenth-century environment. He poured two bowls without asking if she wanted any.

"I'll tell you, I was worried for him when he first decided to settle here with us, with Mariah," he continued. "I just couldn't see him farming like the rest of us."

"No more than I can see him carving little wooden gewgaws," she blurted.

Joe's half smile came back. "Chasing cows," he said, "trying to squeeze milk out of their udders. Can you picture it?"

Kim laughed, heard herself, and was shaken all over again. When was the last time she had laughed? Then she had another disturbing thought. She had probably done it around the last time he had.

"It didn't seem Adam's style," Joe agreed. "Unfortunately, there are limited things we may do here to earn a living, according to the *ordnung*."

"That damned thing again."

Both his brows went up this time. "Yes."

"I thought Adam was rich." She remembered Mrs. Madigan talking of glorious houses all over Texas.

"Not so much anymore."

"So he's carving gewgaws."

"He's opened the shop in the village. He sells them there, as well as quilting and samplers that our women make. It satisfies him most, I think, because he's putting a little independent money in the women's pockets. There won't be another Katya if he can help it. He's joined us, but he's done it on his terms."

Kim nodded. "He's a Wallace." Then she frowned. "What do you mean, another Katya? How can he prevent that?"

"If it wasn't for her courage, she would have been trapped here forever, depending upon others. She had to leave her husband. He was a drunkard and he abused her. But we don't recognize divorce, so there's never been any reason for a grown woman to have to support herself here before. She was trapped between two worlds, between the ugly intrusion of yours and the rigidity of our own. So she was living with Mariah and Adam, living off their charity.'' He was pouring milk into the bowls now.

Where was Susannah? Kim worried. Had Katya fed her, too? She opened her mouth to ask, and found that she trusted Susannah was just fine with these people. It wasn't as though she was off negotiating L.A.'s streets on her own. Had she been sick, Kim knew someone would have told her.

''I think Adam just wants to make very sure that if a situation like Katya's ever arises here again, then the woman in question will have some small income and independence to fall back on,'' Joe was saying.

''And the *ordnung* allows this?''

He hesitated only a moment. ''Yes. In this *gemeide,* anyway. We decided that since quilting and embroidery are acceptable pastimes, there's no harm in selling items to you folks and taking your money. We'd rather have the *anner Satt Leit*s pawing through our handiwork in the village than driving our back roads in their ferocious automobiles, crashing into our buggies and horses.''

Kim's eyes widened. ''Has that ever happened?''

''At times.''

She didn't have to be told that the result had been ugly. She felt a surprising spurt of indignation on behalf of these people and their world. She sat, scooping up a spoonful of the cereal. Cereal, for God's sake. She never ate cereal. It seemed so…wholesome. ''So whatever happened to Katya's first husband?'' she asked at length.

''Ah,'' Joe said as he sat across from her. ''Well, Frank came to our new *gemeide* and repented for a brief while in the hope of getting her back. If she hadn't left the settlement, she would have been forced to return to him once we were forced to lift his *meidung.*''

''You can say you're sorry and have that whole thing removed?'' she asked, surprised.

''Yes. We're not unforgiving, Kimberley, because God is not.''

''I don't know Him well enough to say,'' she admitted.

He watched her for a long time, then he nodded without answering.

"So," she prompted, needing to change the subject. "Katya's first husband?"

"When he realized he'd lost her anyway, that she had run and wasn't going to return, he saw no sense in staying off the liquor, I suppose. We all knew his being sober wouldn't last anyway. If he *had* gotten her back, no doubt he would have immediately returned to his old ways. As it was, he went back to drinking whiskey behind his barn. He missed a couple of Church Sundays, came to one intoxicated, and we threw the *meidung* on him all over again. Most of us were relieved to do so."

"But isn't he a threat to her now that she's come back here?"

"Not as long as Jacob lives and breathes."

She considered that a moment and nodded. Yes, she decided, Jake would fiercely protect what was his. She thought again of their discussion last night, of the sense of responsibility he seemed to feel for their childhood.

His undeserved guilt killed her appetite. She pushed her cereal away.

"Please don't tell me Jake's off on a street corner playing the banjo and selling flowers," she muttered. "There's only so much shock my system can stand."

Joe laughed again. Then his eyes became appraising. "No. At least, I hope not." He paused. "I like your sense of humor."

Kim felt something odd scoot through her. It was pleasure and panic. It was warmth and cold. "I'm surprised it's still there at all," she answered finally.

"It's what saves us, I think."

"Has it saved you?"

His face went hard and pained again. "No. But I haven't truly given it a chance." He changed the subject abruptly. "Jake took your car into Lancaster to get the tailpipe and the muffler replaced."

"What?"

Kim was on her feet again in an instant. She ran into the hall and looked around wildly, as though expecting to find her brother there, with that lopsided grin she remembered from her childhood, the one that said it was just a joke. But he wasn't there and her anger bloomed. She raced to the front door and stormed out onto the porch.

Her car was gone.

She stomped her foot. "Damn it, he can't do this! What's he doing?"

"Unless I badly miss my guess, he's making those amends he spoke of last night."

She whirled around to find that Joe had followed her. He was standing at the inner door. She gave him an indignant look. Joe shrugged.

"You were both shouting loud enough I'm sure people heard you in the next county," he explained. "I wasn't eavesdropping."

Kim's jaw hardened. "It's my car, my responsibility. I don't need him to take care of me! I won't allow it."

"I doubt there's much you can do about it. And would you, if you could? It makes him happy."

Her eyes narrowed. He thought, right before they did, that they threw sparks. He felt something thump in the area of his chest, but he made himself keep watching her, even as he needed badly to run from the way she was beginning to fascinate him.

"Stop it," she said. Her angry voice soon scattered his musings. "Stop trying to make me out to be some wonderful and kind and generous person. I'm not. I don't care about Jake. I don't want to care about his happiness. I want to fix Susannah and go home."

Joe nodded thoughtfully. She didn't want to open up, to care, to leave herself vulnerable to hurt again. But, he knew, there wasn't always a whole lot one could do to prevent it.

"Then tell him so," he said finally, nodding in the direction of the street, crossing his arms over his chest.

Kim snapped around again. Her poor blue Mazda was chugging up the street. But it wasn't burping and sputtering, and the engine didn't sound like that of a 727.

"Oh, damn it," she whispered. "Damn, damn, damn."

Jake parked and got out of the car. And he *was* wearing that lopsided grin. But not because any of this was a joke. He was thoroughly and disgustingly pleased with what he had done for her, she realized. *Tell me what you need, what brought you here. Let me give it to you. I need to give it to you. I need to make amends.* Unfortunately, accepting help and charity had never been her strong suit. She'd learned there was always a price to be paid.

Susannah was with him. She popped out of the car right behind him, and she was glowing. "Mom! Guess what Uncle Jake did."

"What?" she croaked, expecting to hear a recitation of the car's repairs.

"He punched a horse right in the nose!"

Kim's jaw dropped. "I beg your pardon?"

"Goliath," Jake explained, coming up on the porch. "I had to stop by Adam's place to find out the name of a good garage. His horse got out of line. Ate my cowboy hat. Snatched it right off my head." His expression was aggrieved, betrayed. "And here I thought we'd had a meeting of the minds last winter."

"That's a darned fine horse," Joe noted.

"With a swollen nose and a mouth full of good suede," Jake answered. He leaned one shoulder against the jamb of the porch door. "So are we all ready to head into Philly? I told Adam we'd pick him up ten minutes ago, and I want to see if I can buy a new hat while we're there."

Kim looked at him. She looked at her car and at Susannah's grin. She sighed. In the end, she said nothing.

# *Chapter* 7

They *all* went to Philadelphia. The Mazda held four—tightly. Adam and Jake had taken the two front bucket seats. Katya and Susannah shared the left rear one—they were both small enough to squeeze in side by side. Joe took up the right rear one in its entirety. Kim had been the last one to get to the car, and there'd been no other logical place for her to sit—nor had she felt comfortable making a big deal out of it—so she perched gingerly on his lap.

The doorknob pressed into her back. She squirmed uncomfortably. "You didn't have to come with us," she said through gritted teeth.

"Nothing else to do," Joe answered, his jaw equally set.

"You can't expect me to believe that. You have that whole damned farm."

"'That whole damned farm,' as you so eloquently put it, essentially lies fallow after the harvest."

Kim angled her neck to look at him.

"And harvest," he continued tightly, "was last month."

"This isn't your problem," she countered.

"So you keep saying. To anyone who will listen."

She crossed her arms over her chest awkwardly and accidentally thumped him in his chest with her elbow. He gave a small grunt. She tried to move forward a little so she could at least breathe without gouging him. Something happened to Joe's face. His expression twisted, then his eyes widened. And then she felt it, felt him hardening beneath her. Something happened to her breath. And her heart rate. One fell short; the other went wild. For one too long moment their eyes met candidly. Everything in them was naked, without complication. There was just wanting for the sake of pleasure, hunger for the sake of need.

When her gaze finally left him—that almost violet-blue gaze—Joe finally let himself breathe. When she'd first started wriggling, he'd known panic. When she'd kept it up, he'd felt disbelief. Now he was only horrified by how easily and readily and willingly his body responded to her, with absolutely no complicity from his mind.

He had to believe there was no complicity from his mind.

"I thought cars were against your *ordnung*," Kim muttered at last.

Joe latched on to the distraction of conversation, perhaps as grateful as he had ever been in his life. His heart was still thudding. The heat lingered. "To own one, yes," he said, his voice strained. "To ride in one, no."

"Now *that* makes a lot of sense."

"It does. If we owned them, the next thing we'd know the Eitners would be trying to have a fancier one than the Fishers."

"So what? That's America." Her temper flared as she fought against the instinct to move again. She knew that would probably only make things…worse.

"It's the part of America we don't care for," Joe answered shortly. "The *ordnung* states that no one of us should call attention to ourselves, to appear better or more attractive or wealthier than any other. Pride is a sin. We live together, equal parts of the same community. And not once has any of us had the overriding urge to lift a weapon against another."

She felt oddly chastened, which did not improve her mood at all.

"Here we are," Jake announced with jarring cheerfulness.

Kim couldn't remember the last time she had wanted anything so badly as she wanted to get out of that car and off Joe's lap. She scrambled out as soon as Jake braked. Susannah caught up with her as they approached the immense conglomeration that was the University of Pennsylvania Hospital. The Children's Hospital of Philadelphia was attached to the south end of it. Kim deliberately put several feet between herself and Joe as they crossed the parking lot. She hung close to Katya and Jake. Suddenly, their company seemed the better part of the bargain.

"Mom?"

"What, baby?" She looked down at her daughter, her voice automatically softening.

"How come you're not happy? This is what we wanted. This is what we came all this way for."

A million answers came to her tongue: *We'll test their blood, but that doesn't mean they can help. And I hate having to take anything from them, but for your sake, I would beg. Because marrow is one thing and two hundred ten dollars of car repair is something else again. Because that man over there with the dark beard and the depthless eyes has a way of making me acutely aware of things about myself that I don't like and I've always been comfortable enough with myself before.*

*Because he makes me want.*

Kim let out her breath. "I guess I'm just nervous, that's all," she lied. And then Adam reached over and squeezed her shoulder. She jumped; then, preposterously, her eyes filled.

They went inside and traveled an endless maze of blindingly white corridors until they came to the oncology unit. There they were introduced to a Dr. Reginald Coyle, a man Jake assured her was one of the top leukemia and immune deficiency experts in the country. The man had helped him in his search for the little boy and the appointment was a personal favor. They spent an hour in his office. He had Susannah's medical records faxed in from California. He took Adam's blood. He took Jake's. And he told them what Dr. Parra had already told them.

"This is a long shot," he said, folding his hands on his desk as they awaited the results.

"Why?" Jake demanded. "We're her uncles."

Kim thought of how she had protested, only a couple of weeks ago, that she was Susannah's mother. "Siblings are best," she explained, her voice strangled.

Dr. Coyle gave her an appraising look. "Yes. That's correct. Having two identical twins is ideal."

"So this is second best," Adam snapped.

"No. *Parents* are second best," the doctor countered. "Unfortunately, that wouldn't appear to be true in this case. As for more distant relations, an uncle has approximately a twenty percent chance of matching."

Suddenly, Kim was angered by his clinical tone. She searched her daughter's pale face. *Why does he have to talk like this in front of her?* She answered herself in the next heartbeat. *Because he's one of the best in the country and he can do anything he likes. I'm not buying his bedside manner. I'm buying his expertise.* She shot to her feet to pace the room, too crowded now with too many people.

"So if we don't match, then what?" Adam asked.

His voice had taken on a gravelly sound, and she looked at him sharply. She remembered that now, too: remembered that had always happened when he got very upset by something.

"Then we begin an ethnic and racial canvass of strangers, of the donor lists," Dr. Coyle explained.

For God's sake, she thought, Dr. Parra had been doing that. She had come all the way to Philadelphia to hear it again?

"What about a cousin?" Adam demanded.

Kim felt her heart squeeze so hard she lost her breath for a moment. Before she had met her brother's son, Bo Wallace had just been a potential donor. Sometime in the past eighteen hours or so, he had become a kid. She remembered his face at the dinner table last night. His laughing blue eyes, the scar on his chin. He looked so much like Adam.

"I don't..." she heard herself say. "I can't..." But how could she say no? How could she decline when it was her daughter's *life?*

"A cousin is an even more remote chance than an aunt or uncle," the doctor told her. "One more set of unrelated genes has been introduced—that is to say, your wife's."

Adam rubbed his jaw in distress, and Jake tunneled his fingers through his hair. There was a knock on the office door.

"Come in," Dr. Coyle said.

A nurse opened the door and handed him a long printout, the end trailing. The doctor took the paperwork and scanned it. Twice. Finally, he sat back and pushed his glasses up on his head. Finally, he looked human. Kim saw that his eyes were tired and his face showed distress. He didn't have to tell her.

"I'm sorry," he said. "Neither of you is likely to match."

Adam slumped in his chair. Jake swore.

"Granted, this is just preliminary testing. It will take a few more hours to break your blood down completely. But that doesn't usually yield a drastically different result—it might add one antigen, if that."

"What are you saying?" Jake demanded.

"At this juncture, you..." He nodded at him. "You appear to be the closest, with three HLA matches. It's not sufficient. Most doctors will operate with five. I prefer six." His gaze swerved to Adam and he frowned. "You don't have any matches with her at all."

Adam's jaw fell. Kim cried out and turned into the body closest to hers, the one right behind her. The arms that waited for her were Joe's. His chest felt like strength and solidity, and she wasn't surprised. Kim had the sudden thought that he was more than capable of being leaned on, and oh, God, she needed to lean now.

"I'm sorry," he said quietly.

His hand stroked over her braid in comfort, and it sent something shivering down her spine. That was when she became fully aware of what she had done, and she backed off hard and fast.

She moved to Susannah's chair, putting her hands on her shoulders reassuringly and wondered who was comforting whom.

"Oh, no," Katya murmured.

"How can that be?" Adam demanded.

"What about Susannah's father?" Dr. Coyle asked.

"He's passed on," Jake said, sending a glance Kim's way. "It happened right after you left, Kimmie. I—"

"I...we know."

"There must be *something* we can do!" Katya cried. "Some other alternative."

*We, we, we,* Kim thought wildly. She pressed her hands to her temples. *Yes, please help me,* something inside her begged.

The doctor looked at her. "Your husband's parents? His siblings?" he asked. "What about them?"

She didn't bother to correct him about the husband part. "His father's dead, too," she heard herself say in a flat, raw voice. "His mother is in a nursing home. No siblings."

"Do you have the name of the nursing home? I could contact them, have them draw blood there. Where exactly is she?"

"Dallas, Texas, I think."

He scribbled on his blotter. "What nursing home?"

"I don't know."

Jake shot out of his chair. "This I can fix. I can get you the information by the end of the day." Then a grimace passed over his face. "If I could use your phone."

Dr. Coyle turned the one on his desk around and pushed it toward Jake. Give the man credit for trying to be human, she thought.

"What's her first name?" Jake asked, looking at Kim.

"Ah...Gretal. No, wait...it was Greta, Grete, something like that." She looked at Adam. "Do you remember?" she asked. The Guenthers had lived only four doors down.

"Grete," he agreed.

"Guenther, right?" Jake asked. "With a *u-e?*"

Kim squeezed Susannah's shoulders again. "Right."

"Ah," she heard Joe say from behind her, as though someone had just turned the lights on for him.

She looked over her shoulder at him. She knew he was remembering her questions that morning about his German heritage. She met his eyes defiantly and he nodded, passing no judgment. And that made her angry. *Everyone* passed judgment. She wanted to shout at him: *Do it! Tell me I'm single-minded, that I'm only looking at all of you for what you can do for me.*

"I guess there's nothing more you can do for us," she said to the doctor. "Right?"

"I'll feed Susannah's needs into the donor network."

"That's already been done," she said harshly.

"And as of this morning, nothing has popped up," he answered, touching one hand to the fax of Susannah's records. "Dr. Parra was not as comprehensive in the data he entered as I'd like. I'll enter her needs again, in more detail."

"But won't that narrow the possible matches even more?" Katya asked.

"Yes. But neither will we kick out a lot of false potentials and get anyone's hopes up needlessly when we get a potential match that doesn't quite fit."

It was the kindest thing he had said yet. Kim nodded.

"I've heard of people putting pleas out to their communities," Jake said. "Would that help?"

Dr. Coyle nodded. "I wouldn't leave *any* stone unturned at this point." He looked back at Kim. "Where can you be reached, Mrs. Mancuso?"

"I…uh…oh." She gazed at them all helplessly, at Jake and Adam and Joe.

"She'll call you," Joe said. "We should prearrange times."

Dr. Coyle finally seemed to take note of the way Adam and Joe were dressed—Joe in his black trousers, his broad-brimmed hat clutched in his strong hands; Adam in his white shirt and suspenders. Kim realized she had already started taking the dress for granted. She had scarcely noticed it today.

"Amish?" Dr. Coyle said without inflection. "No telephones, then."

"That's right," Joe answered, his voice equally bland.

"That makes this difficult."

Dr. Coyle looked at Kim again and seemed to take in her thoroughly modern jeans, her sweater, the leather jacket.

"You're staying with them until this is resolved?"

As far as she was concerned, it just had been resolved. "I…for now," she said lamely.

"Well." He pushed back from his desk and stood. "I would suggest that you find a convenient phone and call in every forty-eight hours or so." He glanced at his watch. "It's one o'clock. Let's say at four-thirty p.m., beginning tomorrow."

She had no clue where she would be tomorrow. "Fine," she said, because she wasn't up to arguing. She turned for the door, looking back at Susannah expectantly when her daughter didn't rise from her chair. "Are you coming?"

"I'll wait for everyone else," Susannah said. Jake was back on the phone again.

Irrationally, Kim felt betrayed. She hurried out, moving as quickly through the corridors as she could without causing a commotion. When she reached the parking lot, she ran blindly for the Mazda.

*They didn't match.* Adam and Jake didn't match. Her parents were dead, and Grete Guenther was in a nursing home.

"Oh, God," she wept. "Oh, God, help us."

She neither expected an answer nor got one.

# Chapter 8

She ended up on Joe's lap again for the ride home. This time there was nothing titillating or intimate about it. At least, not sexually intimate, she corrected herself. His arm was braced against the small of her back, a steady, warm, even pressure. The contact reminded her of the moment in the doctor's office when she had fallen into Joe's arms. And at least one small part of her craved the contact. At least one small part of her desperately needed that human connection in a world that had been slowly and systematically disintegrating at her feet for weeks now.

Jake tried to improve everyone's mood by teasing Adam. "Do we remember what the milkman looked like?" he asked.

No one laughed.

Kim glanced at Susannah and threw herself into the joke. Suze probably wouldn't understand what they were talking about, but she would recognize the light mood.

"Wait a minute," she murmured. "I do. Wasn't he big and blond?"

Adam finally made a choking sound. "This isn't funny. I don't know why I don't match."

"Dr. Coyle said there was only a twenty percent chance," Katya reminded him.

"For *some* antigens," Adam argued. "But *none?*"

They fell silent for the remainder of the long, two-hour drive.

"I'm tired, Mom," Susannah said when they parked in front of Joe's farmhouse.

Kim felt something inside her scramble in protest. She realized then that she had been planning to go inside, throw everything back into their suitcases and leave for California immediately. There really was no reason to stay here now. There was nothing this Coyle could do that Dr. Parra wasn't already doing. But Susannah's eyes were deeply shadowed. She looked exhausted.

"Go upstairs, baby," Kim said on a sigh. "Catch some shut-eye."

Susannah didn't need to be urged twice. They all followed her as she woodenly walked up to the porch, Katya clutching Jake's hand, Adam's eyes looking troubled and faraway. He was still stuck on the antigens, Kim thought, and felt a twist of sympathy for him.

"Coffee anyone?" Joe asked when they were inside, then he stopped cold, his eyes narrowing, his head cocked. "Oh, no."

Kim listened, as well. A cacophony of female voices came from the kitchen. It sounded like a flock of frenzied sparrows in there.

"They're back," Jake said. "I thought they weren't going to speak to you for a while."

"I didn't think they would."

Joe began walking again. Kim followed him warily—and, she admitted, curiously—into the kitchen. Five women in Amish dress were bustling around. They ranged in age from their early twenties to forty-something as near as Kim could tell. The din was incredible as they all continued to talk at once.

"Look at the leftovers of this roast. It's overcooked."

"Sarah would be appalled. Do you remember how well she did roast?"

"Give me those diapers, Frida, and I'll see to the wash."

"Little Hannah's formula is low. Now, why didn't Joe take care of that?"

"*Enough!*" Joe roared.

The women froze. Only their heads snapped around so they could all look at him. Every face changed color, from varying degrees of parchment white to beet red.

Kim was hemmed in on every side as she took in the spectacle. Adam and Jake and Katya surrounded her. They had all knotted up right behind Joe, as though for protection, she thought. And they might need it. She just wasn't sure from whom.

"I told you yesterday," Joe said, his voice only slightly calmer. "This isn't necessary. You've got families of your own. There's no need for all this. God in His sweet heaven, *think!* Think what you're doing here! No household needs five women to run it smoothly! Please. Go home. This isn't going to bring her back. It's not going to keep her memory alive. At least, not in a good way. You're disrupting our lives. You're tearing us apart with the past. Think of the children. Please, let's move on."

They all stared at him. Finally, the one named Frida cleared her throat and sniffed heartily. "Of all the ungrateful—" she began to protest.

"It's been months!" Joe bellowed, at the end of his rope.

Kim stared at his shoulders, inches from her nose. She could almost see the tension there. He does get angry, she thought. He's not entirely unflappable. And his temper is a force to be reckoned with. She felt something odd scoot down her spine, something not quite alarmed, but not entirely comfortable, either. Men's tempers had always terrified her. But at the moment, Joe's just seemed...appropriate.

For some reason that she couldn't comprehend and could scarcely believe, she found herself reaching up to put a comforting hand on his shoulder. It was as hard as his chest had been in the doctor's office. But this time she felt the restrained desperation there. She heard herself speak, though she couldn't believe she was doing that, either.

"Don't you see?" she asked the women quietly. "All this fuss and bother only reminds him of his loss."

He jerked around to look at her. His eyes were hot this time. They made her shiver, too.

"I can fight my own battles," he snapped.

A little macho ego there, she thought. "Well, I don't mean to rock your boat here, but you're not winning the war."

"Who's she?" one of the sisters asked peevishly.

"What's she doing here?" another demanded.

"Where did she come from?"

"She's our sister," Adam and Jake said in unison.

"Another outsider!"

"In your home, Joe?"

In an instant, commotion descended again, everyone talking at once.

It took the better part of half an hour for tears to be dried, fresh accusations and pleas to be heard and for everyone to clear out. Katya finally poured the coffee the sisters had made.

Joe sank heavily into a chair, rubbing his face with his hands. He took his hat off and tossed it onto the nearest kitchen counter. "I can't take it anymore," he muttered. "Nathaniel can't take it anymore, but he won't go to Berks. Dinah's becoming just like them. My home is a zoo, and nothing's right."

They all stared at him silently. No one knew quite what to say.

But Joe did. And he felt the words come up his throat, a rumbling there long before they became actual sound. He was going to ask because he needed desperately to right his children's lives. Because it was the most obvious answer to all this heartache and commotion, and for some reason none of the Wallaces were seeing it. Maybe they didn't want to see it. Or maybe it wasn't as sensible as he thought. Maybe he was the only one desperate enough to contemplate it.

"Don't run home," he said, looking at Kimberley. "Don't run again."

He thought her beautiful, expressive face went a little pale, as though she was shocked that he knew what she had been thinking. But, Joe knew, it had been as plain on her face as the sun in the sky.

"I need help here," he continued, "and you can give it. Adam and Jake need you, and you need them, too, whether you'll admit it or not. Don't run. Don't disappear again. It won't solve anything. And I need you. Don't you see? This course of action satisfies everyone."

"What course of action?" Adam asked, obviously baffled.

"If she stays here, the sisters will back off. If she stays here, she can get Susannah help at the best children's hospital in the country. Dinah and Gracie can get some sleep again, and I think Nathaniel will go."

"Here?" Jake said tentatively. "*Right* here? In this house? But I thought that was what she was doing."

"No," Joe said flatly. "She's thinking of heading home at the first opportunity."

Kim flushed.

"Home?" Katya echoed. "Where is that exactly?" Then her eyes brightened. "Is it near Texas?"

Everyone's eyes came around to Kim. She realized that with everything going on, no one had ever asked her where she had been living these past many years. She didn't enlighten them now. Joe's words had finally penetrated her daze.

"You want me to stay *here?*" she bleated, panicked. "Live with you? Like some kind of a...well, what? A nanny? A housekeeper?"

"I was going to hire someone," Joe said doggedly. "I want it to be you. I'll give you and your daughter room and board. I'll pay you something. Please," he said again. "I need you."

"Why me?" she asked.

"Because it solves some of your problems, too."

He didn't get quite the reaction he expected, though he realized a heartbeat later that he *should* have anticipated it. Kim turned on her heel with a crazed look, then she fled from the house.

She went out the back door because that was closest. She raced across the grass, deadened now by the breath of oncoming winter. She tried to leap a creek she found at the edge of the property, missed her footing and splashed down into icy water. But she picked herself up and still she ran.

She didn't slow down until she reached a tree line. The forest beyond it was just a little too quelling to contemplate bursting into. She sat down hard on a boulder there, instead, and hugged herself against steady shivers. Her jeans were wet to her thighs. Her boots were splotched with water stains. An incredible wind was blowing up from the west, biting at her, especially where her clothing was sodden.

She heard his voice again: *I need you.* Her own inner voice responded in angry panic: *Not me, you don't even know me—don't you dare need me. You don't know anything about me.*

The man was crazy, she thought. For all he knew, she was an ax murderer. Yet he was asking her to come into his home, to take care of his children. It was naive. It was incredible.

It was also perfectly reasonable.

It was the way he chose to voice the request that had drummed alarm into her blood, she realized. She didn't like being needed. She didn't *want* to be needed. Dear God, she had her own problems right now, she thought for what had to be the thousandth time in the past couple of days. And the simple emotion of need implied a drawing in, a snarling of joined goals, of shared efforts. She was reminded of what she had said to Jake and Adam last night: *Eleven years ago we never paid any attention to one another. It was each of us for ourselves.* And she'd learned to be comfortable with that.

Yet both Jake and Adam had apparently gone on to care about someone else. She felt incapable of it. It terrified her. Was *that* why she had reacted so strongly to Joe's suggestion? Because she liked him? Because she could so easily come to care?

"Kimberley."

She looked up sharply and saw Joe approaching. He held a blanket out toward her. Solicitous. Caring. Ruggedly handsome, with need in his eyes.

"I saw your misstep at the creek," he explained.

"I'm fine." But she reached for the blanket, snatching it from his hand, wrapping it around herself. Her teeth were chattering, probably as much from nerves as anything else, she decided.

He sat on the boulder beside her. Too close. Much too close. Unfortunately, if she inched away, she'd be bottom first on the cold, hard ground.

"I didn't say that very well," he admitted. "I'm at the end of my rope, and finesse is currently beyond me."

She nodded. She didn't entirely trust herself to speak, either.

She cleared her throat. "It w-wasn't you. It's m-me." She closed her eyes, willing the shivers to stop. "It's not *just* you," she amended. "It's everything. It's Jake and Adam. They've gone on. I haven't," she acknowledged. "I can't. I don't want to get all...enfolded here. I can't risk it. Especially not now. There's too much else tearing me up inside."

"It wasn't easy for either of them," Joe said quietly. "They struggled hard. I witnessed both battles."

"I'm cold," she persisted, as though she hadn't heard him.

"We'll go back."

"No, not that way. I mean...*cold.* I'm not what you need."

Perhaps she wanted to be cold, he allowed. He thought he could accept that much. He remained silent, letting her try to convince herself.

"I'm selfish. I didn't come here for some grand reunion. I came to save Susannah."

"You wouldn't overwhelm me with care and kindness," he told her. "Well, I've had enough of that anyway."

She gave a choked laugh. She couldn't help it.

"Kimberley, just think of the practical aspects of this. Think of all those things I said so ineloquently back in the kitchen. And...be selfish. Think of it from the angle of what's in it for you."

She looked at him warily.

"If you go home, you'll be going back to a physician who's inferior to the one Jacob has found here," he stated.

She stiffened. "Not necessarily."

"Is this Parra an oncology expert?" he asked. "Or is he..." What had they called the doctor who had taken care of Hannah after Sarah had died? "A pediatrician?"

"He's a pediatrician," she mumbled. "But I'm sure he could find us an expert."

"But Susannah's chances are better with this man, right? Jacob said Coyle was the best in the country."

"He said *Children's Hospital* was the best in the country."

He watched her with one brow up. "You're splitting hairs."

"There are oncology experts all over the country, Joe," she said, suddenly weary. "I can certainly find one in California. This all just hit me hard, out of the blue. When I took Susannah to the doctor again three weeks ago, for more tests, I wasn't expecting her blood work to come back saying that she was *dying.* I guess I knew it was bad, but..." She took a breath and collected herself again. "I certainly never expected Parra to tell me that my family was the best chance of saving her life. So I just...reacted," she admitted. "I didn't look for a better doctor or a second opinion. I just set out on a wild quest to locate the kin who might help her. That doesn't mean I can't go back now and find a specialist."

Joe said nothing.

"What?" she demanded, searching his face.

"California," he murmured. "So that's where you're from."

She nodded warily, watching him.

"Quite a distance," he observed. "Is it true there are palm trees?"

She frowned. "In some places," she replied.

"Earthquakes? I read that somewhere."

She nodded dazedly. She was reminded all over again that for all his fascinating depth and contradictions, he'd spent his whole life in this cloistered environment.

"An interesting existence."

Then he changed the subject again so suddenly her head swam.

"None of us asked you this. Is there a man you must go back to?"

"A man?"

He was damned if he was going to hold his breath while he waited. "Someone of the male gender who you are...uh, currently romantically involved with."

"I...no. Not for a very long time now."

"A job?" he asked, trying hard not to sound relieved. Telling himself he certainly shouldn't care one way or the other.

Kim shook her head. "I took...well, sort of a leave of absence. My boss had someone who could work temporarily in my place. He'll hire me back when that girl has to return to school. And it wasn't a real coveted job to begin with. Except in the world of cocktail waitresses." It had taken her a long time to inch her way up to the hotel lounge she worked at now, a place with a reasonably good benefits package and substantial perks.

"You serve cocktails?" Joe asked.

"What's wrong with that?" she countered defensively.

"Not a thing. At least, I imagine there wouldn't be in your world."

"Well, then." She let her breath out and decided not to tell him that a lot of people looked down their noses at her.

He changed the subject again. "Adam paid the doctor when we left. They both want badly to help you."

Her spine went ramrod straight. "*Paid* him? But I have insurance through my job. I gave that woman my card on the way in."

"It was a hundred dollars. They called it a...co-pay?"

She wilted, covered her face with her hands and groaned. Between that and what she owed Jake for the car, her expenses here were running sky-high, and she had been here only a couple of days.

She had so little money left. Too little to get them all the way back to California. But that was going to be a problem if she left today or six months from now, she reasoned.

"I'll pay you a salary," Joe said again.

It was almost as though he had read her mind. Kim flinched and dropped her hands. And she heard herself say something she'd had no intention of saying, something that implied agreeing to his maybe-not-so-crazy plan. "That's not necessary," she murmured.

Joe shrugged and let the subject go. They could talk about that part later. "I have one last argument," he said. "A very, very good one, if I must say so myself."

"What?" she asked, sliding her eyes to him again. And she found herself thinking that their shoulders were flush, braced against each other, and that it felt in an odd sort of way as though it were the two of them against the world.

"If you're not going to rely solely on those computer lists," Joe said, "if you choose the avenue Jacob mentioned about canvassing a community, then you're certainly in the right one. How many German people do you know in California? You've already thought of this, Kimberley. You questioned me this morning."

Her heart started thumping too hard. "Susannah needs someone who's German *and* Irish."

"Well, I can't help you with the Irish part. But if you would care to check out a few Germans, I can probably offer you hundreds to choose from. And I can guarantee you, you won't find them listed with any computer registry."

She wanted to laugh at the way he put it. "What are you going to do? Snap your fingers and have the entire...the whole settlement or *gemeide* or whatever you called it line up at the curb to have blood drawn?"

"Something like that."

He wasn't kidding, she realized, her head swimming. "They don't even know me!" she protested.

"As I said last night, that wouldn't matter."

"It should!"

"Should it? There's not one person—in my *gemeide,* anyway—who would not go to hell and back to save a child, Kimberley. Which is not to say the old one wouldn't have proclaimed that your daughter's illness was God's will. But we broke off from them over precisely this sort of issue. We broke away because we couldn't tolerate that way of thinking, that extreme adherence to nonresistance where a child's life and safety are concerned." He paused. "Besides, this isn't about you. It's about Susannah."

She felt her skin go warm, because he was right. "We don't need to be here for the people to be canvassed," she remarked. "And if their marrow matched, it could be flown to California."

"Do you have a good reason to complicate this?"

She scarcely heard him. She was too busy thinking of other arguments. "Even if someone matched, then it would require surgery to take the marrow from them," she said. "An operation. General anesthesia."

"Well, they'd do that, too."

"For a *stranger?*"

"For a child," he said again.

She was overwhelmed. And suddenly, she felt petty and small. Because as he had said, this had so little to do with her own fear and hang-ups. It had everything to do with Susannah's life. There was no way in hell she could turn away from what Joe Lapp was offering. How could she refuse the opportunity to live rent-free within two hours of the best pediatric oncology facility in the country?

"And the way I understood it," Joe was saying. "Dr. Coyle is putting Susannah's antigen list into that computer system to scan against Irish, German, Chinese, Polish and Italian backgrounds—to scan everyone in there. I'm just suggesting that we try some German folks who wouldn't be listed in that network, widening the search."

She swallowed carefully. "That's true."

"So what can it hurt to draw blood from everyone here, while you're waiting to find out what those donor lists contribute?"

Her throat closed. Her eyes filled. "It can't."

He said nothing to indicate that he had obviously just won a point.

"There's still her grandmother. Bobby's mother," she said.

"Yes. Perhaps that will pan out."

"And maybe it won't. And if it does, I should probably have Dr. Coyle perform the surgery." She realized she was arguing *herself* into it now, and she just felt weary.

"How long are children generally hospitalized for something like this?"

She scraped the heel of her boot in the brittle grass. "Awhile."

"Exactly how long is 'awhile'?" he persisted patiently.

She dredged for what Dr. Parra had told her on their second visit after Susannah's diagnosis. "Something like a week for the conditioning regimen—for the chemotherapy and whatnot. And most patients stay in the hospital for one to two months after the engraftment. But in a lot of ways, this Coyle is much more stringent than Parra was."

Joe looked a little overwhelmed. "My Lord, how are you going to manage that co-pay thing on something like that?"

Her eyes filled. She scrubbed at them. "I'll be paying the bills off for the rest of my life, no doubt. But if she lives, you'll never hear me utter a word of complaint."

"Of course not."

They were quiet for a moment.

"No need to run up an immense motel bill while you're at it," he said finally.

Kim sighed. "What would you want me to do here?"

He answered without hesitation. "Help Dinah. I want her to be able to go to a church social now and again. And Gracie. So she doesn't have to get up at night with the baby."

It was such a simple request, she thought, shaken, and it was all for his daughters, not for himself.

"And make those women go away," he finally said.

A chuckle escaped her. "They didn't seem too enamored of me."

"Which is why they'll give you a wide berth. You're an outsider. You might contaminate them with your heathen, worldly thinking."

She narrowed her eyes at him. "Is the whole settlement going to feel that way? Am I going to be treated like some kind of pariah?"

His expression turned pained. "Not at all. It's just that the sisters...you'd be invading Sarah's kitchen. Hallowed ground."

Her heart hitched. "Presumably."

"What do you mean?"

"You're assuming I can cook on that stove contraption." She paused. "What about your children? Aren't you worried I'll corrupt them with my...uh, worldliness?"

He met her gaze. "I thought about it, but no. Unlike a lot of parents here, I *do* want them to be exposed to all avenues of life. I want them to be able to make educated decisions about baptism when the time comes. And I trust myself as a good judge of character. Amish or not, you have solid values."

She snorted at that, but the compliment made her heart skip an uncomfortable beat.

"Anyway, the sisters consider me a heathen, as well," he added. "They've never approved of my Berks County upbringing. As I said, folks are much less stringent there. Then, to add insult to injury, I led that uprising and pulled a hundred or so families from the old *gemeide* earlier in the year. Sarah's family came with me, but most of her sisters consider me a little wild because of what I did."

Kim realized that she'd like to hear that story one day.

"I'll give it a shot," she said finally. "I mean, as long as we leave the arrangement open-ended. I'm not going to commit to any precise period of time, Joe. Let's just see how it works out. It could turn out to be a disaster."

Joe realized he had been holding his breath. "Good enough. Thank you."

"Don't thank me until you've tasted my cooking. And if you think I'm doing all this without benefit of Pampers, you're crazy."

"Pampers?" He scowled.

"Disposable diapers."

"You throw them out afterward?"

"Precisely."

"What are they made of?"

"Some kind of absorbent paper."

"No kidding." He seemed bemused. "That could work."

"Trust me—it definitely works." She got to her feet, took a step, then looked back at him. "You're going to send Jake and Katya home, aren't you? No matter what you said back there in the kitchen about my spending time with my brothers." She figured if he really wanted to get his house back to normal, then booting out that faction of the Wallace clan might be one place to start. There were six of them.

Joe stood, as well. "I'm certainly going to try. Actually, I suspect Jacob is going to have his own mountain to climb, once he realizes that his wife is pregnant."

"That's going to blow him off his foundations, huh?"

"I think so."

They began walking, side by side. Together.

"Disposable, huh?" Joe said after a moment. "I wonder where that fits into the *ordnung*."

## Chapter 9

"I'm not going home," Jake said twenty minutes later. He looked around at them as though they had all just changed color. "Are you nuts?"

"There's nothing you can do here," Kim said. "You don't match."

"I can give moral support if nothing else," he said stubbornly.

"I can handle that end of it," Adam said.

Kim noticed that Joe was exchanging a pointed look with Katya. He finally glanced back at Jake. "It seems to me that you'd be of more use to Susannah in Dallas," he suggested. "ChildSearch has one of those newfangled computer systems, doesn't it?"

"A web site. Yeah," Jake said slowly. "We flash bulletins of missing kids on it. Advertise an E-mail address for people to anonymously send in tips."

"Can you flash a bulletin for a child in need?" Joe asked. "Can you do this to search for an Irish-German marrow donor?"

Jake's eyes narrowed. "I could do that."

"That's a *wonderful* idea!" Katya exclaimed.

"I can do that from here," Jake said. "A few phone calls to tell the staff what I want to transmit—"

"Jacob, *I'm* the staff! Well, for the most part." Katya threw her hands in the air. "I want to go home. I *need* to go home. Especially now that everything is covered here."

He looked at her dumbly. "You don't want to help anymore? You broke your neck dragging us all back up here in the first place!"

"That was three weeks ago, and something has changed." She stood from the kitchen table. "Come upstairs. We need to talk."

Jake watched with an immense scowl as she left the room. "What's going on here?" He didn't wait for an answer, but got up to follow his wife.

A few moments later, they heard his shout from upstairs. It was impossible to tell if he was astounded, overjoyed or terrified. Kim and Joe exchanged looks. Kim's mouth tugged into a smile, though she would have sworn it wasn't possible.

"I'm missing something here," Adam said slowly.

"Katya is pregnant," Kim volunteered.

Adam's mouth hung open. "Katya? Jake? Jake's going to be a *father?*"

"Well, I do think he already is," Joe said. "To Katya's children."

"Yeah, but..." Adam trailed off. He felt stunned. "Wow," he said at last. He looked at Kim. "How did *you* know?"

She thrust a thumb at Joe. "Old Sonar here picked up on it."

"Sonar?" Joe repeated, scowling. And that simply, that quickly, she was overwhelmed again by what different worlds they inhabited.

Maybe she was making a mistake staying here. Maybe she was making a *big* mistake. But she had no time to dwell on it. A sound came from the direction of the kitchen door. She looked and saw Susannah there.

"I thought you were sleeping," Kim said. "What's wrong?"

"Uncle Jake woke me up."

"He just had the shock of his life," Adam said dryly.

"Mom, I don't feel good again."

Kim felt the floor shift under her feet. She'd been lulled into a false sense of complacency, she realized as she rushed to her daughter. Susannah hadn't come down with a fever in over two weeks now. Kim accepted—intellectually—that Suze had a very big problem, but somehow it was easier to cope with without all the little telltale signs barraging them.

She caught her daughter's face in her hands, feeling for fever. It was there. It hadn't really bloomed yet, hadn't taken hold, but it was starting, the way flames licked in a furnace before everything started to really burn.

"Oh, God," she said helplessly. She looked at Adam, at Joe. "We have to go back to Philly."

"Is this the leukemia?" Joe asked.

"Not exactly. The leukemia weakens her resistance against...well, germs. It's just some...bug."

"Well, then, let's see what we can do about it immediately. No sense in making her hold out for two hours until we can get back to Philadelphia." He went to the stairs. "Katya!" he called up.

"What about Lancaster?" Adam suggested. "That's closer. There are doctors. Admittedly not on a caliber with Coyle, but there are doctors."

Kim nodded, shook her head. She was still holding Susannah's face. Susannah struggled away and sat down, a little exasperated, a lot weary.

"The thing is," Kim said helplessly, "this has been going on for enough months now that she's developed a resistance to a lot of medicines."

"Then perhaps this will help," Joe said, coming back into the kitchen. "Katya knows healing."

Kim looked suspiciously at her sister-in-law as the woman came back to the kitchen. Katya's eyes were twinkling and her face was flushed, as though she had just been laughing.

"Healing," Kim repeated carefully.

"Let me just see what I can do to make her more comfortable for the moment," Katya said. "I certainly don't mean to suggest that you not take her to a doctor. But it seems to me, under the circumstances, that it's vital to get her temperature down as soon as possible. A fever taxes the body terribly. She's running one?"

"Yes," Kim said warily, as the woman knelt beside her daughter.

"What hurts, little one?" Katya asked.

Susannah wrinkled her nose. "What doesn't?"

Kim flinched.

"Well, let's see what Sarah kept in the way of herbs." Katya got to her feet again and moved to some potted plants on the windowsill over the kitchen sink. "I think it's safe to say that whatever this is bit you before you got here."

"Why?" Kim demanded.

Katya cast a vague smile over her shoulder. "Because there are very few contagions here. The Amish don't mingle enough to catch them. For instance, none of my children even had measles until we moved to Dallas. Then, of course, they all came down with it at once."

"I've got a stomachache," Susannah said. "And diarrhea. Not measles."

Katya nodded. "I can fix that. Joe, did you plant pumpkins this year?"

"Pumpkins," Kim echoed dazedly.

"Yes. You need one," Joe stated.

"Just the seeds. Could you bring me a handful?"

He went out the back door, and Katya set to work at the woodstove. "I make a tea with them," she explained. "It purges the system."

"She *is* purging," Kim snapped.

"Well, she'll do it one more time. And then that should be that. It will wash the germs right out of her."

"I don't know about this," Kim said doubtfully.

Joe chose that moment to return with the pumpkin seeds. The area around the woodstove began to smell horribly. Susannah began to look green. She went back upstairs to their room.

Kim sat weakly at the table. Oh, God, she was so tired. So tired of it *all.* Out by the forest, talking to Joe, she had actually felt a little stronger. She'd developed a means, a goal, a way to proceed. But now it felt as though everything were shattering again.

Except...if what Katya had said about contagions was correct, then this was a very good place for Susannah to wait for a transplant—assuming she got through *this* bug. That was an added advantage Joe hadn't mentioned.

She continued to watch Katya put together a tray to take upstairs.

"This is for the fever," Katya said, placing a small glass beside the cup of tea.

"What is it?" Kim leaned closer to it and sniffed. There was some frothy white stuff inside. At least it didn't smell quite as foul as the tea. "I need to know exactly what's in it."

"Of course. Egg white, sugar and vinegar," Katya answered. "Nothing complicated."

Susannah had no dietary restrictions. The mixture seemed okay. Still, Kim blanched. "If she drinks this stuff, she'll throw up all night."

"Oh, no." Katya shook her head. "The egg mixture is for the bottom of her feet."

Joe saw Kim's eyes register shock. "Let's go," he said quickly, taking her arm, pulling her to her feet.

"Go? Where? I'm not leaving her."

"There's a phone booth two miles up the road. We'll call Dr. Coyle and find out what else we can do for her."

Kim latched on to that like a lifeline. It was a real, concrete, normal path of action from her own world. "Yes," she said tightly. "Yes. That's what we should do."

She let Joe guide her outside. She got as far as the porch before she had to go back for her car keys. Katya had already gone upstairs.

When she was behind the wheel of the Mazda and Joe was buckled into the passenger seat, she gave him a sidelong look as she pulled away from the curb. "Which way?"

"Keep turning left every time you come to a crossroads."

"You said it was 'up the road.'"

"A figure of speech."

She fell silent, then she let out a shaky breath. "I'll say one thing for you, Joe."

"What's that?" he asked curiously, and didn't like the way his gut moved because there was apparently something about him she liked.

"At least you don't go through a big macho routine about wanting to drive."

He laughed shortly. "Not if we want to get there."

She looked at him. "You've never done it," she said. "Not once in your whole life have you been behind the wheel of a car."

"No."

It was almost too much to comprehend.

"How often have you driven a horse?" he asked.

She gave a short, cracked laugh. "Good point."

He was right about the distance. It was just less than exactly two miles. She stopped the Mazda and looked dumbly at the little building he indicated.

"It looks like an outhouse," she muttered.

"It's not."

It was the shape and size of one. It had a very small window on one side showing a neat white curtain. The walls were covered to midheight with ivy. And scattered all around the base were the remains of last summer's garden.

She thought it would probably be very pretty in the summer, and she got out of the car shakily. She dug in her jeans pocket for change. She had to call information first to get the number, because she hadn't remembered to bring it with her. She'd gone through all the coins she had with her before Coyle came on the line. The operator was whining for more money. She told the doctor quickly to call her back, gave the number and felt guilty for cheating the Amish settlement out of whatever share of money the call would have earned them. She was losing her mind.

The phone rang and she snatched at the receiver. "Susannah's sick," she blurted.

"Yes, that's a natural side effect of her cancer."

"I *know* that. What do I do?"

"What are her complaints?"

Kim told him.

"Give her some children's ibuprofen for the fever—I've found that works more immediately than acetaminophen. And an antidiarrheal."

"What else?"

"Nothing else."

"Her other doctor gave her all sorts of antibiotics!"

"And they're not working much anymore, are they?"

She wanted to hate him for his flat tone. But she found she was comforted by his knowledge. "No," she said quietly. "Of course not."

"Mrs. Mancuso, the only thing that is going to fix your daughter at this stage is a transplant. My concern with the infections these children pick up in the meantime is that they weaken the immune system even further. The human body has to put up a tremendous amount of energy to sustain a fever. Susannah does not have large reserves of energy to draw on any longer. That's why whenever one of these bouts passes, she sleeps a great deal, probably even more so than usual these days. Am I right?"

"Yes," Kim whispered.

"And those periods grow longer with each subsequent fever."

"Yes," she said again.

"So we must get this fever down as soon as possible. I'm much less concerned about her other symptoms."

"That's what Katya said," she agreed absently.

"I beg your pardon?"

"Uh...nothing."

"Very well. Give her the ibuprofen. It should work within half an hour after ingestion. If it doesn't, call me back."

"How much longer will you be there?"

"My office will page me if I've left for the day."

Good enough, she thought. "Thank you."

"I'll speak to you tomorrow," he said, almost kindly. "Around this time."

"Right. Oh—wait. What about what my brother said when we were there? What about canvassing the community for matching donors?"

"As I said, it's a good idea. It's been done before, and it's often yielded fruit."

*Often.* She liked that word. Oh, yes, she definitely liked it. "That's what we'll do then."

"You're thinking to canvass the Amish settlement?"

"Yes. It's been pointed out to me that these people wouldn't be registered with any donor lists. They don't have much to do with the outside world.'' Her eyes went to the little window and beyond it, to Joe waiting in the car. Her heart and eyes both filled. ''Someone here will help me.''

''It's certainly worth the effort,'' Dr. Coyle said. ''In fact, let me know when you want to do it. We'll send technicians out from the hospital to oversee it. They'll bring a van equipped to deal with such things. That will avoid contamination and maintain a clear identification of the samples.''

Katya almost asked what something like that would cost, then she realized it didn't matter. If insurance didn't pay for it, then she'd find a way to come up with the money. Eventually.

''Okay,'' she said, and hung up.

''Well?'' Joe said when she slid behind the wheel again.

''He said pretty much what Katya did.''

To his credit, he didn't gloat. She might have been able to dislike him if he had.

''But if you don't mind, I'd like to run into the village and buy some children's ibuprofen just to be on the safe side,'' she said dryly. ''Pumpkins and eggs notwithstanding.''

''Of course. If one world's methods are good, then two are better.''

Her eyes narrowed. ''Do you believe that?''

''No. I'm reasonably happy the way I am.''

She let out a bark of laughter and started the car. ''You're good for me, Joe.''

''I'm hoping we'll be good for each other.''

Kim drove, and ignored the coiling warmth in the pit of her stomach.

They ended up having to go all the way into Strasberg to find a drugstore that carried children's ibuprofen. Kim decided to stock up on it so she wouldn't have to make the trip again. She filled her arms with all the little boxes she could carry and started for the cash register, only to realize that Joe wasn't coming with her. She turned back to look for him. He was filling his arms with the last of the ibuprofen.

Kim took a shaky breath. She just wasn't used to people *helping* her, she realized. And, surprisingly, it was the little things—like this—that had the most impact on her. A helping hand. An extra set of arms. These rattled her. ''That's not necessary,'' she called back to him. ''I've got seven bottles here.''

''Then twelve is better,'' he replied, coming to the register. ''Twelve will last until she's eighteen.''

''You'll be here for a while.''

Her heart kicked. ''Not that long.''

''Do you want to risk running out?'' he asked. ''You can't always get this sort of thing close to our villages. What if there's another emergency?''

There probably would be, Kim thought. It was the premise that had had her buying seven bottles to begin with. Five more bottles didn't seem worth arguing about.

Kim gave the cashier her credit card. The woman ran it through her little gadget and handed it back to her.

''I'm sorry. It's been declined.''

''Declined?''

The woman grinned sympathetically. ''I guess you hit your limit. Happens to me all the time. Got another card?''

''I...no.'' *This couldn't happen now. She needed this medicine.* She flipped open her wallet frantically. She had seventy-two dollars in cash left.

''How much is it?'' Joe asked.

''Eighty-seven dollars and eighty-seven cents,'' the cashier said. ''Including tax.''

''Oh, God,'' Kim muttered. ''Okay, okay, give me half of them.''

The woman started to collect half the boxes.

''That's not necessary,'' Joe said. ''I have some cash on me.'' He took a roll of bills from his pants pocket.

Kim's throat started closing. ''I don't want your money.''

''You need it.''

''Six bottles will be fine. That's almost what I was going to buy to begin with.'' Then something else occurred to her. ''And what in the world are you doing walking around with all that cash anyway? People have been mugged for less.''

''We don't believe in banks. They're—''

''Against the *ordnung,*'' she said for him.

''Well, no. Not exactly. They're just part of the *anner Satt Leit* world, and therefore to be dealt with cautiously.''

Kim closed her eyes. ''Oh, God,'' she said again.

Joe peeled off several bills and handed them to the woman.

"Please...you've got to stop this," she pleaded.

"What is it, Kimberley? Why is it so hard for you to take anything from anyone?"

"I take care of myself!"

"That's fine, as far as it goes. But this is for Susannah."

"I know! Will you stop saying that?"

"Will you take my money?"

"I already owe Jake and Adam over three hundred dollars!"

"Then we'll consider this an advance on your salary."

"I told you I don't want your salary and damn you will you stop being so *reasonable?*" she shouted on one breath.

The cashier's eyes went back and forth between the pair. The line of customers was growing behind them. "Should I take this or what?" the woman asked, waving the money Joe had given her.

"Yes," Joe said.

"Or what," Kim snapped at the same time.

The cashier bagged the ibuprofen and Joe grabbed it. "You," he said quietly, "are being ridiculous. I'll meet you outside."

Kim stared after him as he left the store. She fought a childish urge to stomp her foot. Then she laughed, shakily at first, a little soggily, and wiped her eyes again. "Damn him," she whispered, reaching absently to take the change the woman offered her.

"Hold on to that one, honey," the cashier said, winking. "A guy like that is hard to find. Ain't many out there you can shout at and not get a reaction from."

"Oh, he reacts," Kim managed to answer. "But," she added in a smaller voice, "he's not mine."

She followed after him. He was already in the car when she went outside. She got in and sat staring out at the parking lot for a long time. A cold rain was beginning to fall, and dusk was gathering hard.

"Snow by morning," Joe said mildly.

"It's only November," she muttered.

"It snows here pretty much from November through March."

"Terrific. Something to look forward to." She gnawed on her lip. "Thank you."

He watched her face, and her expression touched something deep inside him. He knew from both Adam and Jake that their childhood had not been an easy one. But he wondered if maybe the scars within this woman were the deepest of all.

"It's just..." she began, then trailed off. She wasn't used to explaining herself, she realized. "It's just that I'm afraid that if I get too used to other people helping me," she began again, "then I'll topple when I'm back on my own. Anyway...I'm sorry...if I made a scene back there."

"Apology accepted."

"I just panicked."

"I know." Still, he thought, she seemed braced for some subsequent reprimand.

He needed to touch her, he realized. He needed it badly. It would be as much for himself as for her, because he was the kind of man who enjoyed giving and what she needed now was to be reassured. He kept his hands to himself. Because she had agreed to stay. Because this wasn't going to work if he touched her. Because he'd never be able to live inside himself again if he liked it.

She finally started the car, and Joe breathed once more. Carefully.

The house was silent when they got home. Kim felt a flutter of panic. Had Susannah gotten worse? Maybe they had rushed her to the hospital without her. Maybe there had been no time to wait for her return, no minute to spare. Maybe that crazy goop of Katya's had had some adverse affect on the leukemia.

Before she could begin racing through rooms, looking for someone, anyone, who knew the answers, they found Jake on the living room sofa. He was staring at the wall, at nothing.

"Hello," Joe said tentatively.

Jake's eyes came around to them almost vacantly.

"Where is everyone?" Joe asked.

"Where's Susannah?" Kim demanded.

Jake spoke as though reciting. "Adam went home for supper. I made Katya lie down for a little while. She won't be cooking tonight. I'll go get takeout somewhere. The kids are…I don't know. All over. Outside, I guess."

Kim's mouth watered involuntarily at the thought of real food, of anything that wasn't wholesome and Amish. "And Susannah?" she asked again. "Where's Susannah?"

"Upstairs. Asleep. Oh, Katie says to tell you her fever broke."

Kim stared at him. "She hasn't had any medicine yet."

"Katie's stuff worked."

"On her *feet?*"

Jake shrugged. "It worked," he said again.

"He's still in shock about the baby," Joe told her in an undertone.

"Yes, I think so. Can his Katie do anything for *him?*"

"She's doing it. She's resting. I reckon that will last until they get back to Texas. If he's lucky."

"We're not going back to Texas," Jake said sharply. He finally stood. "I need your car keys if I'm going to get food."

"Oh, sure." Kim handed them over and went upstairs.

Susannah was asleep in Joe's big bed. Kim sat gingerly beside her, trying not to jostle the mattress too much. She put a hand to her daughter's forehead. Cool as a cucumber. Her head spun. "I'll be damned," she murmured. She decided then and there that Katya could smear goop all over Suze's body if she was so inclined. This bug, at least, had never had a chance to dig in and take hold. She got to her feet and went out into the hall, closing the door quietly behind her. She heard voices downstairs. Katya's was one of them. Kim managed a tired smile. Apparently, as soon as Jake had gone, his wife had popped right out of bed.

Jake, bless his befuddled soul, came back with Mexican food. Kim figured he was pretty much like a homing pigeon. He'd always had a huge appetite, and no doubt his stomach and his instincts had led him directly to the only Mexican take-out place within a hundred miles. Then they had guided him safely home again.

It wasn't great, she thought, biting into a burrito, but at least it was real food. She finished the burrito and reached for a chimichanga. Maybe it was nerves. Maybe it was relief.

Maybe it was two days of Amish food and good all-American cereal. She was famished.

"What?" she asked, realizing Joe was watching her.

"You enjoy this…variety?"

"Well, sure. I was raised on it." Then her throat closed over the food. The comment had come out so easily. Just as two weeks ago it had been effortless not to speak of her past at all.

"It's fine," Katya agreed. She was doing just as she had last night—sitting back from the table a bit. She had her own separate little bag of spicy goodies. "Then again, I could eat a horse right now if you just knocked the hooves off it," she added on a sigh.

Jake paled and swallowed carefully.

The kids—all the many kids except Susannah—were down at the other end of the table, reserving judgment but eating heartily. Susannah was still feeling washed out and had settled for a bowl of rice in bed. Katya had recommended it after the pumpkin tea purge.

Jake roused a little. "By the way, I filled your tank up, Kimmie. Your gas gauge was on empty."

That put her up to about four hundred twenty dollars she owed all of them, Kim thought, but she was too hungry to care at the moment.

"Thanks," she said stiffly, chewing.

"For the record, I also located a Chinese place, a pizza place and a fried chicken joint down in Strasberg," Jake continued.

"Good to know," Kim said fervently, eyeing the woodstove again.

"Perhaps I ought to develop a taste for this stuff," Joe said.

"Perhaps you should." Kim realized she was smiling at him and wasn't sure how it had happened, when her emotions had felt so depleted just a short time ago.

The back door banged open. Adam, Mariah and Bo streamed into the kitchen. Adam took one look at the food and said, "Wow."

Jake slid his chair to the side to make room for him. "Dig in. I bought plenty."

"But you've already had supper!" Mariah protested.

Adam sent her an apologetic look. "But this is Mexican," he said, as though that explained it all.

"You can take the boy out of Texas," Jake observed, swallowing a bite of taco, "but you can't take Texas out of the boy."

"Speaking of Texas," Adam said, helping himself to a chimi, "I called ChildSearch back. I figured you were incapacitated, Jake. They found Grete Guenther. She's in a place called Peace Valley. She's reasonably senile, but she's clear on one thing. She's sure she doesn't have a granddaughter. After that she got confused, cried, lamented poor Bobby."

Kim lowered her fork carefully. Though she thought she was calm, resigned, the sound she made was like a soft wail of pure despair. She felt Joe's hand close over hers. This time, unconsciously, she twined her fingers with his and held on. "No," she said. "Mrs. Guenther didn't...not even Bobby...I never had a chance to tell any of them I was pregnant."

"Well, I figured that," Adam said quietly. "But even in her current state, Texas law says we can't draw blood against her will. If she had a guardian, if someone had power of attorney for her, that person could give permission. But she has no one."

Jake threw down his fork and swore. It skittered across the table and landed on the floor. Katya jumped and Kim gasped. Joe watched him evenly.

"So go do something about it," Joe said.

Jake's eyes swerved to him. "Like what?" he demanded. "Bludgeon her until she agrees?"

Joe stated the obvious with such patience that Kim was impressed with him all over again. "Go home, Jacob. Go see her. Talk to her. Try to reach her. Convince her she has a granddaughter, and that granddaughter has cancer."

"Please, Jacob," Katya said. "We can come back. There's no reason we can't go home for a few weeks, then return."

"You shouldn't be traveling. Period," he snapped.

Something amazing happened to Katya's face. Color came high to her cheeks. Her eyes blazed. Normally she was so demure that Kim stared at the transformation.

"Jacob, would you kindly look down the other end of the table?" Katya asked in clipped tones.

"Huh?" But Jake looked at the kids.

"I gave birth to four of those babies, Jacob. Without a doctor. With just a midwife on three of them. Delilah—well, Delilah just burst right out and took us all off guard."

Jake went white.

"I'm not an invalid," she continued. "God help me, there are few enough things in this world I've had the chance to gain experience at, but having babies is certainly one of them." She shot an apologetic glance at Joe. "I'm sorry," she said quietly. "I would have saved this until we were alone again, but he's being so stubborn." Katya looked back at her husband. "Jacob, the vast amount of time, *nothing* goes wrong. I'm young, I'm healthy. And forgive me, but you're being absolutely silly about this. The only special consideration I want right now is my own bed. I'm tired a lot, but that, too, will pass."

He frowned at her.

"As I said, I know these things," she added.

Mariah had taken a seat with the children. She rested her hands on the immense swell of her own pregnancy. "She's right, you know," she agreed.

"All right," Jake said wretchedly. "I don't like it, but we'll go home for a while. *After* the wedding."

"That's fine," Katya said. "That's the day after tomorrow, and I wouldn't miss it for the world."

# Chapter 10

If anyone had told Kim three weeks ago that she would be attending her brother's wedding before the month was out, she would have laughed in his face. If he had told her that on the morning of Thursday, November 27, she'd be chopping a chicken into pieces for Amish roast instead of shoving a turkey into her perfectly normal electric oven, she would have had that person committed. But here she was.

Adam had delivered the birds to Joe's house at dawn. As near as Kim could tell, it was some sort of Amish wedding tradition that the groom should bring a bunch of flapping, clucking fowl to the bride's family, or whatever the bride had that passed for one. Joe had kindly decapitated them before he'd carried them inside in a big tub.

Then even the children had been pressed into service, Susannah included. She was feeling much better. She had gone with all the other kids to Adam's property, where they were pulling up weeds, scooping up the inevitable horse piles, even painting fences that didn't particularly need to be painted.

Kim finished the chicken she was working on and put a sloppy hand to the small of her back, groaning. She felt Joe's presence before he spoke.

"Tired already?" he asked. "You *anner Satt Leits* have no stamina."

She looked at him incredulously. "Us *anner Satt Leits* have the good sense to plan weddings months—even years—in advance." She couldn't even comprehend an American bride leaving everything go until the last day.

"Can't do that here," Joe responded. He turned his back to the counter and leaned comfortably against it, crossing his arms over his chest to watch her.

"Why not?" she asked.

"Because probably 150 weddings will take place in the Lancaster settlement alone between...oh, say, the end of harvest in October and the early part of December."

Kim grabbed the next chicken and felt her stomach heave just a little. "Well, there's your first mistake," she said. "Smart people spread them out all year." She paused, thinking. "Although a lot of us seem partial to June for some sentimental reason I could never really fathom."

"Because you're not sentimental." Or, he thought, she tried hard not to be.

"Probably," she agreed, then she looked down at the bird in front of her and screamed. As she'd gotten ready to hack in to this one, it had...moved. Not a lot. Not emphatically. But it had put up a small protest. Its legs were kicking.

"Sorry," Joe said, laughing. "They do that sometimes. I should have warned you."

"Is this a wedding or Halloween?" she cried.

He moved quickly to take the bird away, though it had stopped twitching. "We'll save this one for later."

"Real later." Kim pulled back sharply as he passed her, holding the chicken high. Then she realized she still had a handful of feathers. She shook her hand wildly until most of them fell off into the sink.

"Haven't you guys ever heard of Frank Purdue?" she demanded.

"Who?"

"Never mind."

His mouth quirked. "I take it he sells chickens."

"Smart man," she muttered, and shot a look at him.

"Do you know the cost of buying chickens in stores as opposed to raising our own?"

"I don't want to know, Joe. I really don't."

He'd tossed the more tenacious bird out the back door somewhere, she realized. She wished it good riddance, though she suspected it would find its way back to the tub eventually. Joe fished out a new one for her. Kim swallowed, closed her eyes and hacked at it.

"Better watch what you're doing there," Joe said. "That knife is sharp."

"I don't want to see what I'm doing."

He chuckled, a warm, deep sound.

"Anyway," he said, "we can't spread weddings out here. It's written—"

"In the mighty *ordnung,*" she interrupted.

"Yes. It's written that weddings can only take place between the harvest and Christmas. There's too much work on the farms any other time. Weddings would interfere with that."

"By all means, let's keep our priorities straight." But actually, she thought, it made sense.

"Given enough time here, you, too, will start thinking in terms of the seasons," he said mildly. He wished he hadn't said it as soon as he heard the complacency in his words. As soon as her eyes widened in that trapped-animal way again.

"Joe," she said carefully. "I'm only going to be here a short while."

He forced himself to meet her eyes. "Yes. We certainly hope so. For Susannah's sake."

"Right," she said unevenly, and attacked the chicken again.

"Anyway." He pushed on past the awkward moment. Because he didn't want to think about how much he enjoyed having her here, or how quiet and, well, dull his house would be when she had gone. "And weddings can only be held on Tuesdays and Thursdays."

She looked at him. She worked very hard to make her own voice mild again, too. "And what's the reason for that?"

"So we can all collapse in exhaustion the day after."

"That's the first thing I've heard all day that makes sense."

A smile got away from him. "We certainly wouldn't want to have to face weddings two days in a row. Or the day before a Church Sunday. Or the day after. So you see, with so many people getting married on limited Tuesdays and Thursdays during a couple of months in the autumn, and many of the same people involved in each wedding, it would be very difficult to start all this months in advance. People would be running around like—''

"Chickens with their heads cut off,'' she interjected grimly. "You know, I never truly appreciated that saying before.''

"Exactly,'' he said, his grin lingering. "It's far easier to concentrate on one at a time, at the time it's to take place.''

"Actually, I can live with that. It's these birds that get to me.'' She was grateful that the rest of them weren't moving.

"Let me help.''

"No, I—''

But he did. No matter, she thought, that by his own admission the kitchen had always been alien territory to him until his Sarah had died. No matter that she was reasonably sure he had never butchered a chicken before in his life. It would be women's work in his world. He took one and began cutting at it with more determination than finesse.

"You guys don't do Thanksgiving around here, huh?'' As soon as the words were out, she realized that that really bothered her. She wouldn't have considered herself so much of a traditionalist.

"Of course. If no wedding falls on that Thursday. It's a moot point anyway. What we do for weddings and what we do for Thanksgiving are virtually identical.''

"Ah. So...uh, how many people are coming to this shindig?'' This was a whole lot of chicken, she thought. "Something tells me it's more than the average Thanksgiving dinner.''

"Well, yes,'' he acknowledged. "There should be somewhere around 350.''

She stopped cutting to stare at him. "People?''

"The cows and horses don't count. They're vegetarians.''

She swatted him with the dish towel she had slung over her shoulder.

"We'll feed them dinner and supper,'' he said. "There'll be singing and snacks and festivities. And a three-hour service.''

Her hands went still. "You people really get into this wedding stuff.''

He glanced at her. "The bride's family—Mariah's family—stayed with the old *gemeide* when I helped break this one off. Her father's the bishop over there. The holiest of holies, so to speak. Very devout. Very rigid. Since she was shunned, they don't see her anymore. Normally, they would do all this work, so we're all stepping in for her."

Kim's heart hurt for Mariah. "They don't even see her on the day she's to be married?"

"The *meidung* is absolute. Besides, according to them, she's been living in sin ever since she and Adam had that civil wedding and moved in together. Worse, she *didn't* marry the man they more or less chose for her ten years ago."

Kim's skin got a crawly feeling at that notion. "You know, there's a lot about this place I don't like, Joe."

"There's a lot about it that I don't, either," he said.

She was startled to hear him actually admit it. "So why stay?"

"If you mean the Amish faith, the good far outweighs the bad. And if you mean in this particular county, this settlement, then, well, I came here for Sarah."

She knew he didn't talk about her easily and this time her heart rolled over. "But...she's gone now," she ventured.

"Yes. She's gone," he said flatly.

He had no chance to say anything more. They heard the front door burst open. More women poured into the house. This time, Kim noticed, Sarah's sisters weren't among them.

"I still say Adam's beard is too short," one of them complained. They were carrying sacks and bags brimming with more food.

"He'll have a full stand by springtime communion," another answered complacently. "Give the man a chance. He only just took his baptism."

The throng stopped talking and eyed Joe. He rubbed a hand over his own short beard and grinned. One of them elbowed him affectionately in the ribs.

They love him, she realized. She got the strong feeling that Joe Lapp could have run naked down the road and they would have found a way to forgive him. He had saved them from something terrible. That feeling was palpable in the air. She looked at him again curiously. He'd gone back to finishing his chicken. Calm, as always. A little troubled, as always. A complicated man with many layers. She dragged her eyes off him.

"Uh, now what?" she asked of no one in particular, dropping the last of her chicken pieces into another huge tub on the counter.

One of the women came to inspect the chicken. "It needs bread and butter, celery and onion."

"Point me at 'em."

"The bread is outside in Marthe's wagon. That has to be torn into little pieces, too."

"Okay." Kim washed her hands and headed for the front door. Several buggies were piled at the curb, hemming in her Mazda. Only one of them was the open kind. She went to it and peered in. There were easily fifty loaves of bread in the back—home baked, wrapped in paper towels. Very large loaves. "Good God!" She groaned and turned away quickly, then leaned her back against the wagon and slid down slowly until she was sitting against the wheel, cradling her head in her hands.

Susannah raced by on her way home from Adam's. "Mom! Isn't this *great?*"

"Terrific," Kim muttered. She vowed in that moment never to complain about cooking on Thanksgiving again.

By noon, somehow, miraculously, everything was done. The sheer number of things they had accomplished boggled Kim's mind. Then again, easily fifty people had chipped in.

The "roasts"—mixtures of Adam's chickens and the bread, butter, celery and onions—had been poured into casserole dishes. One by one, they'd departed Joe's home to be taken to various woodstoves elsewhere. Joe's own stove held four of them. Kim stood idle for the first time since dawn and looked around the kitchen dazedly. That was when Joe burst in.

"I can't find it," he said. "I can't find it!"

Kim's jaw fell slowly. Then her pulse kicked hard enough to leave her dizzy. He had on trousers, but he was barefoot. He wore no shirt. The chest she had leaned against a few days ago in the doctor's office looked no less strong when it was naked. It was broad, muscled, impossibly toned. A fine vee of dark hair tapered down between his nipples and dove into the top of his pants. She had seen a lot of men wearing a lot less on

California beaches, but as she stared at him, her pulse thumped so loudly she was sure it echoed in the room. She couldn't swallow.

"What?" she croaked finally. "Can't find what?"

"Adam's letter."

"He wrote you a letter?"

"It was signed by all the elders."

"What elders?"

"Me, the rest of us. Well, not me. Not yet."

"Joe, you're making no sense." What he was, she thought, was as rattled as she had ever seen him.

That made two of them.

He took a deep breath. "Adam had to have a letter signed by all the elders, stating his good standing in this *gemeide.* It was no small feat, either, after he just lived with Mariah all those months. Well, they lived together with the civil marriage license. But he repented for that and he got baptized, and finally they all signed the letter. I've got to present it at the service."

"And it's missing."

"It's missing," he said miserably.

"Joe, there are more kids around here than in your average kindergarten class."

"So?"

"Eye level—a *kid's* eye level. Wherever their little hands can reach—that's where we have to search."

He gave her a look that could have been either dubious or awed.

"I raised a toddler in a one-room apartment," she explained wryly.

Twenty minutes later, they found the letter stuck into the Bible in the keeping room. "Delilah," Joe muttered. "It must have been Katya's Delilah. She's the only one who's precisely that short. This house is a zoo."

"Well," Kim said, "they'll all be leaving tomorrow." She turned away from him, suddenly uncomfortable again. That would leave just her and Susannah, alone with him for all intents and purposes. *His* kids would mostly be off at school. She glanced at his chest and away again.

Joe rushed out of the room. She had a headache.

She followed him upstairs at a good distance to find the one dress she had brought with her. Something told her that if she showed up in her beloved jeans, she'd get booted out of the ceremony. She paused and thought about that. And then she decided that she wanted to be there. She wanted to see Adam married. After all, she was the one who had chopped up most of those chickens. It was nothing more than that. Nothing at all.

Kim rode to Adam's small spread with Joe and Nathaniel. Dinah had gone ahead with the other children in the open buggy—not to be confused with one of the wooden wagons, Kim had realized. The one Dinah had taken was sleek and trim and black. They rode in an enclosed one. It startled her as soon as she climbed inside. The dashboard was teak. The horse's reins trailed in through small slots there. It was carpeted and the bench seat was of some pretty nice upholstery.

"So much for finer automobiles," she muttered.

Joe glanced at her. She liked that he didn't have to be reminded of their conversation of the other day, on that uncomfortable ride to the doctor's office.

"They're all the same," he answered. "Abe Miller makes them for us. The only differences are brass or silver hardware, and the color of the upholstery and carpet. Personal choice, you know." Then he thought about it. "Actually, there's not much difference there, either. They're all some shade of blue or purple."

"Like your shirts," she blurted. Well, she had awoken every morning for days now with the things hanging on the wall in front of her, she thought.

"Yes." He cleared his throat and took up the reins. "You look...very fine."

Kim blushed. *Blushed.* She never blushed. "It's...uh, okay, then?" She looked down at the plain burgundy dress she wore. It was knit, with a full skirt that fell to midcalf. She'd had to wear her boots with it—she had never thought to bring heels. The dress itself had been an afterthought, thrown into her suitcase at the last minute just in case. Still, the ensemble wasn't entirely unfashionable. At least not in the real world, as she was increasingly coming to think of it.

"It's perfect," Joe said. What he liked about it—and what he hated—was the way it clung as far down as her hips. He decided not to think about that.

"It's not blue," she said. "Or purple."

He shrugged. "You're not Amish. And there's no rule about color anyway. Just prints."

"Prints are bad," she guessed.

"Too varied. Someone could get a leg up on somebody else. You know, if Frida had flowers and poor Gretchen just had plain old stripes, for instance."

"I see."

"As for the blue and purple bit, they just seem to be the fashion lately. For, say, the past century or so."

She laughed. She liked the way he almost mocked his own culture—fondly so, as though he were talking about a beloved but recalcitrant child. Then she felt Nathaniel staring at them. She glanced over at the young man, then looked forward again fast at his sharp expression.

"Jake and Katya are leaving tomorrow," Joe said.

"I know that, Pa," Nathaniel answered.

"They're going to rent a car in the city to get back to the airport. They'll be glad to drop you in Berks on their way."

Nathaniel's face hardened. "Berks isn't on the way to Philly—not last time I checked."

"Just the same."

Kim jumped when the boy punched a fist against his thigh. "I don't like this, Pa. I don't like it at all."

"But you won't do anything to disrupt Adam and Mariah's wedding," Joe said. "We can't argue about it now."

Nathaniel's face became mottled. "That's plain unfair."

Joe gave a small, pained smile. "I know."

"You can't make me."

"No. Of course I can't. But I can tell you that if you remain, you'll break my heart." He let that sink in. "Nathaniel, Kimberley will be staying with me awhile."

They hadn't told any of the kids yet, not even Susannah. There had been too much commotion with the wedding. Inside the tiny vehicle, Kim could feel Nathaniel's confusion and uncertainty.

"Susannah needs to be close to that new doctor fellow in

Philadelphia for a bit," Joe explained. "So Kimberley has agreed to take care of the house while she's here." He paused before he added, "And the baby."

"Her name's Hannah, Pa."

"I know that," Joe snapped.

Kim was suddenly aware of how horribly difficult it was for him to send his son away. When he continued, his voice was even more strained.

"This will give Dinah some more free time. And Gracie should be able to get some sleep now. The sisters will go. Crops are in. Farm's just sitting."

"Cows still need to be milked and tended," Nathaniel said stubbornly.

"Seems to me I've been milking cows for thirty-nine years. I'll handle it."

"What about spring? What about the planting?"

Joe let out a sigh. "What do we ever do, Nathaniel? We all help one another come that time. For that matter, you can come home to help, too."

They had reached Adam and Mariah's house. The whole rear paddock was already crammed with buggies. They were also squeezed in beside the small barn in the back. A few of them were stuck in front of the house. The horses were gone, presumably out grazing somewhere.

"Okay?" Joe said to his son.

"Don't have a choice, do I?"

"No. But—"

Joe broke off. Something about his voice made Kim's skin actually pull into gooseflesh this time.

"I will tell you this. It's one of the hardest things I've ever done."

With that, Joe got out of the buggy. Nathaniel went after him. Kim watched them walk to the house side by side, one of them angry, both of them pained, but...together. She rubbed her hands over her arms. His voice, she thought. Oh, the pain there. And the strength and the kindness.

*Don't think about it. Don't you dare let him get to you!*

"He's still in love with his wife," she whispered. "And Suze is so sick." *And I can't give him anything,* she thought. He gave so much to others, and she couldn't give anything at all. Especially not now.

That, she thought, was the whole thing in a nutshell. Oh, she could keep his house for a while and change his baby's diapers. She could stick a bottle in the kid's mouth when she woke up hungry in the night. But she couldn't *give* him anything. So it was just senseless to get too cozy, too comfortable, too involved with them and their problems.

She had tried to give something to a man. She had tried to pretend, with Mark, that she was whole and that the past was past. That the unset bone in her arm didn't still throb sometimes when it was damp. *Don't trust him,* an inner voice had always said. *Mark could go off like a rocket at any time, too. Don't let your guard down or he'll hurt you.*

Men were not to be trusted. She knew that. Her father had been a maniac. Even her brothers had saved their own hides first. They were willing to help now because their own hides were safe and sound, and she didn't blame them for that.

*They've moved beyond it,* an insidious little voice in her head said again.

"No!" she protested aloud. Damn it, she'd moved beyond it, also, in her fashion. She'd created a solid, safe world for herself and her daughter. She'd done it alone. She'd done it well, with what little she'd had to work with. And they would weather this, too, she thought. They'd found Dr. Coyle. Susannah would be okay. She had to be. And together, just the two of them, they would go on. Safe and sound.

Joe had reached Adam's front door. He looked back for her quizzically. Kim got out of the carriage on wooden legs and went to join him.

The people ate first. That was tradition. Close to four hundred of them milled between the house and the barn in the cleared part of the yard. Adam's small property was straining at the seams.

The food was everywhere. There were the roasts, and mashed potatoes and gravy. There was creamed celery, pepper cabbage and steaming rolls. There were home-preserved pears and peaches, and puddings and cakes and pies.

Joe watched Kimberley as she wandered about. His heart still hurt from his conversation with Nathaniel, but he found that watching her lightened the pain a bit. Though there were rows upon rows of tables set out, she didn't sit. She remained basically outside, her leather jacket hiding most of that dress. She watched, avid, curious and nonjudgmental.

Of all the *anner Satt Leits* Joe had met over the years, only two had simply accepted what they saw in this settlement or his old one in Berks. Both Adam Wallace and his sister seemed to look around and say, well, if this is how you choose to live, then go for it and be happy. Adam, at least, had never anticipated the peace he would find here, or that he would end up staying. Kimberley knew she would be staying—for a while, anyway. And she fought that peace tooth and nail.

Jacob, Joe thought, had been another story altogether. From start to finish he had pretty much bucked their culture, bending willingly and without reserve only so far as was required to save the missing children. And Jake hadn't stayed here.

One by one, his eyes found all three Wallaces, then they went back to Kimberley. Someone offered her one of the chicken casseroles. She shook her head and backed off fast. Joe heard himself laugh quietly. He'd been just about as impressed as he could get when she had actually rolled up her shirtsleeves that morning to butcher the birds. Like the willow, he thought again. Tough…but pliable.

He felt his throat close painfully. There was no good sense in coming to like her so much, he told himself. He had allowed himself to be swept away by his idea that she should stay awhile because he needed a solution so desperately. Because *she* needed a solution. But now that the issue was settled, he thought that a reasonable man would keep his distance. A reasonable man would cohabitate with her on a polite and proper basis.

But as he watched, her jacket slid from her shoulders. She was holding a plate, and could not move quickly enough to catch the garment. And Joe felt something heat inside him at the way the burgundy knit clung to her high, round breasts and nipped in at her waist. He decided that his hands could span her waist entirely.

He wanted to look away and couldn't. She put her plate down quickly on the edge of the nearest table and dove for the jacket.

Her long, midnight hair spilled forward over her shoulders, and his heart pounded and his hands itched to gather it.

"Inside, please, everyone," called a voice from the back door.

Joe glanced that way, and he felt his face flame. It was Paul Gehler. Their bishop. Sarah's father.

The older man gazed at him and their eyes met. *Does he see inside me?* Joe wondered. *Does he know I'm thinking about another woman, with his daughter not in her grave half a year yet? Dear God in heaven, how could I* want *Kim? How could I want anyone after my wanting, my selfishness, killed Sarah?* Sarah had been the only woman in his thoughts for half his lifetime.

Joe put his own plate down quickly and hurried inside. He meant to continue to keep his distance from Kim, but it wasn't possible. The people couldn't all fit inside for the ceremony. Adam and Mariah had no keeping room. The ceremony would take place in the living room. Immediate family was ushered in first, but that only amounted to Bo, Jake, Katya and Katya's kids. And Kim and Susannah. Mariah's family was conspicuously absent, as Joe had known they would be.

Adam and Mariah's closest friends came next. Which meant him and his children and the Stoltzfuses. Joe found himself squeezed in next to Kimberley on a bench close to the front of the room.

Others poured in behind them. The furniture had been moved out to make way for the benches, and Kim sat carefully, giving Joe a weak smile. His responding one was just as wobbly around the edges. She wondered why, and told herself she shouldn't care. She faced forward again. It occurred to her that this bench was going to feel damned uncomfortable three hours from now.

She was right. It was uncomfortable after *half* an hour. And she learned something else, another reason it was feasible for this whole thing to be pulled together in just a couple of days' time. There were no bouquets. There were no rings. No pianist or organist, photographers or ornate white gowns. Except for the incomprehensible meal they had just partaken of, Adam and Mariah could just as easily have eloped. But even that, she thought, would have required rings in the…well, in the real world.

Mariah wore a deep purple dress not unlike any other Kim had ever seen on her. And yet, somehow, she was the most beautiful bride Kim had ever known. She was radiant. She never stopped smiling. Her pregnancy seemed a bit jarring, but from the snatches of conversation Kim had overheard outside, she realized that everyone was celebrating the fact that Adam had accepted the church and that they had gotten married in it before the baby arrived.

As for Adam, he looked pretty magnificent, too, she admitted. And happy, so very happy. She was getting used to his beard, although it was coming in in about five different shades of blond and gold. He wore a black coat and a vest, and a small bow tie.

There were four…well, attendants, Kim decided to call them. One could hardly call them bridesmaids or groomsmen. They, too, wore their customary clothing—except the two men also wore bow ties. They consisted of Nathaniel and Dinah, and a young man and woman Kim hadn't met yet.

She'd meant to keep some emotional distance from Joe, but she found herself leaning into him a little. "How come Jake and Katya don't stand up for them?" she whispered.

"They're married, and attendants must be single. Not to mention the fact that Jake isn't Amish and Katya's been shunned."

"Ah," Kim said. She looked at her other brother and his wife. Except for Jake, there was a little gap of isolation around Katya. No one looked at her, at least not when anyone else might notice. There were a few surreptitious glances of pure bafflement and utter horror. It didn't seem to bother her. "I hate that," Kim whispered fervently. "I hate that they do that to her."

"It's unfortunate," Joe agreed. "But she's a strong woman. She can handle it. She lost a lot when she left here, but look at all she's gained. And I think she's wise enough to balance it."

They sat through another two and a half hours of what was essentially a worship service. They sang—in German. They prayed—in German. A handsome man with blond-gray hair gave not one, but two sermons. Kim imagined he was the bishop Joe had spoken of.

Her bottom hurt abominably.

After a long time, Joe got to his feet and stepped up beside the bishop. He handed over the letter that they had hunted for so frantically just a few hours ago.

"*Psst.* Mom."

Kim leaned the other way, closer to her daughter. "What?"

"Promise me if you ever get married, you won't do it this way."

"Not a chance."

"Of getting married? Or doing it this way?"

Kim caught her daughter's face in her hands and made her look at her. "Either one. We're fine the way we are, Suze. Aren't we?"

Susannah hesitated too long. Don't do this to me, Kim thought helplessly. Please don't do this to me now.

"Yeah," Susannah said finally. "We're cool. I guess."

"Good," Kim whispered hoarsely.

"It's just nice having all these cousins around. It's like...a family, you know? I never knew I'd like it so much."

Kim was still searching for a response to that, when she realized the ceremony was over. People all around them were getting to their feet. She jerked around again to find Joe. He had come back to sit beside her while she had been speaking with Susannah. "That's it?" she demanded.

He stood, as well, and stretched. "That's it."

"Three hours of services, and just five minutes of 'Who gives this woman'? I missed it!"

He looked at her blankly. "Who gives what?"

She groaned. "Never mind."

"God blesses their union. That's all that matters."

Suddenly, she felt an overriding need to get away. Why hadn't she realized before how claustrophobic this living room was? How hot? So many bodies, so much heat. Kim moved quickly for the door. Joe moved with her.

"Susannah wants cousins," she blurted, stepping outside, breathing deeply of the cold, clean air.

"Well, she has several of them."

"But—"

"But you're still not convinced you'll stay in touch with your brothers once this is all over," Joe said for her.

She didn't answer, and that was answer in itself. She refused to let him make her feel guilty over it. She brought her chin up a notch and looked at him defiantly. But...he didn't look remorseful, she realized. It had just been a statement of fact.

"Why don't you just take one thing at a time?" Joe suggested.

Reasonably, as always, Kim thought, and couldn't stop herself from asking, "Are you always so...so calm? So sensible?"

His face hardened. "No. It seems I'm only able to give such good advice to others."

He moved off then and left her. She was relieved, of course. Of course, she was. There was no sense in getting too cozy here, too dependent upon his company, his friendship. In fact, if she had half a brain in her head, she would gather a few *new* friends here at the wedding. She looked around at the throng dismally, then she went to a reasonably isolated area of bench and sat by herself. She watched helplessly as Susannah raced off with her cousins.

It was dark and the moon was high before Joe climbed up on one of the tables to stand head and shoulders over the crowd. They'd eaten—again—although the second meal had been comparatively lighter. Kim had listened as much speculation was bandied back and forth when several of the young people paired off. She was a little amazed to learn that this was their first public "appearance" together, that they'd actually been sneaking into each others' keeping rooms all year after dark. It was, she ascertained, some kind of courting ritual.

She was also staggered to realize that these kids would be expected to marry, as well, now that they'd taken this step of going public. They seemed like such babies, she thought. They were barely out of their teens, and some of them weren't even that old! Did they even know what they were getting into?

"There's something I need to speak to you all about before any of you begin leaving," Joe called out.

Kim snapped her attention to him again. She knew what was coming.

"As I'm sure you're all aware, Adam and Jacob's sister has been staying at my home. I wanted to be the first to tell you that she'll be staying for a little while longer. Her daughter is gravely ill and needs our help, as well as proximity to a hospital in Philadelphia."

Voices murmured. She heard several people offer whatever they could—just like that. She felt faint. He had warned her. Still...

"The first thing we need to do for her is give blood samples. An *anner Satt Leit* doctor will come to my farm at a time I'll notify you of later. He'll take a small amount of blood from each of you who would like to help. Susannah needs special blood, and there's only a slim chance that any of us will match. But I think God would want us to try, just as we sought outside help earlier in the year to look for our children. It's my heartfelt belief that helping Susannah Wallace is no different, and I hope you'll agree with me."

A chorus of voices sang out yes at that. Kim went hot, then cold. Just like that, she thought wildly. Just like that, they would help. Her eyes filled.

"What if we do match?" someone shouted. "What then?"

"Then she'll need some of your bone marrow."

Another uproar followed about this, but mostly it was just questions about how such a thing could be removed from the human body.

"I'm sure the medical people will explain all that when they come," Joe said. And that was good enough for the crowd.

His eyes met hers. *I told you so.*

Hers clung to his. *I owe you so much.*

This was so much more than money, she thought, so much more than holding a few bottles of ibuprofen or her hand when the news was bad. Even if no one here matched, it didn't negate his gift, this effort.

"Thank you." She mouthed the words at him.

He came down off the table and gave her arm a quick squeeze. "See? It gets easier to say that all the time."

# Chapter 11

Kim awoke earlier than usual on Saturday morning. It took her all of ten seconds to realize why. Something felt different. The house was inordinately quiet. Everyone had gone.

Jake and Katya had left yesterday afternoon. They had taken Nathaniel to Berks County. Yesterday morning, fourteen people had been crammed into the various bedrooms. Today there were only seven.

The sun was just up, its light new and pure and thin. Kim sat up and put her feet warily to the floor. She was learning. She'd taken to shoving some wood into the stove each night before she slept. Not enough, obviously, to keep it burning through the night, but the chill was somewhat less today, so this fire had lasted the longest. She got up, collected her clothing and toiletries and headed downstairs to the bathroom.

As soon as she reached the ground floor, she heard a steady thumping from outside. Curious, she reversed direction and went to the front door, then out onto the porch. Joe was already up on the roof of one of the barns across the road, hammering away. She decided to leave him be and went to take a bath. Twenty minutes later, she came out and heard the baby crying upstairs. It was time to start earning her keep.

She went to Dinah's room. The door was closed. The baby's hungry wails came loud and clear from the other side. Kim knocked once and got no response. She knocked again, harder.

"What?" Dinah shouted.

"Can I come in?"

"I don't care."

Kim cracked open the door. Only Dinah and Hannah were inside. The baby was howling in her cradle while Dinah hurriedly finished dressing.

"Where is everybody?" Kim asked.

"Susannah is in Gracie's room. I guess that's who you mean."

There was something defensive in Dinah's voice, Kim realized. "I meant everyone in general," she said quietly.

"Oh. Well, I guess Matt's still sleeping. Pa's outside."

"Yes. I saw him."

The girl tied her apron on with quick, hard tugs. "Then what did you ask me for?"

Kim held her tongue. "Would you like me to feed the baby?" she offered.

Dinah looked up immediately. Her eyes were angry. "I can do it. I always do it."

Kim started to turn away. She felt incapable of dealing with the girl's resentment right now. She wasn't entirely thrilled with this situation, either, but it was necessary on a lot of fronts. She got as far as the door and stopped.

Dinah was only a few years older than Susannah, she realized. She was just a kid, really. A confused, bereaved kid with too much responsibility on her shoulders. And now there were more changes—two strangers in her home, trying to edge in on the one area that had been allowing her to cope. Kim took a shaky breath and turned back to her.

"If you take care of the baby, that means I have to cook on that stove," she said. "And I don't know how to."

Dinah narrowed her eyes suspiciously. "Katya showed you yesterday."

"She did. But I haven't tried it yet. How hungry are you?"

Dinah went to the cradle and gathered the baby. "I'm okay."

"She's not."

There was a long, stiff silence.

"Please cook. Feeding the baby is something I can handle. As for the stove...well, at least let me watch how it's done one more time before I attempt it myself."

Dinah looked at her uncertainly. "I guess that would be okay."

It wasn't quite a concession, or at least it wasn't a big one, but Kim took it as one. "Thanks."

Dinah handed her the baby. It had been more than nine years since Kim had held an infant. It all came back to her in a flood—the pure fragility of a child so young, the dependency, the sweet and simple responses. A finger to hold on to brought a smile. A soft breast to nestle against brought sleep. Hunger brought complaint.

She carried the baby downstairs behind Dinah. The girl went to the woodstove, poked around at the embers inside a bit, then she laid two small logs upon them.

"This stove in the kitchen always stays low," she explained, still somewhat rigidly. "The ones in the rest of the house we burn hot for heat."

"Okay."

"Too much heat in this one would scorch the food."

"Sure."

"It takes longer to cook things, but at least nothing gets fried."

"Your aunts were complaining that the roast was overcooked the other night," Kim volunteered, filling a bottle with the last of the formula. She'd have to go into the village to get some more, she thought. She could call Jake while she was there and see if he had had any luck with Grete Guenther yet. Probably not. He'd scarcely been home twelve hours.

"What?" she asked, realizing Dinah was still speaking.

"I said the aunts will find something to complain about in heaven," Dinah repeated.

Kim laughed. "I gathered that."

"Mom wasn't like them."

Silence fell abruptly. Dinah turned back to the stove again quickly, but Kim saw her eyes fill just before she moved. "This has got to be hard on you," Kim ventured, trying to chip out an opening for communication.

"It's hardest on Pa."

Dinah wasn't cooking. She'd crossed her arms over her waist. Kim saw her shoulders shake. She ducked her head. Kim's heart spasmed with sympathy. Oh, God, she didn't know the right thing to say now. She was so *bad* with emotion. Giving comfort to virtual strangers was so alien to her. She had so rarely received it and didn't know how to offer it.

"Why did he have to do it?" Dinah burst out, spinning around again. *"Why?"*

"Who?" Kim asked carefully. Was Dinah talking about the God who was such a big part of their lives or her father?

"Pa," she sobbed. "*Pa.* They *knew* she couldn't have more babies. I...I heard them talking once. They said it was dangerous for her. But he did it anyway, and now everything's horrible and *I miss her!*"

"That's enough, Dinah."

Joe's voice lashed into the kitchen like a whip. Kim gasped and whipped around to look at him. His eyes were as tormented as she had ever seen them. And for once he was not wise, not kind, not seeming to care for his daughter's pain. He had enough of his own. What had she walked into here? Kim knew she should come to Dinah's defense. But the girl shoved past both of them before Kim could think of what to say. Dinah raced from the room. Joe only stood rooted.

"Well, great," Kim muttered. "Who's supposed to cook now?"

"I'll do it." Still, he made no move to cross to the stove.

"No, thanks," she answered shortly. "I saw that mess you threw into the sink the other day."

He took off his hat and raked a hand through his hair, then he plunked the hat back on again. "What do you want from me, Kimberley?"

*I want you to be the man I was getting used to knowing. I want you to be strong so I can be weak.* Kim felt her skin heat. "Here," she snapped. "Take Hannah. I'll give the damned stove a shot."

He jerked back so fast his back hit the door frame. He swore, and this time it wasn't mild.

"Joe, for God's sake—"

"Forget breakfast," he growled. "Give them cereal. I've

got to get back to that roof.'' And with that, he was gone again.

Kim moved out into the hallway to stare after him. She heard Dinah crying softly from behind her. She had gone out the back door.

''Well, hell,'' Kim mumbled. She went after Dinah. It seemed safer.

The girl was sitting on the single step that led down from the back porch. A water pump stood right beyond it. Dinah jiggled the handle up and down, up and down, nervously. Kim sat next to her, still cradling the baby. Old habits came back instinctively. She braced the bottle with her chin to tuck the little blanket tighter around Hannah. It was cold out, colder even than it had been yesterday.

''He didn't mean that,'' she said finally. ''You know, to be so...harsh.''

Dinah wouldn't look at her.

''I think he's just...'' She closed her eyes, feeling overwhelmed all over again by this situation. And inadequate to the task. ''If what you say is true, if they knew your mom couldn't get pregnant, then I think he must feel guilty about it all,'' Kim stated. And, she thought, that went a long way toward explaining his behavior toward Hannah. Poor babe. She touched her lips to her cheek.

''Pa's too smart for that,'' Dinah said tightly.

''You blame him,'' Kim declared bluntly. ''And you seem smart.''

Dinah finally glanced her way, then her eyes shot away again. ''It's just...you know...if you know something's gonna hurt you, then don't *do* it.''

''It's not always that easy,'' Kim murmured.

Dinah averted her eyes. Tricky ground here, Kim thought. She took a deep breath. ''When I was a kid,'' she began, ''there was always a box of doughnuts in the bottom drawer of the fridge. They were off-limits. They were for my father. Sometimes they would sit there for days at a time, going stale. It didn't matter. He'd rather see them tossed out than have any of us eat one.''

Dinah gaped at her, clearly shocked. ''That's mean!''

Kim winced, then forced herself to nod. ''Sometimes it

drove me nuts just knowing they were there. I'd sit upstairs in my room, and I could just *taste* them. Sometimes I just had to take one, even though—'' *I was going to get beaten within an inch of my life for it* ''—even though…he'd punish me for it,'' she said less graphically for Dinah's sake. ''Do you get what I'm saying here?''

Dinah jiggled the pump handle harder.

''Sometimes you can want something even more than you fear it,'' Kim continued. And her own words sent an uncertain tingle down her spine.

Dinah sniffed and dragged a hand over her cheek.

''Granted, I don't have a lot of experience with men,'' Kim said carefully, ''but I'd almost bet that that's what happened with your dad. The men I've known haven't been like your father, but….'' She trailed off as the enormity of that statement [illegible], [illegible] she rushed on, around it. ''But anyway, it makes sense to [illegible].''

Dinah covered her face with her hands. ''What're we gonna do? Everything seems so sad all the time.''

[illegible] ''I don't know,'' she admitted. She stood again. ''But for now, let me just lay the baby down and I'll pour out some cereal. That I can handle.'' Her bottle mostly finished, Hannah was already dozing, impervious to all the tension around her. Oh, to be a baby again, Kim thought.

''I'd better wake up Gracie and Matt,'' Dinah said. ''Make them get ready for school. Gracie takes *forever.*''

''Dinah.''

''What?''

''It's Saturday.''

And just like that, the girl started crying again. Kim sat beside her one more time and put an arm around her awkwardly, cradling the baby with the other.

So much for having her own problems.

It was nearly noon before Kim saw Joe again. On the one hand, she was relieved. At least it seemed clear that he wouldn't be hanging around all the time, close by, making her think, making her…feel things. Asking for emotion, for the kind of altruistic, honest reactions that she'd buried so deeply so long ago. On the other hand, she was pretty sure he was avoiding her. Or maybe it was just the house. After their spat this morning, maybe it was even Dinah he was steering clear of, although he had been out on the barn roof long before Dinah came downstairs.

Kim managed to boil some eggs on the woodstove with reasonable success, and she made egg salad sandwiches for lunch. She battled her way through two cloth diapers. That was going to be the end of *that,* she thought again. She set plates out on the table. Dinah came downstairs from whatever she had been doing in her room. Susannah and Gracie came inside from playing in the side yard. Matt didn't come back. And Joe was still stubbornly out on the barn roof.

"Where's Matt?" Kim asked the girls.

"Playing with Bo. He went there as soon as chores were done," Gracie answered, biting into a sandwich. "Hey, this is pretty good."

Kim longed for a telephone so she could just call Mariah and make sure Matt was okay. Five kids was a little more than she had ever thought she would have to take care of. Instead, she looked at Dinah. "Hold the fort for me?" she asked.

"I always do."

So they were back to that again. But it seemed to her that maybe there was a little less resentment in the girl's tone this time. Kim turned away and started rummaging through some stuff on the counter, looking for her keys.

"Where're you going?" Susannah asked, snapping her head up from her plate when she heard the telltale jingle.

"I have some errands to do. Hannah needs formula. And I want to call Uncle Jake." She would swing by Adam's house on the way, to check on Matt. "Do you feel okay?"

Susannah rolled her eyes. "Yes."

*Please, God,* Kim prayed, *let her just keep thinking I'm a nuisance and always answer just like that.* Then she realized what she was doing, and her throat squeezed shut.

"Well," she answered tightly, "I won't be long."

She went outside. She felt as though she was escaping, and that made her feel guilty. Then she looked up at Joe on the barn roof. She'd crossed the road when she hadn't meant to, moving past the Mazda. She stopped beneath him and stared up. When it began to seem that he was going to pretend she wasn't there, she called to him. He finally looked down.

"I'm going to run into the village and get some more formula," she said.

"Do you need money?"

"I still have my own," she said. "The money you wouldn't let me use for the ibuprofen."

"That's yours."

"Yeah, well, I owe you for the medicine."

To his credit, he sidestepped that argument.

"You can't get formula in Divinity," he said. "You'll have to go into Strasberg for that, too."

"That's okay. I can pick up something for dinner while I'm there. We can heat it up later."

He appeared vaguely alarmed. "Dinner? You mean supper? Tonight?"

She frowned. "Well, yes."

"What kind of supper?"

"I don't know. What do you feel like?"

Beef, he thought. A mountain of it. With gravy. And mashed potatoes. Corn. Maybe some of Deb Stoltzfus's beans. That Mexican stuff Jacob had bought earlier in the week was still burning a hole in his gut.

"Chinese?" she suggested when he didn't answer.

"What's in it?"

She eyed him strangely. "Well, vegetables. A lot of vegetables."

"Can you get some with meat?"

"Sure."

"Uh, okay. That would be fine."

She nodded and started to turn away. Then she looked back. "Joe," she said again.

He hadn't started working yet. He was just holding the hammer, watching her. She couldn't read his expression.

"None of this is Dinah's fault," she ventured.

Color burned into his face. He began hammering again. Hard.

"Joe!" she shouted over the clamor.

"What?" he growled.

"Lunch is on the table."

"It's called 'dinner,'" he snapped.

"Not when I do it." She turned back to the Mazda.

"What did you do?" he shouted after her.

"Do?" She paused and looked back.

"What did you make to eat?" he asked. "For this lunch-dinner-whatever."

"Egg salad sandwiches."

"*Sandwiches?* I need fuel, woman. I've got three more roofs to do."

Kim looked around at the buildings. Their shingles were clearly visible in the sun. They were even, in neat, perfect lines. In good condition. She shook her head.

"No, you don't. Go have lunch, Joe."

She found Matt eating leftover fried chicken with Adam and Mariah and Bo. Admittedly, it appeared a lot more appetizing than her sandwiches. Kim made sure Matt wasn't being a pest and left that branch of the Wallace clan munching happily.

She went back to the drugstore in Strasberg, and was relieved to find that the cashier who'd witnessed her scrap with Joe the other day wasn't on duty. She bought three packages of disposable diapers and a carton of formula, and pretty much wiped out her money. Afterward, she stopped at a pay phone on the street—one that *looked* like a pay phone—and called the 800 number Jake had given her. Katya answered. He hadn't seen Grete yet. He was going to drive out to Peace Valley this afternoon. He'd put Susannah's bulletin on the web site that morning. Kim thanked her and hung up.

She didn't want to go back to the farm, she realized. Here was civilization. Here was normalcy. Automobiles. Horns. Voices. If people had problems, they kept them to themselves the way she had done for too many years to count. At least, she thought, until fate had finally landed her a good one, a problem she couldn't fix on her own, and she had landed in Joe's lap.

She put that out of her mind.

She found the Chinese restaurant Jake had mentioned and spent the last of her cash. Finally, reluctantly, she drove back to the settlement.

Joe was no longer on the roof when she got home. He was whitewashing a fence that already gleamed in the sun. She got out of the car and crossed to him, jiggling the keys nervously in her hand.

"Get everything you needed?" he asked without looking up.

"This isn't going to work, Joe."

He put the paintbrush down carefully. "What do you mean?"

"You can't keep avoiding me like this. It's me, isn't it? It's not the house. And it's not Dinah."

"It's you," he said bluntly. "And God help me, I have to. I can't let myself...want...like...grow fond of you." He fumbled with the words.

They both felt it at the same time. For Kim, it was a leap of something warm in the area of her heart. Part of it was purely a feminine response to the meaning in his words. There wasn't a woman alive who wouldn't be flattered at being desired, she thought, especially by a man like him. She was just...normal. It didn't mean she had any intention of following up on it.

But it was more than that. The warmth burned fast into heat, and it left her with a breathless feeling, as if everything inside her was suspended and waiting. She thought she might actually have gasped.

For Joe, there was a moment of embarrassment that he had spoken so honestly. He thought painfully that if he lived to be ninety, he would never learn to be suave and clever with women. Then relief washed through him, because he *had* spoken, because there it was, on the table. He found her attractive. And he was damned if he was going to do a thing about it.

They both began talking at the same time.

"What changed?" she demanded. "Why? We were fine—"

"Were we?"

She flushed, remembering too many moments—the car ride to the hospital, his strong arms closing around her in comfort that wasn't quite just comfort. No, she thought, they hadn't been "fine" at all.

"As long as there were other people here," she began. "Being alone—"

"It's awkward."

"Like throwing the barn light on a bull making his rounds at midnight."

They both broke off. They looked at each other, then away. It certainly wasn't the analogy she would have used, and that was so typical, she felt absurdly like crying. It just proved why any attraction between them would be...hopeless.

"As long as we're aware of it—" Joe began again.

"We're two grown adults," she interrupted. "We're not a couple of hormone-wild kids."

"No, of course not."

"I mean, it's not like we...we haven't even..."

"No," he said again.

"Of course not."

She let out a sigh.

He rubbed his beard.

Change the subject, she told herself, before she started to imagine those big, work-roughened hands on her skin. He was a farmer, for God's sake, an Amish farmer! They hadn't a thing in common in the world. But his *hands*...

Think of something else to say, he ordered himself, before he could start to imagine the soft warmth of her against his straining body. She was an *anner Satt Leit* woman. A cocktail waitress! And even if it wasn't too soon, even if he hadn't killed his own wife with his selfishness and wasn't bitterly ashamed at that, this particular woman couldn't possibly want him back.

"So," she said awkwardly.

"I...uh, I was thinking."

She latched on to the opening. "What about?"

"While I was working. I was thinking about this business of taking blood from the community. Tomorrow is Church Sunday. But next Sunday everyone will have free time. We only have services every other Sunday and we only ever spend off Sundays with our families. Friends. Visiting, you know."

"Oh. Well, sure. That sounds like a good time to do it."

"I think so."

"I'll tell Dr. Coyle when I call him this afternoon."

He looked up at the sky. "What time is it?"

Kim glanced at her watch. "A little after three. I'm going

to do some laundry, then I'll run down to the phone booth to call him.'' She started to turn away, then she froze. ''*Please* tell me you have a washing machine.''

''Behind that door that's on the east wall of the kitchen.''

''Thank God.''

''It's powered by the generator just outside that wall there. I'll go give it a kick to start it.''

''Thanks.''

He fell into step beside her. It was better, much better, than having him avoid her, she thought. Things were all cleared up between them now. This arrangement was going to be just fine.

''No dryer, though,'' he added.

She missed a step. ''Of course not. That would be too easy.''

''There's a rope strung off the side of the house to that willow tree.'' The one that reminded him of her, he thought. ''Sarah hung everything there.'' Never knowing that she was going to die, he thought, that another woman was going to come into her home to take care of her children and hang clothing there and make her husband feel randy.

They collected the various bags from the trunk of Kim's Mazda and headed into the house.

''We're going to be fine, Joe.'' This time Kim said the words aloud.

''Sure.''

He believed that until he reached the kitchen and opened a carton of the Chinese food to sneak a peek while she wasn't looking. He found only slivers of meat amid the vegetables—not even a decent mouthful.

## *Chapter 12*

On Sunday morning, while Kim was struggling and swearing at the woodstove again, she heard the bathroom door creak open. She looked up as Joe stepped into the kitchen. This time, at least, he had a towel slung around his neck. She was going to have to talk to him about wearing a shirt, she thought as frissons of a now almost familiar heat shot through her. Then she rubbed her temples. Mentioning it, admitting that it made enough of an impression on her that she *would* mention it, had its downside, too. Especially after what had happened yesterday afternoon.

How had this gotten so complicated?

She dropped her hands with a sigh. "'Morning," she said, reminding herself that everything had been ironed out between them.

Joe nodded and stated the obvious. "It's Church Sunday."

"Yes. You said." She wondered inanely if he wandered around half-naked on all days that involved services.

"Is everything okay?" he asked, scowling.

"Fine. Good. Right as rain."

"Would you like to join us—"

"No!" It came out too quickly. She turned back to the

stove, embarrassed. "God already knows the mess we're in, Joe. Either He's going to lend a hand here, or He's not. Bugging Him about it isn't going to change anything."

He thought about that for a moment. "It wouldn't be possible for you to join in. You're not Amish. But you could...I don't know, observe."

"I said no." She flipped bacon irritably.

"How bad was your childhood?"

He blindsided her with the question. She never saw it coming. She jabbed at the bacon. It had been on the stove for a small eternity, and it was still pink and rubbery.

"Admittedly, I haven't known your brothers long. But in this settlement, you get close to people in a hurry. I know Jacob seems to have carried some guilt around for a long time now, and Adam was damned if he was going to trust anything that seemed too good. And you—you seem determined to shut everyone else out, no matter what it costs you."

"I guess they teach pop psychology in those Berks County schools of yours," she muttered.

"You didn't answer my question."

She didn't intend to. She just never talked about it. It was a habit she'd gotten into, and she considered it a good one. But she turned around. And she heard herself being honest, too honest, letting him in.

"I could tell you stories that would make your beard curl," she whispered. "And I learned my lessons well. The more people you let in, the more opportunity there is for disaster. You can't control other people, Joe. You're always, *always* at the mercy of their moods. Well, I won't allow it. People can fly off the handle all they want, but they're not going to do it in my world. Twenty years ago, I *had* to take it. If I tried to defend myself, I only got hurt worse. Now I've earned the right to fight back." She hugged herself. She hadn't meant to say all this. And yet it just kept coming.

"Eleven years ago, my father used to say that as long as I lived under his roof, I lived under his thumb. By his rules. He used to say that as long as he paid the mortgage and put food in my mouth, then no, I had no right to argue with him or try to defend myself. Now I pay my own rent. I pay my own way.

And nobody, *nobody* better try to take away my right to protect myself."

Ah, Joe thought. It was as though someone had just lit all the lanterns in the kitchen. Light illuminated everything. Now he understood why she'd seemed so frantic over taking Jake's or Adam's money. Why she didn't want a salary from him. She'd said it was because she didn't want to grow accustomed to accepting help, then have it removed from her. And maybe that was true, he thought, as far as it went. But he supposed he'd known, even then, that there was more to it. He wondered what she hadn't been permitted to defend herself against. He decided he preferred not to know.

"Well," he said finally. "I'd better go finish dressing."

*Good idea.* Kim rubbed her eyes, still shaken by what she had just said, what she had revealed. "Are you taking Hannah?" she asked numbly.

"Of course." Then he paused. "Dinah will look after her."

"Joe, leave her here."

His eyes narrowed as though someone had just offered him a million dollars and he was trying to figure out what strings were attached. Kim wondered helplessly if she was just aiding and abetting him in his heartache. What was the word they used in rehab centers? A girl she'd worked with had been in and out so many times she spouted the phrase like a mantra. Enabling him, she thought. That was it. Then she decided that she'd had her fill of pop psychology for one day.

"You said something about church socials," she told him. "Give Dinah a chance to pal around with her friends today, and tonight, too, if that's what she wants. I mean, assuming there's food and singing and stuff, like at the wedding."

"There is." Then his voice softened. "Yes, that would probably be best. Thank you."

"You won't have to torture yourself about taking care of the baby so Dinah has a chance to go off on her own."

"I said okay!"

The guilt was there again, hot and ashamed in his eyes, enough to bubble up in temper.

"I said yes," he repeated quietly.

Then he turned on his heel and left the kitchen, naked chest and all.

* * *

Three hours later, Kim heartily regretted her offer. Hannah wouldn't stop crying.

"What's wrong with her?" Susannah asked. They had brought the cradle downstairs and put it in the living room. They both stood over it, looking down at the squalling baby.

"I don't know," Kim muttered. "I'm a little out of practice here."

Everything that had come back to her so readily yesterday had flown right out the window today. The baby had had a bottle less than an hour ago—it couldn't be that. She was dry and clean. Kim had no qualms about changing diapers more often than necessary since she had bought the disposables and she could toss the dirty ones in the trash afterward. A wintertime chill had penetrated the house, but this room was the warmest, and Hannah was dressed adequately. So she wasn't cold. Overly warm didn't seem like a viable explanation, either.

Kim didn't know what else to do, and there was no one to ask. She knew without being told that everyone within miles would be at that church service. Maybe, she thought, Hannah was just pain colicky. "Okay," she mumbled. "Let me try walking her again. Or—I know! When you were a baby and you got real antsy, I used to take you for a drive in our landlady's car."

"Well, we've got a car now," Susannah said.

"But no car seat."

"So I'll hold her."

It would have to do, Kim thought. She was only going to be crawling around the settlement roads, after all. And there would be no other cars on the road. She ran upstairs for a warmer blanket for the baby. Five minutes later, they were in the Mazda, moseying along. Still Hannah cried.

"This is ridiculous," Kim said through clenched teeth.

"Maybe she misses Dinah."

"Babies that young don't know the difference," she argued. "Well, maybe they do, but all they really care about is warmth, a full tummy and a clean diaper."

"She's got all that," Susannah reminded her.

"Yeah." Even the Mazda's heater was cooperating for a

change. It was belching something very close to hot air. "Okay, this isn't working. Let's go back."

When they parked, Hannah was still howling.

"Mom, do you care if I lie down for a little while?" Susannah asked almost guiltily as they went inside.

Kim looked at her quickly. "Of course not. Go upstairs. Take a nap."

"Well, I mean, I don't want to leave you alone with her like this."

*She was such a good kid.* And on the heels of that came the other thought that never quite left her: *Please, God, don't let me lose her.* "Baby, if you can shut out the noise, I can take care of the kid," she assured her.

Susannah nodded, still uncertain.

"Scoot."

She went upstairs. Kim kept walking the baby. Through the living room. To the front door. To the back. Around the kitchen. She held Hannah on her shoulder. No good. She cradled her in her arms. No better. She rocked from side to side, heel to heel. Nothing.

The house was a disaster. She felt like crying herself. She had undertaken a commitment here, and she was damned well going to live up to her end of the bargain. She wasn't going to owe Joe Lapp anything. She closed her eyes and gave a little snort of pure despair. She already owed him everything. He was going to bring the whole settlement here next Sunday to have their blood drawn to try to save her daughter's life.

She set her jaw. She'd at least keep this house looking as good as Sarah's sisters had kept it. As soon as Hannah calmed down, she would whip through the place with the vacuum and a dust cloth.

*What vacuum?* Vacuums ran on electricity. "Oh, God," she moaned.

She veered back through the kitchen. The sink was full of dirty dishes. Soggy bacon still sat in the frying pan. *That* had been a bust. After an hour, it still hadn't cooked enough to be edible. Joe and the kids had been in a hurry, and there had been no more time to defy Dinah's advice and throw a few additional logs into the fire. Kim hadn't even had a chance to make her own bed, and now Susannah was in it. Finally, at the end of her rope, she went to the foot of the stairs.

"Suze?" she called softly. There was no answer. She went back to the kitchen and found paper and a pencil, juggling the squalling baby to her other arm to write.

"Ran down to the pay phone a minute," she scribbled. "Won't be long."

She strapped the baby into the passenger seat, jury-rigging the seat belt. She went back to the phone booth at a crawl. She couldn't believe she was doing this. Katya answered the phone at ChildSearch on the second ring.

"Thank God, I found you." Kim all but whimpered. "You have to help me."

"What's wrong?" Katya asked, alarmed.

"What kind of tricks do you have up your sleeve to stop a crying baby?"

"Does she have diaper rash?" Katya asked.

"No, no. I know all the *motherhood* secrets. She's absolutely fine from head to toe. I need some of your Amish hocus-pocus."

"Try chamomile tea."

"*Tea?* Won't the caffeine just wire her up more?"

"No. Anyway, it's either that or chopped yellow dock, burdock, dandelion root, black snakeroot and sassafras steeped in wine. And something tells me you can't handle that." There was amusement in Katya's voice.

"I'll try the tea," Kim said quickly. "Where can I find some?"

"The cupboard to the right of the woodstove."

"Joe's already got some? Great," she said, relieved.

"Kim..."

Something had changed in Katya's voice. Kim felt her body succumb to an overall stiffening. "What?" she asked warily. *What now?*

"Jake had some luck getting blood out of Grete Guenther. She still didn't understand why she was giving it, but she gave it."

"And she doesn't match, either," Kim said hollowly.

"Well, it's too soon to tell with absolute certainty..." Katya let out her breath and trailed off. "No," she said honestly.

"She doesn't seem to match. Jake had most of the sample sent to Children's Hospital for Dr. Coyle's people to test, but from this end, just on the blood typing, it doesn't look good. I guess Dr. Coyle will be able to tell you conclusively, but I...I thought it kinder to warn you."

There was a moment of quiet. The long-distance phone line crackled. "What am I going to do?" Kim whispered finally, helplessly.

"There's still the web site. There's still the Amish community. Have faith, Kim," Katya urged.

*Faith.* Kim murmured something noncommittal and hung up.

The chamomile tea worked. Damned if it didn't work, Kim thought, amazed all over again.

At half past one, Hannah finally stopped crying. Kim started to set her down in the cradle again, then she thought better of it. Better not rock the boat, she decided. She'd keep holding her for a while, just to be safe.

She settled down on the sofa and pried off each boot with her opposite toe. It was a struggle. She put her feet up on the coffee table and closed her eyes, giving a heartfelt breath of relief.

Joe found them that way at three o'clock, both sound asleep.

When he stepped through the front door, he was startled, then pained, at the sheer quietness of the house. Once, five short months ago, the house would have been alive with laughter and voices as they all burst in after church.

He assumed the cradle would be upstairs, because it always was. But as he moved slowly and curiously past the living room, he caught a glimpse of it out of the corner of his eye. He stopped cold. Then he forced himself to walk over to it, to peer down into it. His eyes didn't swerve, didn't move, remained glued to that small mahogany basket with the frothy white bedding inside. He stared at it as though all the demons of hell would burst from it once he got close enough.

It was empty.

He breathed again and looked around, and found them on the sofa. It was like a slap in the face, and it made him reel backward, one step, then two. He stared at them the way he had stared at the cradle, and he had the blasphemous thought that God was getting even with him for sitting through that service this morning, mouthing the prayers and singing the hymns, when all along a big part of his heart agreed with Kimberley: *God already knows the mess we're in.... Bugging Him about it isn't going to change anything.*

He'd prayed and he'd tried to tell himself that God had already made up His mind to take Sarah. That his own will and desires had had nothing to do with it. Because he was a rational man, and on some level he knew that, although he was having a very hard time making his heart buy it. And if it was true, then he was having a very hard time forgiving God.

Now, here on his living room sofa, was a woman he wanted in the same carnal way. Oh, not with the adoration and the pure, uncomplicated love he'd felt for Sarah. This was much different. But, he admitted, he craved the heat of this woman—emotionally, and oh, yes, physically. He wanted to feel it sliding over his body, closing over him. That need had grown tenfold in the short time since everyone had left, leaving them alone together in this house.

His blood suddenly pounded at the idea that their bodies could meet purely for the sake of need. It was a sin, certainly, but he had lived a good life, had always been an honorable man, and look where it had gotten him. He made a strangled sound.

Kim stirred. "Joe?" she said groggily, opening her eyes. Then she added, "*Damn* it."

"What?" He was startled by her reaction—as though she had read his mind and was disgusted, he thought.

"I wanted to have everything cleaned up when you got home, but all hell broke loose and..." She trailed off, finally seeing the torment on his face. "What's wrong?"

"Nothing," he said roughly, turning away.

"Where are the others?"

He paused. "You were right about Dinah. She stayed for some singing the teenagers are gathering for at the Eitner farm."

"Singing," Kim repeated.

"Uh, they all get together around someone's kitchen table and...sing."

"Sounds like a good time," she said dryly.

"They flirt." His heart jerked a little, not so much at the thought of his daughter doing so, but more at the reminder of his own needs in that department.

"Gracie?" she asked deliberately, watching his face. "Matt?"

"At Adam's. A person would be hard-pressed to separate Matt and Bo for any length of time. Gracie stayed at the Byler's farm after church."

"I see." She got to her feet. Hannah awoke at the jostling and began crying again. Kim closed her eyes in defeat. "More tea," she decided. "But first let's make sure everything else is hunky-dory." When she opened her eyes and looked again, Joe was gone. "Coward," she muttered, going upstairs.

She took Hannah to Dinah's room because Susannah was still asleep in her own bed. She laid her on the one in there to change her. As soon as she unwrapped the little receiving blanket, she felt her fever.

"Oh, no." There was concern first. Then the kick of real fear. *Susannah.*

It was, of course, the same bug that Susannah had had. Nothing else made sense. Hannah was so tiny, so vulnerable. Her little body had accepted the germs without fuss.

Katya had left instructions for the pumpkin tea and that egg stuff. And where there was children's ibuprofen, there was infant's ibuprofen. What scared Kim, what made her heart thump and her head suddenly pound, was the fact that Susannah had held the baby in the car just this morning, smothering her little face in comforting kisses. And Susannah had no defenses left against germs at all.

Suze was going to get sick again. And this time... *No, I won't think about that.*

There was no immediate hope on the horizon. Grete Guenther hadn't panned out. *No!* They wouldn't even do the community thing until next Sunday! And as of yesterday afternoon, the national donor lists hadn't produced anything. Maybe this time a fever would prove too much. *No, no, no!*

Susannah had already been sleeping far too long, she real-zed, glancing at her watch. This wasn't her usual catnap. Kim :hanged Hannah's diaper quickly. She picked her up again and ushed out into the hall. Joe was just coming up the stairs. 'Here,'' she said, shoving the baby at him blindly. ''Don't argue about it this time.''

She knew his first instinct would be to step away and she only hoped to forestall it this once, perhaps even to startle him nto holding Hannah without thinking. But his back hit the wall again. He stared at her as though she had somehow betrayed him.

''Damn it, Joe!'' she cried out, at the end of her rope. ''Please!''

''This is not your problem,'' he growled. ''I didn't ask you to stay so you could fix it.''

And just like that, her temper snapped. She felt it come up from the pit of her stomach, something red-hot and fiery. At the same time she felt something pop in her head, like a rubber band, some flimsy thing that had been holding her control together during this whole terrible day.

''No,'' she answered, her voice trembling. ''You certainly didn't, did you? You asked me to stay so you could keep hiding from her. Well, you're right. That's not my problem. I don't give a damn—unless and until it threatens *my* daughter!''

''This isn't any of your—what are you talking about?'' he asked, at least looking uncertain now.

''She's sick! Hannah's *sick.*'' She thumped him in the chest with her free hand. ''I need to go check on Susannah. She was holding Hannah all morning. And I'm not taking this baby in there with me to expose Susannah all over again, if by some miracle she's dodged the bullet so far!''

''Just...put her in the cradle...''

''She's sick! She's crying!'' she shouted. ''Damn it, Joe, have a heart!''

His face went white.

Oh, damn him! she thought. Why did she feel guilty? Why did she feel that she was putting him through absolute hell? This was his daughter! And she had to take care of her own!

But her heart went out to him, though she wanted to stay

furious. Underneath his fear, underneath his own hurt, he did have a heart. A big one. And she was battering it.

Kim stepped around him unsteadily. She took Hannah downstairs to the cradle. Then she headed for her own room again, dragging an angry hand under her eyes, disgusted by the tears that were threatening.

"Grete doesn't match, either," she whispered when she passed Joe a second time—a halfhearted explanation for falling apart. "I found out this morning that Grete Guenther doesn't match. I can't take much more...you know, the hope, then the defeat. It's like being on a roller coaster. And I'm getting so tired of the ride."

He wasn't paying attention to her, she realized. He was too caught up in his own nightmare, the one she had plunged him back into with her angry words. Any other man would probably have throttled her, she knew, and that shook her even more. Because Joe was just staring down the stairs, where Hannah was crying from the living room. Kim gave a hoarse sound that was supposed to be a laugh, but it came out more like a gasp.

"What a pair we are," she muttered, turning away. And maybe they were, but even contemplating that terrified her. "Let me check on Susannah," she continued, "then I'll go get Adam. He can take care of the baby while I run back to the drugstore. Hannah can't take the same medicine we got for Suze. She's too little."

Joe finally looked up. "Mariah can—"

Kim shook her head. "No," she interrupted. "Leave Mariah out of this. She doesn't need to be exposed to this thing, either, not in her condition."

He blanched even more. "No, of course not."

Kim cracked open the bedroom door. And she could have sworn she *smelled* the fever in the room, like some kind of vile presence, laughing at her, mocking her, before she even stepped inside.

"Kimberley," Joe said.

She looked back at him. And somehow, without meaning to, she fell right into his eyes. His depthless eyes, filled with too much sorrow and shame for her to bear. And yet, it was a warm place there, she realized headily, as if her head were swimming. Maybe they *did* make a crazy pair, but there was something strong and bolstering about having company in the middle of all this hell God had created.

"I'm sorry," he said finally.

She took a shaky breath, her mind clearing. "I'm not the one who needs to forgive you, Joe," she said softly, then she went into the room.

# Chapter 13

The day was interminable. Barely fifteen minutes after Kim had determined that Susannah was indeed ill again, just after she finished pouring ibuprofen down her throat, Gracie dragged herself listlessly home.

Kim met her on the stairs. "Oh, no," she groaned with one look at her face.

"I don't feel so good," Gracie complained.

"Okay. Okay," Kim said, rallying. She looked at the bottle of ibuprofen she still held. "Go crawl into bed. Just let me grab a clean spoon, and I'll be there in a sec."

She found Joe in the kitchen. He did not have the baby. She could still hear Hannah crying from the living room. He appeared panicked.

"Did I just hear Gracie?" he asked.

Kim nodded. "I've already sent her to bed. She's sick, too."

"What's going on here?" he demanded.

She glanced at him over her shoulder as she got a spoon from the drawer. "Calm down, Joe. It's not the plague. It's just some virus. Look how quickly Susannah bounced back."

*The first time,* she thought. How much more could Suze withstand?

He stared at her. "How can you be so calm?"

"Because of the thought of what might happen if I fall apart. *You're* sure not going to win any awards in the common sense department right now."

She amazed him, he thought, stepping aside so she could pass through the door again. Half an hour ago, he'd thought she would crumble, and he wasn't sure he could have blamed her. Guilt had been slamming through him ever since their altercation on the stairs.

He started to go after Kim, when Dinah came wandering in the front door. And his first reaction—pure relief because *she* would take care of Hannah now—made him feel ashamed, too.

"Why's the baby screaming?" Dinah asked immediately.

"She's sick."

"Oh, no." Then her face hardened. "So where's Miss I'll-Fix-Anything?"

"Dinah," Joe warned sharply.

But she was already following the sound of Hannah's cries into the living room. "She's dirtied herself! Why didn't Kim change her?"

"It's the same bug Susannah had," Joe snapped. "And Susannah has it again. Right now Kimberley is taking care of Gracie."

"Oh. *Oh.*" Dinah's face flushed a little.

"She's here to help us, Dinah."

"I'm sorry, all right?"

"The least you could do is show her a little support, a little *gratitude*—"

"I said I was sorry!" Dinah cried. And Hannah just kept howling.

"Stop it!" Kim shouted from the door. "Both of you, just...stop it."

They snapped around to look at her.

"Why did you come home?" Kim asked, diverted from whatever she had been about to say by the unexpected appearance of Dinah.

Dinah looked sheepish. "I don't feel so wonderful, either."

Kim sank into the nearest chair. "Well, that's great. That's just great.'' Then she startled both of them by laughing. It was an edgy sound, but it was still a laugh. She raked the short part of her hair back from her forehead. ''Okay,'' she said. ''We need a plan of attack here.''

''What if we all come down with it at once?'' Joe asked worriedly.

''Then we'll be a sorry bunch, indeed.'' Kim sat forward and rested her elbows on her knees, still holding her head. ''I won't get it,'' she said finally.

''You don't know that,'' Joe argued.

''As a matter of fact, I pretty much do. I never get what Suze brings home. At least, not after the first few weeks of it, you know, when she started getting sick all the time. I think my body's just toughened up to the assault,'' she added with a weak smile. ''Either that, or that God you keep touting has a few streaks of kindness in Him.''

Neither of them answered that.

''Anyway, let's look at what we've got here. Susannah and Gracie have both had ibuprofen and that antidiarrheal stuff. If that doesn't work within the next half hour, we'll move on to pumpkins and eggs. In fact, I'm going to start with that on Hannah.'' She gave another giddy laugh at Joe's surprised expression. ''Why give a baby chemicals if you don't have to? Besides, if one world's methods are good, two are better,'' she quipped.

He felt dizzy. She was incredible. He echoed her response of last week. ''Do you believe that?''

''No, but at this point I'm willing to try anything.'' Kim got to her feet again. ''I'll take care of the baby, Dinah. You go take some medicine yourself. It's only for kids up to twelve, so you might want to increase the dosage.''

''I'll make the tea, too,'' Dinah said. ''I can manage that much.''

''I'll go get the pumpkin seeds,'' Joe offered.

''Now we're cookin','' Kim muttered, heading for the stairs again, taking the baby this time.

''We're what?'' they asked in unison.

Kim closed her eyes for just a moment. ''Never mind.''

* * *

Sometime after midnight, the worst of the crisis had passed. Kim wandered dazedly into the living room to find Joe sitting on the sofa, looking just as dumbstruck as she felt. At least he hadn't gotten sick, either—so far.

The cradle had been moved back upstairs to Dinah's room. Everyone was asleep. Kim dropped down beside him. "Do you hear that?" she asked, her voice a reverent whisper.

"What?" he asked, gazing at her dully.

"The silence." It was broken only by the gentle tick-tocking of the old German grandfather clock.

One corner of Joe's mouth managed to lift into a smile. "Oh. Yeah."

For several more long moments, they just appreciated it. Then Kim cleared her throat. "Susannah's fever broke," she reported. She didn't think that the ibuprofen had done it. Suze seemed to be building up some kind of resistance to that now, too. The egg goop appeared to be the victor yet again. Kim shook her head in disbelief. "Assuming Matt or you or I don't come down with it yet, we should be back on an even keel by morning," she added.

"It *is* morning," Joe grumbled.

She peered at the clock and wasn't quite able to read it in the darkness. She'd take his word for it. "I made Adam swear he'd send Matt home at the first sign that he's gotten it, too." Matt was still staying with Bo.

"Matthew is an island," Joe answered. "He spends more time there than here."

"So I've noticed."

They fell quiet again.

"Thank you," he said finally. "I don't know what I would have done if I had been here alone."

She stared at him incredulously. "None of this would have happened if you had been here alone. You heard what Katya said. There's not much in the way of communicable germs here. Susannah brought them."

"Of course there are germs here," Joe snapped. "We don't live in a bubble."

"Close enough."

"Jake and Katya's kids could have brought it."

"They didn't get sick and they were here for weeks before Suze and I turned up."

He lifted his head from the back of the sofa to look at her again, cracking one eye open. "Why are we arguing about this?" he asked quietly.

"We're not arguing." Then she thought about it. "I have no idea," she amended. "Maybe because I'm just not comfortable with you thanking me. I managed to do *something* today to earn my keep. That's all."

Joe stiffened and sat up. "Don't start that again. I'm not going to transform into some kind of monster and make you pay for it if you take anything from me."

"You might," she said flatly, though she'd meant to be flippant. "You never know."

Joe let out a strangled sound of disbelief. Kim rubbed her eyes.

"We're tired, Joe," she continued. "Just drop it."

But he couldn't. For some reason, he just couldn't. Not this time. "I've never hit a woman in my life," he said angrily. "Is that what you expect? That you're here, in my debt, so I'm going to take advantage of it, use you to let out some kind of latent, truculent male impulses and—"

"I am *not* in your debt!" she shouted.

Her voice rang in the room. They stared at each other.

Their shoulders were touching. They both jerked away at the same time.

"You're right," he said finally. "You're not."

"Damned right I'm right. I mean, I'm not." And if the comment was ridiculous, deliberately contentious, she didn't care.

"Just for the record," he added, "I have no truculent male impulses—"

"You've got male impulses raging all around your body or we wouldn't be arguing like this! It's called 'frustration,' Joe. How long did you think you could keep pounding at the barn roof, ignoring what's going on between us?"

Joe jerked off the sofa as though she had slapped him. "Nothing's going on between us."

"And it won't, either, if you keep biting my head off! Makes things safe, doesn't it?"

"I'm trying to be a man I can live with!" he shouted back.

"There's nothing *wrong* with you, Joe! You're the only one who thinks you should feel guilty!"

"I told you before, this isn't your problem."

"That's *my* line. And it seems to me you've pointed it out a time or two!"

"Because *you* need help. I don't."

"Let's look a few facts in the nose here, pal. I'm living here. I'm the one tiptoeing around your guilt. Me and Dinah. If you've got some misguided sense of responsibility for your wife's death, don't take it out on us!"

She knew in an instant that she had gone too far. His face became mottled. He took a step toward her and threw his hands up in frustration. She didn't see the emotion in the gesture, only the jerk of his arms. Terror—old, instinctual, never far away—simply bloomed. It billowed up from the bottom of her soul. It was irrational and she was powerless against it, had always been powerless against it. Next there would be pain. And humiliation. The humiliation, the demeaning crouch to ward off the blows, was the worst. She hurtled up off the sofa with a squeal of pure horror.

The sound knifed its way clear through to Joe's soul. He realized at the same time she did that she couldn't run forward because he was in front of her. Dodging around either side of him would mean moving close enough to him that he could grab her. Her eyes widened in fear.

Before he could move to get out of her way, she scrambled over the back of the sofa. It was freestanding, in the middle of the room, facing the hearth, and she put it between them, her hands clenched into fists at her sides.

He'd thought he'd learned all about a woman's fear, all about the special vulnerability of the fairer sex, from Katya. But Katya had spent her adult life dodging a man's blows, he realized. The early part of Katya's years, where fears were formed, had been blessedly normal.

Not so here.

"Kimberley," he said finally, very carefully. His voice was raw with shock. "I would never hurt you."

Everything seemed to go right out of her. She gave another little cry, this time of embarrassment and confusion. She sank to the floor where she stood. He lost sight of her behind the sofa.

He didn't know what to do. He circled around it warily, the pull of her sobs stronger than his wariness against getting too close to her right now. She was sitting on the floor, hunched forward, her hands covering her face. He stopped just short of her.

"God, I am so *stupid,*" she said at last. Her voice was muffled, thick.

"No." He sat on the floor beside her.

She lowered her hands. Her arm throbbed, as though he *had* struck it. Just memory, she thought bitterly.

"I *was* angry," he confessed. "But I would never take that out physically on you or anyone else. Kimberley, it's against my religion, if nothing else."

She finally looked at him. "You're still angry," she whispered.

He felt the heat simmering in his gut. "Yes," he admitted.

Her chin came up. "I won't take back what I said."

"No. I don't imagine you'd ever do that." He thought that for everything that had just happened between them, she still had a kind of ferocious courage.

"It had to be said," she snapped. "You're hurting Dinah."

He opened his mouth to argue yet again that it was none of her business. But of course it was. She was right. She was living under his roof, in the thick of it.

She opened her mouth to tell him again that nobody blamed him, but that wasn't quite true. Dinah did, if only in her own confusion and innocence and pain. And he blamed himself relentlessly.

They spoke each other's names at the same time, then they broke off, embarrassed. Joe was the first to clear his throat.

"This...this cohabitation business would be difficult under the best of circumstances," he said at last. "Two people, two strangers, coming together in the same house."

Except that he had never really felt like a stranger, she thought, her heart kicking.

"Add to that all the emotional baggage we both carry, my problems and yours..." He trailed off.

And Kim thought, add to *that* the fact that we like each other anyway, we want each other, and we're really lost.

He'd said once that they needed each other, she remembered. And maybe they did, for so much more than comfortingly holding the other's hand.

Their mouths came together before either of them could say anything more. It happened fast, with explosive release. Suddenly, with raw and emotional need. His hand caught her long hair, the hair he had wanted a handful of from the first moment he'd seen her. He used it to drag her closer, like a barbarian, he acknowledged helplessly, like a man out of control, like everything she seemed to think he was moments ago.

She didn't fight him. Her hands were no longer clenched into fists. That, a part of his mind thought, might have saved them. Might have stopped what he was too weak to prevent. Then there was no more room for thought because tasting her for the first time was like something igniting in his head—white-hot lightning shattering all sense. The heat of her hit him first, as he had always known it would.

Something happened to her when their mouths made contact, and it obliterated any rationality Kim might have possessed. She caught the pine-forest scent of him again. It filled her head now, leaving room for nothing else. He was holding her hair so tightly it hurt, but oddly, it didn't frighten her. His mouth bruised hers. His tongue moved through her mouth with deep and searching sweeps, as if he sought salvation.

With each plundering of his tongue, he drew back a little, as though for breath. With each breath, he kissed her again, relentlessly, encompassingly. He was all smooth motion, a steady, constant assault. She heard a groan, and didn't know whose throat it had come from. She found her fingers threaded into his hair, tightly, fiercely, as though to hold him, dragging his mouth back each time it slid away.

And then something changed. Some of the wildness ebbed, and pure pleasure crept in. Her hands slipped down to his shoulders, then around to his back. And he was so broad, so male, the warmth and solidity of him alive and real. How long? she wondered. How long since she had felt so wanted, so necessary? How long since she had touched something that was so fascinating, so *good?* How long since she had needed so completely and without fear?

He finally let go of her hair and dragged her still closer. Filling himself greedily with the pure essence of her—femininity and strength, temper and tears. Needing it, the way he needed air to breathe. In that moment, if only in that moment, there was no sense in fighting it.

He found himself lowering her to the floor. Someone's foot—he didn't know whose—hit the sofa. He was vaguely aware of the scraping of its legs across Sarah's burnished oak floor. But he didn't think in terms of Sarah this time. She was only a hazy image at the back of his mind.

Immediate, much more immediate, was the realization that he had been right. Kim's soft body gave beneath him, accommodating him, as his own strained. And he kissed her again, thinking that if he tried hard enough he could find his way clear to her soul and everything would be good there. His hands searched and sought to find the path, one under her thigh, lifting it against his hip so she could accommodate him more fully, then up to her own hip, to the side of her breast.

Then he heard a hushed, confused voice from behind them, from beyond the sofa.

"Pa?" Dinah asked sleepily. "You in here? I thought I heard shouting."

Everything inside him froze. But he was reasonable, sensible—so damnably sensible—after all. And as he felt Kim's chest rise in a gasp, somehow he had the presence of mind to stifle the sound with his hand.

He felt her jump beneath him when his palm covered her mouth. They lay still, barely breathing. The clock ticked, then tocked.

"Guess not," Dinah said finally. "Guess you went to roam around outside again." Then came the blessed sound of her footsteps retreating.

Slowly, carefully, Joe took his hand away. Kim drew breath in raggedly—once, twice, then more easily. They stared at each other. He spoke first in an undertone, his voice as jagged as the pieces of self-restraint that had just splintered inside him.

"Sweet Jesus, what have we done?"

* * *

At least he had said *we,* Kim told herself as she approached the hated woodstove in the kitchen five hours later. This, at least, he wouldn't take all upon himself. And though she wasn't sure why, the relief she felt at that was too big to be contemplated.

Joe dressed in the bathroom as he always did. He listened to the sounds of her movements in the kitchen. The clanging sound of the woodstove door opening and closing. A frying pan hitting the top with a bang. A mutter here, a curse there. Outside of her occasional and mild swearing, something no Amish woman would do, they were all sounds of home and hearth as he knew them, so very misplaced and mixed-up right now.

He hadn't slept. At least not much. He'd spent the hours of darkness, after she'd gone upstairs to his bedroom, prowling the house and outside as had become his habit lately. He'd told himself they could just go back, retreat, start over. But now, as he stepped into the kitchen door, as he took in the curve of her spine as she inspected the fire, he knew he was lost.

He cleared his throat. Kim jerked upright and hit her head on the little metal lip at the top of the stove. She swore and clapped a hand there, pivoting to find him, then a hundred shades of pink crept into her face.

They both spoke at the same time.

"I think I have it right this time," she said hoarsely.

"Don't worry about me. I'll just take some coffee out to the barn."

Their eyes met briefly and slid quickly away again.

"I…uh, didn't make any yet. Any coffee," Kim explained. "I'm running behind this morning." Then her face went beet red.

A sense of urgency rushed through Joe, not unlike what he had felt last night when he had finally done it, when he had finally kissed her. But this time it was a need to get them past this, around this. Dear God, they couldn't spend the next weeks looking at each other and remembering, looking at each other and yearning. Somehow they had to move on.

Then he heard his own thoughts and he was staggered. *Each*

*other...remembering...each other...yearning.* That was when it truly hit him that everything that had happened between them last night had been entirely mutual. She had wanted him, too. Just as desperately as he wanted her.

He took a few steps into the kitchen without realizing it, without knowing what he intended to do once he crossed to her. She backed up a little, this time hitting the base of the stove with her heel. She swore again.

"Look, we had a rough day yesterday," she gasped.

He took her cue. Grabbed for it like a lifeline. "It was just reaction," he agreed. "To everything."

"My nerves were all wired up," she blurted. "I was so worried about Susannah."

"Of course."

"We'll just put it behind us."

"It didn't happen," he said.

The hell it didn't, they both thought.

Neither of them heard the back door open and close. Mariah stepped into the kitchen doorway and felt it instantly—the heat, the frustration, the sizzling tension. Her eyes widened slowly. They slid between Joe's back—his shoulders were rigid—and Kim's face. Her sister-in-law's eyes were huge. Just wait, she thought, amused yet somehow troubled as she read the situation. Just wait until I tell Adam about *this* development.

Mariah cleared her throat. Joe almost literally jumped in the process of jerking around to face her. Kim's immense eyes darted to her face.

"Good morning," Mariah said easily. "How's everyone feeling today?"

They both spoke at once, a torrent of words.

"Better, much better," Kim said. "Susannah's still wiped out, but these things hit her so hard."

"Dinah's right as rain," Joe said. "Gracie says she's fine, but she looks pale."

"The baby's still sleeping—"

"She slept most of the night—"

"And neither of us seem to have gotten it."

Mariah smiled, amusement winning out. "Well, that's good. I didn't think Gracie would be going to school, but I stopped anyway to tell you that Matt came through fine, also. I thought it prudent to lend him some of Bo's clothes. There was no sense in sending him back here until I was sure that the germs had settled down."

"They have," Joe said.

"I think so," Kim echoed.

"Well, then." Mariah turned for the hall and the back door again. "Oh, one other thing. If everyone's feeling better, you're invited to supper."

Joe's eyes lit. "Supper?"

Kim almost swayed with relief. "I don't have to cook?"

Mariah grinned. "Five o'clock. Bye now."

Joe moved after her as though someone had set his tail on fire. "Wait. I'll walk you out. I'll hitch up the buggy. I'll give you a ride to school. I'll..."

His voice trailed off. Kim stood at the stove, watching him go. She stood there for a long time after he was gone. Then, finally, she moved for a chair and she sat hard.

What had they done? she asked herself, as he had asked last night.

Then she thought of another better question, much more intimidating. What were they going to do?

# *Chapter 14*

Kim bounced back and forth all day on the advisability of taking everyone to Adam and Mariah's for supper. She wanted to. God knows, she wanted to. She wanted to escape the woodstove. She wanted to escape the warm pleasure and companionship of facing Joe across the supper table, at least for tonight. Suddenly, that companionship had become volatile and dangerous.

So she watched the kids critically, but by four o'clock she still hadn't come to any real decision. She finally wandered out onto the porch. Joe was working across the road. He was no help, she thought irritably. Somehow she was sure he would go whichever way she decided on this. Just leave it all up to the little woman.

Her heart thumped. It felt entirely too much as if they had been living together for an eternity, she realized. As if they had been juggling these kids side by side through a lifetime instead of just a few weeks.

Matt had finally come home after school and a quick game of field hockey. Along with Bo, he was helping his father bring in the cows—*cows,* for God's sweet sake—and once she even saw Joe laugh when Matt's heel hit a slick spot of mud.

The boy didn't fall so much as he did a graceful slide, a good seven or eight feet until he lay under a cow's belly. The animal stepped over him unperturbedly. Kim felt one spasm of fear that he would be hurt, then she smiled, also.

With the cows in the barn—she knew they had already put hay in there for them because she had watched that, too—Joe took his hat off and waved the boys into the house. He followed at a much slower pace. When he found her on the porch, he stopped short.

"What's wrong?" he asked immediately.

"You're turning into a real pessimist, Joe. Why should anything be wrong?"

He grimaced and put his hat back on. She watched and remembered how those hands had felt on her body last night, so briefly, too briefly, before Dinah had interrupted them. She shivered, her tummy rolled over, then she got angry with herself.

It had been a *kiss*. That was all. Well, okay, technically it had been a lot of kisses. It was still no big deal. Unattached men and women kissed all the time. They were two adults living in proximity and they both had needs that they'd ignored—obviously for too long—in the face of their own problems. She had worked hard all day to convince herself that making more of what had happened would be a very big mistake.

Joe watched her eyes move and try to find a place to settle. Sometime during his long afternoon in the barn, he had convinced himself that the fact that she had wanted him, too, wasn't all that amazing. Though he had not looked into a mirror since he had married Sarah and moved to this settlement, he knew he had never been *un*attractive. It was entirely possible that that had changed, but apparently not. He had just begun to accept that a mutual attraction was not so overwhelming after all, when he found her here on the porch with her eyes just a little bit wide. Amazement and wonder hit him all over again. He brought his mind grimly away from it. "Did you talk to Dr. Coyle?" he asked. "Did you learn anything new?"

"Yes. And no," Kim answered, gratefully distracted from

her thoughts. "I called him, but there's nothing on the donor lists yet."

Joe leaned his back against one of the porch posts. "With so many people in this country, that's hard to imagine."

"Not too many people actually take the bother to register to donate marrow. Or anything else for that matter," she noted. "Only a small segment of the population is listed."

Joe scowled. "That's what's wrong with your society. They tend to be selfish."

Kim stiffened. "At least we have most general appliances," she snapped.

"Still, the more I learn of your world, the more content I am with my generators."

She wasn't sure why that threatened her so. She turned away abruptly.

"Are we going to Adam and Mariah's?" he asked, following her, aware that the *we* had come far too easily.

Kim stopped and shook her head. "I don't know. Dinah's fine, Gracie is showing signs of life and the baby has stopped fretting. I'm pretty sure the period of incubation is over. I doubt if it's contagious any longer."

He waited. None of his own children was the most important consideration, and they both knew it.

"It's a double-edged sword, Joe." Kim sighed, reading his eyes. "On the one hand, I so desperately want to protect her. I'd put her in a bubble if I could. And on the other..." She had to swallow carefully. It struck her in that moment that she had never spoken the words before. She took a deep breath. "I keep thinking, what if she doesn't have much time left?"

He felt the pain for her, a horrible protest pushing his blood right up the surface of his skin. "Then you want her to be as happy as possible right now," he said quietly.

"Exactly." She realized almost distantly that she was shaking again. "She loves spending time with all this...with her...our...family."

"Well, then." He slung an arm over her shoulder as they went back inside. If most of the day had been awkward between them, now she was only a woman on the verge of intolerable loss, and he was only a man who had already lost the person he'd thought had mattered most. "I think we should go to Adam and Mariah's."

Kim leaned into him, needing him, telling herself it was okay for just this one second. "You just want some decent cooking," she accused.

"There is that."

They both startled themselves by laughing.

Kim would not have believed it possible for two adults, one teenager, four kids and one infant to fit into that buggy. But fit they did. She hadn't noticed the first time she had ridden in it, but there was a...well, a back seat. It was sort of a bench-berth, flat, upholstered. Dinah, Matt, Bo and Gracie were more than comfortable back there. Bo had opted to wait and come home with them. Kim held Hannah and Susannah sat in the front between her and Joe.

The impact of being part of their family hit Kim. It made her feel claustrophobic for a moment, almost dizzy. She wondered when she had last been part of a...well, a group. She wondered if the people she worked with counted and decided they didn't. Oh, she had felt a certain camaraderie there, but it was still each man for himself. Just as it had been when she was growing up. Try as she might to shake it, there was a certain uniformity of goals to her time with Joe. They both wanted the same things. An orderly existence, peace, a healing of wounds and to be able to trust in a future. And, of course, the well-being of their children.

Their *respective* children, she corrected herself.

She listened with half an ear while Joe reprimanded Matt for bouncing on the back seat. Dinah talked about the fact that the generator had had a brief spell of irritability that morning. Kim heard herself volunteer the information that the hen with the red spot on her beak seemed to consider herself above laying one egg a day.

"Then she's getting old," Joe said, turning into Adam's drive. "She should be supper one night soon before she toughens up too much."

Kim felt her stomach roll over. "I'll have a talk with her," she said quickly. "I'm sure she'll do better."

He laughed.

"I mean it, Joe, I'm not cutting up another half-dead chicken. And I've gotten to know this one. I can't eat her."

"Well, now, I've been meaning to speak to you about that."

"Why?" she demanded as they stepped down out of the buggy. If he wanted chicken that badly, she would damned well find a supermarket and steal one if she had to.

"You do know that we're going to have to feed all those people on Sunday?"

"Feed them? On Sunday? When they come to give blood? Those roast things? We've got to make them? Hundreds more again?"

The pure panic in her voice, rising with each question, made him laugh again. "It's the easiest way to feed hundreds of people," he remarked.

"No, that's not so. Seventy-five or so pizzas would be even easier."

"Well, we've got a few days left yet to decide what we're going to do."

Matt and Bo bulleted along ahead of them.

"Hi," Kim said tentatively.

Adam gave her a quick hug. She worked hard not to jerk back, and actually managed it.

"Come on in," he said. "Mariah has a great idea for feeding everyone on Sunday. We were just talking about it."

Was that all anyone could think about? "Please don't tell me roasts," Kim responded.

"Fried chicken," Mariah called out from the kitchen. "We can set up sort of an assembly line. Deborah Stoltzfus said she would help. Just run them through the batter, into the frying pans and out again. Fried chicken is good even when it's cold."

Kim found her way to the kitchen door. "Correct me if I'm wrong, but this still involves dismembering them, right?"

"Right. But not in teeny, tiny pieces."

Good enough, Kim thought. She figured she would just volunteer for the batter end of things.

The kids had already gathered in the kitchen and Mariah wasted little time in getting dinner—supper, Kim reminded herself—on the table. Another difference from the real world, she thought. No cocktails first, no TV. The kitchen was at the heart of the family.

She had just been getting used to the table at Joe's—seven people, most of them young and boisterous, passing food, chattering nonstop. Now they were back to ten again, and it was even more boisterous.

Kim put one slice of meat on her plate and carefully trimmed the fat. She glanced unobtrusively at Joe. He said not a word as he piled food on his plate. He chewed. And chewed. He swallowed and chewed some more. His expression was downright blissful. And slowly she began to understand.

He was sitting beside her. She turned a little in her seat to look at him. "You don't like Chinese," she accused.

He didn't glance up from his plate. "It's fine. Mariah, would you please pass the biscuits?"

"I've never seen you eat like this," Kim persisted. "I mean, admittedly my cooking isn't the greatest, but you just picked at the Chinese food, too."

"You weren't watching me at the wedding," he said, then he could have kicked himself. He finally looked at her to see her eyes blazing.

"Joe, for God's sake, why didn't you *say* something?"

He put down his fork. "What is it that you would have liked me to say?"

"How about, 'I don't like Chinese, Kim. Why don't we try something else'?" Then she realized that he—and he alone—always called her "Kimberley." Her head got that swimming feeling again. Her full name was somehow more intimate for its formality.

"And then what would you have done?" Joe countered.

"I would have bought pizza!"

"Kimberley, I can't afford takeout every night with a farm full of food right beyond my doorstep!"

"*Kim.* My name is Kim!"

They had both turned in their chairs. They were nose to nose now. The rest of the table plunged into wide-eyed quiet, watching them.

"'Kim' doesn't suit you," he said levelly, but there was an underlying heat to his voice.

"You don't know me well enough to say," she argued.

"Oh, I think I'm coming to know you pretty well."

"That...incident...was a mistake."

"I won't disagree with you there."

"So drop it, Joe. Just drop it."

"Can you? My guess is that you've been thinking about it all day, too, no matter what you said this morning."

Kim paled. Her heart went crazy. Even her skin felt suddenly hot. And she knew, God help her, she *knew* that if they had been anywhere else, if they had been alone, their mouths would have found each other all over again.

So much for letting off a little of the frustration, she thought.

The wanting in Joe's blood was so fierce, so delightful and new in that moment, it almost overpowered him. He almost didn't care where they were, who they were with. How in the world did they expect to keep ignoring this...this tension? It couldn't work. No matter what he had shared with Sarah, this was different, this was something he had never experienced before in his life. Because Sarah had never pushed him. Sarah had never provoked him. Sarah, God rest her soul, had never gone nose to nose with him.

And he liked it. He realized that he liked it very much.

"I thought we were talking about Chinese food," Bo said, confused.

Kim felt her breath rush out of her. She inched backward in her seat cautiously. "We were."

"You know, Pa, every time your kin gets involved, things get weird," Bo added.

"Don't they, though," Adam murmured.

Joe felt as if someone had just doused him with cold water. He picked up his fork again very carefully.

"The biscuits, Joe?" Mariah was holding them out to him. He wondered crazily if she had been sitting like that, extending the basket, the whole time.

By the following weekend, Kim and Joe had fallen into a pattern of cautious and exquisite avoidance. They were, quite simply, never caught alone. They had the buffer of Dinah and Susannah, Matt and Gracie. And, to some extent, there was Hannah. Their arms couldn't easily go around each other if

Kim's were holding an infant. They used the kids with a smooth vengeance.

Somewhere along the line Susannah had decided that she wanted to go to Mariah's school. Kim suspected that it had less to do with her love of learning than with the fact that she was bored out of her mind staying on the farm all day, waiting for the others to come home. Kim thought that as long as Susannah was able to nap when she chose, it was probably good for her. And it worked. It worked well. Outside of the fact that Susannah was gone from 8:30 until three o'clock, she began to get up early enough to...well, to cover Kim in the mornings.

Where once Susannah had languished in bed until everyone else was gone, now they took to using the bathroom together, since there was only one and a good many people had need of it when the day began. That way, when Kim emerged to tangle with the woodstove, she had Susannah's company. Susannah set the table while Kim struggled to make something for everyone to eat.

They subsisted on a lot of boiled eggs until Kim discovered that poaching them was easier, given the slow heat. Then she settled into a routine of eggs Benedict. Even the hollandaise sauce worked out okay, again because high heat would curdle it. She was learning that those things that naturally cooked slowly were her best bet.

By the time the kids streamed out the door for school, Joe was invariably on his feet, as well. He seemed to make it a point to time his departure perfectly.

She took lunches out to him at the cattle barn so he wouldn't have to come inside at midday. She usually left a tray for him at the big, sliding doors. When she went back an hour or so later, the plate was always bare. At first she worried that some of the ever present animals were getting to it—the horses more or less grazed freely. Then she realized that the utensils were always used. And though she had suffered a lot of shocks to her system these past weeks, it seemed safe enough to assume that a horse was incapable of using a fork.

Matt rarely came home until four o'clock, just in time to help his father with the last of the chores. He and Bo always did that together, since Adam did not have a farm and he didn't need his son's services there. Dinah generally waited to reacquaint herself with her friends until he and Susannah and Gracie came home. Then Kim took care of the baby, and gladly gave the girl her freedom once so many of the other kids were around.

Someone was *always* around. They were never alone. And things were going well.

There was even something to be said for the lack of electricity, Kim figured. When dark fell—usually sometime during supper—she cleaned up the kitchen by lamplight and used the excuse to go directly to her room. She read. She started keeping a journal. And she found the writing to be surprisingly healing—a slow, steady, daily outpouring of emotion. The only thing that troubled her was how often she found herself spelling out the letters *J-O-E.*

He had no more spats with Dinah. But, then, he avoided her as much as he avoided Kim. And he had no more scraps with Kimberley, because they were both unfailingly polite, even though it often set their teeth on edge. Everything worked fine until it came time to draw blood from the community.

Part of it, Kim knew, was her own desperation. The donor lists still hadn't kicked off any matches. She was acutely and painfully aware that they were getting down to their last chance. If this didn't work—and she had every reason to believe it was a long shot—then she had no clue what she would do next, how she would proceed to save her daughter's life. And that was, quite simply, intolerable.

Joe felt her panic and terror in the air around her. He didn't have to be alone with her to sense it. It was palpable, something thick and tightening that built as the days went by. And he was tormented, because he needed to comfort her as badly as he needed to keep away from her.

On Sunday morning, as he watched her dismembering her share of the chickens to feed everyone with later, something hit him. He knew the hell of having lost Sarah. But they had had years and years after the birth of Matt to think that everything would work out okay. She would take the pills. There would be no more children. Even when she had conceived, they had both clung to the possibility that everything would be all right this time around. Even the doctors had told them that there was only a small chance that the horror of Matt's birth would be repeated. It was nothing they would have deliberately taken a chance on, but the slim possibility had been there all the same.

There had been no real terror until those final moments, when everything had gone wrong. There had been fear, certainly. But not the terror of knowing well in advance that, barring a decisive miracle, Sarah would die.

He could barely imagine Kimberley's almost sure certainty that Susannah's death was right around the corner. My God, how did she even begin to hold up? Where did she keep dredging courage from? It was the single thing that had him coming into the kitchen that morning, when he had vowed to keep going straight to the bathroom to wash up.

"I can do that," he said quietly, coming to stand behind her. He needed to help somehow, any way he could.

Kim had been lost in thought and she hadn't heard him enter. She jumped, wielding the butcher knife as she came around to face him. "I can handle it," she snapped, because she had pride, and she refused to give in to her need to get these birds off her hands. So much for her idea of doing the cooking part of things. Joe had brought the birds in to her first thing this morning. "Mariah was right," she continued. "This is better than tiny pieces. And this time, at least, they were dead for a while."

"I just want to help."

"You have. You are. And *damn* it, will you *please* put a shirt on? There are no services today!"

"What?" He looked at her dumbly.

She realized what she had said and her face flamed.

"I was on my way to wash up," he explained slowly when she didn't answer. "And what does that have to do with church?"

"Nothing," she muttered, turning back to the chickens. "I've already got feathers stuck to every inch of my skin. I'll finish. No sense in both of us getting garped up."

He didn't want to imagine feathers stuck all over her skin. The image should have been ludicrous. Instead, he imagined taking them off. One by one.

*Why wouldn't he leave?* He was breaking the rules, she

thought desperately. He never came near her anymore when the kids weren't around. And where the hell were the kids? The house was stone quiet.

"Kimberley," he began again.

"Go away," she whispered.

But he didn't move. Instead, she felt his hand in her hair. After the initial leap of her heart, she spun around again, fully prepared to lay into him and bite his head off. And the sobs came out of nowhere, clogging her throat. She threw the knife down, and herself into his arms.

Joe caught her because he couldn't do anything else. Nor did he want to.

She clung, and he felt the tremors of each of her ragged breaths against his chest. He closed his eyes and stroked her hair. And he needed, and he wanted, but at least half of it this time was a strong desire just to make everything right again for her and her daughter.

"What if—" She broke off, started again. "What if this doesn't work, Joe?"

"I don't know," he said honestly. They both knew the odds. *Irish and German.* They both knew it likely wouldn't work. There wasn't any Irish gene to be found in the community, except hers and Adam's.

"I...can't...let her...die. I *can't.* In all...my life...she's all that's...mattered. She's all that's been...good."

"I know."

But he didn't know how to help her. He didn't know how to save her from this.

She drew in one last, rough breath. She tried to pull back. He wouldn't let her go. He decided there was no real need for her to stand on her own two feet right now. He thought it entirely possible that she might hit him for it. That would be okay, too, if it helped vent some of what was inside her. But she didn't. She struggled a little more, then she went limp against him again, just holding on.

"Let it out," he said inanely.

"I am." And she hated it, *hated* it. "I'm not weak."

"I know."

"I can handle anything."

"I know that, too."

"Anything but this."

He didn't tell her this would be a damned good time for prayer. He buried his own hatchets with God and prayed for her.

By nightfall, it was pretty much over. Kim was vaguely astonished by how seamlessly the whole process had gone. Two white minivans from Children's Hospital had pulled up in front of the farmhouse at noon. The community began descending upon them at the same time. There was one brief, easily fixed glitch when the technicians told her that everyone should have a glass of orange juice after giving a sample. Not that they were taking all that much blood from any one person, but those who had never done it before—which was the entire community—might feel a bit woozy.

Adam had saved the moment, thrusting some cash at her so she could run into the village and clean out the refrigerator of the small market there. She'd cried again, hating herself for it, when she'd thanked him, and had vowed to pay him back.

She'd counted the people as they fell into line, one by one, rolling up their sleeves. Joe had gone first, and her throat had slammed shut. She knew he was doing it to show everyone how easy and painless the process was. He'd told her that he had done this once before, when Sarah had needed blood after Matt's birth. When the technician inserted the needle into his arm, she knew he had to be remembering.

She counted up to 170 people in the line, before her eyes crossed and her brain fogged and she lost track. They rolled up their sleeves for a child because they felt their God would want them to do so. Because, Joe told her, community and family were inviolate here.

"This doesn't make sense," she murmured finally, sitting on the top porch step. Joe had come to stand on the walk in front of her. The people who had already given blood were inside eating. Some were simply carrying their plates around with them as they greeted friends. Neither Joe nor Kim had any appetite.

"How so?" he asked.

"If I understand everything you've told me, then God's will is that my daughter should die," she said flatly.

"Not necessarily."

She looked up at him, her eyes hot. "Well, *I* didn't give her leukemia."

One corner of his mouth crooked, but it wasn't a pleasant smile. "No. He did that, all right. But He has also given us this means to remedy it. That's His will, too. That's what this *gemeide* chose to believe when we branched off and looked for our missing children."

Kim gave a guttural sound of distress. "Wasn't there a philosopher somewhere who said that the human mind can rationalize anything, twist any theory to its own purposes?"

"I don't know," he answered honestly. "I never encountered philosophers in high school. But I do know that if God gives you the means to fix something, you should probably grab it."

She watched him steadily for a long time. "Like birth control pills?"

He paled. His eyes went doggedly back to the people. "Something like that."

Maybe she needed to push him because it took her mind off her own fear. Maybe she needed to save him because she might not be able to save Susannah. Maybe she needed to heal him because she cared.

She went on stubbornly. "God gave you the means to save Sarah. You took it, didn't you? The doctors must have given her pills, and she took them, right?" She had to wait a long time before he nodded.

"She had the pills," he agreed. He had never admitted it aloud before. The threat of the *meidung* still haunted him.

"And she got pregnant and died anyway." She watched his jaw go rock hard. But he nodded again. "Sounds to me like that's God's will, Joe, at least as you just explained it."

She reached up for his hand and tugged him down to the step just beneath her. He resisted a moment, then he sat and rested his arm on her updrawn knee.

"Hannah looks like her," he acknowledged finally, bitterly, and could scarcely believe it when he heard his own voice.

"She's starting to look just like Sarah, and I can't stand it. I think that's what gets to me most of all."

"Maybe that's God's way of letting you keep a piece of her."

"Either that, or He's cruel, making sure I never forget my mistakes. I can't decide." It was a blasphemy to say so out loud, and he winced as soon as the words were out. They were bald, anguished, honest. But then he looked at her.

She wasn't shocked. She wasn't offended. Kimberley just nodded understandingly.

# Chapter 15

Kim knew that it would take at least a week for all the results to come in on the community blood tests. Dr. Coyle had warned her. But that didn't stop her from going to the pay phone every day now to ask about the results and any potential donor registry matches. Susannah was pretty much down to her last chance.

By Tuesday, the hospital had completed testing on roughly twenty percent of the community samples. There was no match. On Wednesday, Joe began dropping whatever he was doing to ride to the phone booth with her. On Thursday, forty-five percent of the samples had been tested, and there was still no match.

On Friday, Kim fell apart.

Oddly, it wasn't so much the waiting or the fear that did it to her. It was a phone call she made to California. Maybe it was the straw that broke the camel's back. She needed to tell her boss that her situation was still far from resolved and she wouldn't be back anytime in the near future. He argued with her. The extra girl he'd hired was about to go back to college on Monday. Either Kim could come back to work by then, or they would have to hire someone permanent to replace her.

"I can't do that," she said desperately. "My daughter..." She trailed off before she could embarrass herself by begging him. Besides, it was even more than Susannah, she thought. She had made an agreement with Joe. Joe still needed her. But how could she explain that to this man?

He fired her. Sometime during his shouting, Kim realized that she'd been gone a whole month already.

She went back to the farm feeling overwhelmed and shell-shocked. She had no more savings. Now she had no income to go back to, either. All along, she realized, she'd been clinging to the idea that she could go home, back to work, and collect tips—cold, hard cash. She could do that whenever she chose. It was one thing to take charity when she knew she'd be paying everyone back. It was something else to admit that she was as destitute and without prospects as she had been eleven years ago when she had fled Dallas.

Joe saw it in her face as soon as she stopped the car in front of the house. At first he was angry that she had sneaked out to call Coyle without him. Why did she always have to be so stubbornly independent with her fear? He came across the road, still wearing the heavy apron he used to shoe the horses.

"Who do you think you are?" he demanded. "Wonder Woman?"

Her eyes took a moment to focus on him. "What do you know about Wonder Woman?"

"I went to public high school in the seventies."

She shook her head absently. She started toward the house.

It wasn't quite the reaction he'd expected. "Aren't you even going to tell me about it? What did he say?"

"Who?"

"The doctor!"

"I didn't call the doctor. I called the place where I work. Used to work. I've been fired."

"Fired." He struggled to find the importance of that. "So? You don't need a job here."

Her temper finally sizzled. "I'm out of work, Joe. Out of money. Out of any means to support myself. Are you following me now?"

"You said your job wasn't that great."

"It was mine! It was all that stood between me and welfare!"

"What's 'welfare'?"

She drove both hands into her hair, tears finally threatening. Again. "I can't stand this."

"I need to understand, Kimberley. I need to know why this bothers you so."

She gritted her teeth. "'Welfare' is what the government does to help people out when they're dead broke."

"But you don't need that. You're here. We take care of our own."

"I'm not your own!"

She started to run for the house. She saw Dinah on the porch with Hannah. No, she thought, she didn't want to go there. She didn't want to be nice. She didn't want to be responsible. She didn't want to take care of anyone.

She swerved the other way, crossing the road, racing right past Joe once more. He pivoted to watch her go. She veered into the first barn she came to. At least, he thought, it was the one for the horses, and smelled a bit better than the dairy barn. He went after her, untying his apron and dropping it over the paddock fence as he passed it.

He found her on the bales of hay stacked at the back of the center aisle. They were a small reminder that Nathaniel was missed. Bo and Matt were too small to help him get them up into the loft. He'd been meaning to ask Adam for assistance—it was decidedly a two-man job—but he hadn't gotten around to it with everything else going on.

He'd thought she'd be crying again, and he had spent every step bracing himself for it. Somehow her absolute silence was worse. She sat cross-legged, with her face in her hands. He sat quietly beside her and waited.

"I didn't realize I've already been gone so long," she finally admitted without looking up. "All that talk—we'd talked that this might take months, do you remember? But the reality of that just never really registered with me, I guess. Too much else to think about."

"I remember."

"I never thought of the *practicalities* of such a lengthy stay."

"As you said, your mind's been full."

At last she looked at him. Her eyes were so bleak it hurt him.

"I'm going to lose my apartment. The rent's due."

"Yes." But there was a question in his voice.

"I've gone through all my savings. I can't even get back there to arrange to have my furniture moved. I'll lose that, too. Even if I *could* go back, I couldn't afford storage for it."

He knew better than to point out that one of her brothers would likely float her a loan. For that matter, they'd *give* her the money.

"It's all gone," she said dazedly. "Ten years of eking out a living with my dukes up. Ten years of standing on my own two feet. It's all gone." She'd lose her health insurance along with the job, she realized. They would take that away, too. And she couldn't afford to extend it. How was she going to pay for Susannah's care?

She had to go back there. She looked at Joe, thought of Susannah, and knew that she couldn't. It wasn't because of Joe. She'd been lying to herself. It wasn't because he still needed her, hadn't resolved his own problems. She'd never made any promises to him about how long she would stay here. It was just that suddenly she couldn't even contemplate going back to L.A. and coping with this horribly dwindling hope on her own.

As the enormity of that hit her, she began to tremble. What had happened to her? What had she done?

"Everything's gone," she repeated, her voice thin, on the edge of hysteria, and this time she meant so much more than just money and material goods.

"No," Joe said quietly. "Susannah is alive, over at Mariah's school. And you've still got the heart and the courage that carried you this far in the first place."

She stared at him. Her eyes finally filled. "I...am...so... tired, Joe. The thought of...the thought of starting over again...I just can't..."

The thought of starting over again was what did it, she decided. It buckled her. It overwhelmed her.

She couldn't quite say the words—*help me.* She said them

with her eyes. She said it with arms that reached for him. And sanity had no place in his response.

There was no fervent collision of their bodies this time, though the desperation was still there. Her arms snaked around his neck slowly. His went around her waist easily. They eased together rather than dragged each other closer.

"We'll find a way," he said quietly.

*We,* she mused again helplessly. With him, it was always *we.* And it was so easy for him.

Their mouths met slowly. They touched with exquisite, thoughtful care. They'd found an excuse for the last time they'd touched, though they'd had to dredge hard to find one. They could probably manufacture one this time, too, she decided. But she knew there was only one excuse that mattered—the searching, blind hope in their kisses.

She thought again that she loved the way he kissed. Slowly, deeply, consistently, with that unique breath he took in between. She didn't realize she was still crying until he caught a tear with his tongue, then dove back to her mouth again.

And that undid her.

He thought again that he loved the way she melted and went soft. That for all her prickly independence, her body gave and clung. He didn't realize he was shaking until he couldn't quite find the hem of her sweater. He hadn't meant to find it anyway. But then he did, and his palm moved up the smooth, hot skin of her back.

He leaned into her. She relented. Gave. Eased back on the hay, and he found himself on top of her. Again.

"Dinah..." she whispered, with one last, licking flame of common sense. Maybe that last, licking flame of common sense was just looking for a way out. Before it was too late.

It was already too late. This wasn't a sudden bursting through a barrier to find what was on the other side. They both knew what they were doing, where they were headed. His answer proved it.

"Dinah hates the barn."

"But..."

"Never comes in here," he continued, against her mouth this time, his words getting muffled. "If she can help it."

"We can't take the chance."

"We've got to."

How many days had they spent building toward this, homing in on this moment, like heat-seeking missiles with only one place to go? She thought that it had started when he had first kissed her behind the sofa, and knew that that other physical contact had nothing to do with this at all. It was the little things, the necessary things, that had brought them here. It was the friendship that had bloomed under all the sexual tension. She had never really had a friend before. She needed one. She needed him.

She pushed the suspenders off his shoulders, and didn't even stop to think how amazing it was that she could want someone who wore suspenders. He shrugged one arm to help her, but his other was taking his weight and that side got tangled. So they rolled, and the hat that had fallen off his head in the first moment they came together was crushed beneath him.

Joe didn't realize it. He was riding a wave, and he wanted to tell himself that it didn't allow him time to think. But the truth was that he had thought. He had thought well and carefully about this for days now. He had thought about it when she looked at him with those blue-violet eyes, and when she didn't. He'd thought about it when she passed close to him, and when she stayed steadfastly on the opposite side of the room. When she laughed and when she scowled. When she fought with him and when she smiled. He'd thought and thought.

He was alive. He hadn't died with Sarah. He was only a man, only human. And he needed to give as desperately as he needed to take. They both did. And if there was something deeper than physical gratification in that, then they would both ignore it. For now.

He pulled his hand out from beneath her sweater. Something in his chest nearly exploded when she grabbed his arm and tried to pull him back.

"I need this," she murmured. "I need—"

"Wait," he told her. "Just wait a minute. Let me—"

"No."

He thought that, in spite of everything, her independence was alive and well. And he heard himself laugh, though he would have sworn it was impossible. Or maybe it was just a groan that trembled.

He pulled his arm free of her grip and managed to push the leather jacket off her shoulders. She hadn't zipped it. He wasn't sure he could have gotten it undone at the moment if she had.

She dragged his shirt free of his pants and wondered if she was going to regret this. She decided not to give herself the opportunity. When her fingers fumbled with his buttons, she jerked at the fabric, frustrated, until they popped free. They hit the hay soundlessly.

She wasn't sure how he had ended up on his back, how she had come to be straddling him. Even as she finally, *finally*, skimmed her hands over his hard chest, threading her fingers through that fine vee of dark hair there, she realized that she was too far away, cold, needed to be closer to him.

He saw it in her eyes—a vague flickering. He reached up and caught her hair again, pulling her down to him. Their mouths met again, clung. And he rolled again, driving her back against the hay. His hands streaked under her sweater again, and this time she grabbed the hem herself to pull out of it.

He'd liked her jeans from the start. The lacy scrap of her bra nearly undid him. He fell to it like a starving man offered bounty. He caught her nipple through the fabric, and she seemed to arch up off the hay. The cry that escaped her was like nothing he had ever heard before. A plea, a promise. She drove her hands into his hair and held his mouth against her greedily.

He ran his tongue over the fabric and fought with the zipper on her jeans. He was astounded by how tight they were, how hard to get off. Desperate, he rolled with her again, taking her weight on top of him, thinking that might make it easier. They teetered on the edge of the bales for a moment, then went over.

"Ouch," she gasped.

He didn't feel it. He'd gotten her jeans off.

More lace. Little swatches of it, front and back. Glory. But gone before he could really appreciate it. She twisted against him, and he saw the small piece of fabric go sailing.

In thirty-nine years, he had never before found himself on the floor of a barn, with a naked woman pressed on top of him, her mouth hungry and hot, her skin slick and smooth. He never would have imagined it possible. His hands found her hips, cupped her bottom.

It was amazing, she thought, how instinct took over when everything else was gone. She'd never known before because she'd never let everything else go. Always, always, she kept a part of herself back. Warily. Cautiously. But she couldn't find the barrier now or anything to erect it with, and she didn't want to put the energy into searching.

There were still things between them that kept flesh from flesh, and they both began homing in on them blindly. He dragged her bra away, filling his hands with her breasts now. She got his pants off, encountered boxer shorts, and made a delighted sound in her throat. She got rid of them, too. And somehow her legs were around him and they were rolling again. Her hands were fisted in his hair as she dragged his mouth back to hers.

There were so many parts of him she wanted to explore, that she *needed* to explore, but now that she could, now that she had the opportunity, only his heat, her need and the void inside her that only he seemed to be able to fill mattered.

"Now," she murmured. "Oh, please. Joe, *please.*" She was begging. She didn't care.

He found her mouth again, instead. And he used his hands. They delighted, urged, tormented. She had never thought him imaginative. Intelligent, yes. Intuitive, certainly. Solid and strong, beyond question. But she would never have expected him to bring her to the brink again, yet again, backing away each time. Killing her with the wanting, the waiting.

She'd had enough.

She rolled into him with a strength that amazed him, forcing him onto his back. She'd always thought his body was so solid. He looked solid. But his muscles, his wonderful, hard-working muscles, rippled and moved under her hands. She closed one of them over his hardness. Then he went stone still.

He felt something guttural and inarticulate rip from his throat. He felt himself unraveling inch by inch, felt the flimsy control he'd been clinging to slipping, sliding, as her hand moved, stroking. He reminded himself that he was bigger, stronger than she was. He could do something about this turn of events. But his muscles felt like putty. With one last effort that came all the way up from his soul, that was more willpower than strength, he caught her hips again and pulled her back on top of him.

And found home. It had been gone so long, had been ripped from him, stolen from him, leaving him bereft. Back again, improbably, impossibly, just when he'd thought hell was all he'd ever know. If he hadn't been a proud man, he might have wept.

She was prepared for the physical pleasure. For the eruption of satisfaction when he finally filled her. Instinct took over again, her body seeking, needing, and she moved against him. She didn't expect the way each thrust touched her heart, pummeling it, changing it, making her feel things she had never expected to feel.

He took the upper hand back, rolling with her again. He braced his weight on his hands and pounded into her, but his eyes never closed, never wavered, looked straight into her soul.

Climax barreled into her, making him swim out of focus. She hadn't expected it, hadn't dared hope for it. She turned her head away, gasping.

He caught her chin and brought her face back. "Look at me," he rasped. "This is us, together."

She couldn't speak. She thought she nodded.

He watched the wonder in her eyes, and felt a surprising rush of victory, though he had never considered himself a man who had to win. Then again, no one had ever challenged him before.

He plunged one last time as something close to pain crashed into him. He'd never known release could hurt. Had never known how necessary it could be. Had never felt as though his very soul and every wit was emptying from him. It seemed crucial to find her mouth again. As he lowered himself on top of her once more, she wrapped her arms around his neck, the way she had when this had all started. And she whispered his name like a prayer.

* * *

Dinah didn't come into the barn. Kim considered that a very good thing. She wasn't at all sure she was capable of movement. Maybe, she thought, maybe that was what had made it so good. Maybe it had just been the added little kick that they might have gotten caught. But she knew it wasn't.

Joe had finally rolled off to her side. His arms were flung out. He looked like a casualty of war.

She tried to say his name, and something inarticulate came out. He turned his head to the side to look at her anyway. His eyes were questioning.

Kim cleared her throat. "What would your deacons say?"

Somehow, impossibly, his eyes got hot again. "I *am* a deacon," he reminded her. "And I say it's fine."

A single bubble of laughter burst from her throat. "And your God?"

"Be fruitful and multiply."

His words echoed in the barn for an impossibly long time.

Kim flinched. Joe dragged an arm up quickly to rest it over his eyes, shielding them. And still his words rang in their heads. They had to be addressed, she thought.

Suddenly, something angry blazed through her. She would not let this be ruined. She would not let it be tainted. Not by his ghosts, nor by her own horrors. She suspected she was going to have little enough to remember fondly when this whole ordeal was over. She wasn't going to lose the memory of this afternoon.

She sat up shakily and grabbed his arm, pulling it away from his face. "Don't hide, Joe. Please."

He caught her hand, then he opened his eyes and looked at her.

"You didn't kill Sarah," she blurted.

"I know that."

"Getting her pregnant didn't kill her," she continued.

"Technically, that's not true."

"I just meant…it was God's will. You keep throwing that at me. It works just as well for you. You didn't kill her by making love to her. You didn't kill her by doing…this."

"No. I never did this with Sarah. Not…like this."

She stared at him uncomprehendingly, then the enormity of that hit her. Her pulse roared.

"Kimberley," he said quietly. "I'm going to try very hard not to allow myself to regret this. I get tired of all the heartache, too. I just want something...good."

She nodded slowly. She decided to believe him.

## *Chapter 16*

Things had definitely changed between them, Kim realized three days later. More often than not, it started to show in subconscious ways. Joe's hand would find the small of her back when he came into the kitchen before supper to wash up. He'd peer over her shoulder to find out what she was cooking, and his little sounds of distress were far more honest than his quiet and grim consumption of Chinese food had been.

She'd stopped creeping upstairs to her room at the first hint of darkness. They'd sit together in the living room. He'd read some agricultural magazine, and she'd scribble in her journal or do a crossword puzzle from the newspaper she bought religiously in the village every day. She bought them with his money, but she'd renewed her vows to pay everyone back just as soon as she could find another job.

There was peace. And there was fear, because the community blood samples would be finished at any time now, and there was still no match. And there was a new kind of tension between them, coiling tighter with every day that passed, because they had not found their way back to the barn again.

Joe told himself it was because there was just something so base and crude about making love on a barn floor. But he knew that excuse was just his last bastion of defense against the inevitable. What was he going to do when she left? Where, he wondered, was he going to find the calm sense to accept it? If they didn't go over to that barn again, if they didn't touch again, maybe he would find a way.

Kim told herself that she didn't follow him across the road and ambush him in the barn because there was no future in it. They had to draw the line here. Once had been necessary. Once had been vital. Twice, three times, four...well, that got into the realm of making things hopelessly tangled. Of creating a situation that was going to create a painful void when everything was fixed and she went home. She was just too sensible for that.

"Kimberley," he said as they sat on the sofa Monday night.

She jumped a little as his voice intruded into her thoughts. "What?"

"What are you going to do?"

She relaxed. "Finish this puzzle, then I guess I'll go upstairs."

"I meant about your apartment. Your job."

She'd known that. She put the paper down carefully. "I guess I keep thinking that if I ignore it, it will go away." She laughed shakily, self-consciously.

"That's the problem, isn't it? It might all go away. You might lose it all."

She closed her eyes. "Yes."

"That medical insurance? Will you lose that, too? You said that was part of your job."

"I...probably. There's something called COBRA...it's this program that allows you to pay your own premiums for a while so you don't abruptly lose your health insurance when you lose your work. But I have no way of paying it."

"How much would it cost?"

"Off the top of my head? I just don't know. Probably about three hundred dollars a month." She opened her eyes again to see that he looked shocked.

"So much?" he asked.

"I think there's a ceiling on it anyway."

"What do you mean, a ceiling?"

"After Susannah's medical expenses reach a certain point, the company won't pay any more."

"Then how do they justify taking your money in the first place?"

She grinned mirthlessly and lifted a shoulder. "That's America."

He thought about it, then filed the information away for the moment. He'd deal with that later. "What will the apartment people do with your furniture?" he asked.

Kim shrugged. "Nothing right away. I probably have thirty days before they'll auction it to pay the rent for this month. Though they'll likely only get a drop in the bucket, because I don't own much. Then they'll take a judgment against me for the remainder, and they'll rent the place to someone else." She'd been through this before, just after she'd left Texas.

"That's heartless," Joe protested.

"That's life in America." Suddenly her throat closed. She couldn't pretend anymore. "It's not the furniture so much," she admitted, her voice strangled now. "It's Suze's baby shoes. It's the pictures, the personal stuff, because if I lose her and that's gone, too, then, dear God, Joe, there's *nothing* left. It would be as though she'd never existed at all, and I can't bear to think about that, can't even push my mind in that direction, because I can't stand it."

She threw the newspaper aside and jumped to her feet. Joe stared at her. He'd thought he knew her, that he was coming to understand her. But it staggered him that she was willing to lose all that before asking for help.

He put his magazine down very deliberately. His voice vibrated with anger. "That's not going to happen."

"I can't stop it!" she cried. "Haven't you been listening? I can't even afford to get back there and get the stuff out of there before it happens!"

"Well, for God's sake, woman, call these people and tell them to put the personal stuff aside!"

"If I try to get it out of there, that's like admitting she's going to die!"

There. She'd said it. She looked around wildly as the sound of her own voice rang off the walls.

"It's like admitting that that's all I'll have left. Baby shoes. Pictures," she whispered this time. Then she began crying.

Pain bloomed in his chest, along with the agony of indecision. To try to nudge her into collecting that stuff would be like making her admit that she was going to lose her daughter. Not to try would mean letting her lose such precious things. So he took another avenue.

"And if you ignore the situation," he said, "then you can always pretend you're going back eventually, and everything will be fine."

She looked up, dashed her tears away. "Damn it, I *am* going back eventually. One way or the other."

"If you ignore the situation, you don't have to make any decisions."

"*What* decisions? Everything's been taken out of my hands!"

"That would make it easy, wouldn't it?"

"What are you saying, Joe?" she demanded.

"Just that you have a third option, but it's easier for you not to look that way. You're ignoring it. You have people willing to help you, but you refuse to see that."

She stared at him as though he had somehow betrayed her.

"What are you going to go back to, Kimberley?"

She made a choking sound but said nothing.

"Is it better than what you've found here? Family? Friends? A lover? Are you that scared of trusting anyone again that you'll go alone to a place where you have no one, that you'd prefer to deal with this nightmare by yourself rather than accept someone else to lean on?"

Damn him, she thought. Damn him! How could he know that the idea of that had suddenly become so uncomfortable?

"She's not going to die!" she shouted.

"She might," he said cruelly, trying to reach her. "Here you've got comfort, family." *Me.* "Here you've got something to bolster you if and when it happens. What's in California besides earthquakes and palm trees?"

"What do you want from me?" she cried. "I told you from the start I wasn't the kind of woman you keep thinking I should be!"

"You're a coward," he said relentlessly. "You're hiding behind your excuses."

She came at him like a bullet, all fury, all heat. He caught her wrists.

"You're not cold, Kimberley," he continued. "You've given me pleasure and comfort and companionship. You've given me sensations I never knew I could feel."

"Don't say that!" This was spiraling out of control. She had to fight back. She needed to fight back, to get this off her shoulders and onto his. She felt cornered, threatened. "I haven't noticed you cuddling that baby, Joe," she accused. "You haven't put anything behind *you.* So don't talk to me about excuses!"

She had the pleasure of seeing his face go white. But only for a moment.

"Fine," he said, biting off the word.

"Fine what?" she demanded.

He let go of her arms. "I'll stop avoiding Hannah if you go ask Adam."

"Ask Adam *what?*" Kim cried, but her heart was thundering.

"For his help. For money."

"I'm not asking him for money!"

"I'd help you out, but I don't have all that much to give you."

"He doesn't, either. You said so."

"He has more than I do."

"Stop it! This is crazy!"

"No, it's not."

He left the room. She stared after him. He wouldn't do it. But she heard his footsteps on the stairs.

*"Joe!"*

He didn't answer. She ran after him. She caught up with him in front of Dinah's door. She grabbed his arm as he raised a hand to knock.

"Don't do this because of me," she gasped.

He turned back to look at her. He held her eyes for a long time. "Am I?"

Dinah's door opened at the sound of their voices, and she and Gracie popped out. Then Susannah opened the one behind them. Finally Matt stuck his nose out into the hall from his own room, as well.

"What's going on?" Dinah asked.

"Nothing," Kim snapped.

"I'm crossing bridges," Joe said. "I'm trying to put the pain behind me."

Dinah frowned, clearly not understanding.

Kim tried to swallow and failed. It would shame her into asking Adam for help. Which, she thought angrily, was just what he intended. But she didn't believe that was all it was. She didn't believe it in her heart.

Joe took a step into Dinah's room.

"Mom?" Susannah asked quietly. "I don't understand."

"It's time to start fresh," Joe said, "to start over." Then he looked at Kim again. "None of this is Hannah's fault, Kimberley. And none of your trouble was Jacob's and Adam's. You're only breaking their hearts by not reaching out."

Kim's eyes darted to her, and when she looked back, Joe was gone. She flew into Dinah's room after him. He was at the cradle.

"Didn't you hear me?" she asked.

"I heard you." He looked up at her and met her eyes. "It's time, Kimberley. Things are always easier when you do them together."

"I don't want to be together! How many times do I have to tell you that?"

"You stopped being alone on Friday. Apparently, you're too stubborn to open your eyes to that."

"You can't offer that infant your love just to make me see things your way," she whispered fiercely. "You can't do that, then snatch it back from her!"

"No. If I didn't love her, then that would be cruel," he agreed. "But I do, and I have to start making all this up to her somewhere. And my point is valid, Kimberley. I've never set foot in California. I don't know how it's done there. But where I come from, something like Friday changes all the rules. It means you've got someone to wade through things with you."

"I only...I don't generally do that...I mean, I'm not the

world's utmost authority on the subject.'' Her words were tumbled, tangled, tortured. Her face flamed.

''I'm not that ignorant,'' Joe said slowly.

She couldn't believe they were talking about this with Dinah and Gracie, Susannah and Matt all standing there staring. She looked at them crazily and Joe read her expression.

''Clear out, kids,'' he said levelly.

''But—'' Dinah began.

''This is private.''

The girl's expression became hopeful and confused and angry all at once. But one by one, the children all wandered off.

''I wasn't the first,'' Joe said carefully when they were gone. ''Are you trying to tell me I was?''

Kim shook her head helplessly. ''No. Of course not. It's just…I don't take it as lightly as you seem to think. Once,'' Kim whispered, ''there was someone. Once I got to California. I can't…I can't give anything,'' she said for what seemed to her like the thousandth time. She couldn't imagine why he wouldn't hear her. ''I stopped trying. I couldn't even…you know, before.''

His eyes narrowed. ''You couldn't what?''

''The, uh, grand finale, was a first for me.''

He stared at her as he understood. And in that moment, he understood a lot. Now he knew what she meant by *giving.*

His whole face changed. Neither of them realized he had picked up the crying baby, that he was holding Hannah against his shoulder.

''Don't look at me like that!'' she cried.

''Like what?''

''Like you're going to beat your hands against your chest and grunt in triumph.''

''I might.''

He grinned. Like a fool, she thought. From ear to ear. ''You're crazy,'' she whispered.

''Feels good, though. It's a great improvement.''

She pivoted unsteadily to watch him leave the room. After a moment, she went after him. He was standing in the living room, in front of the sofa. He was still holding Hannah, and she thought he had only just realized it. Amazement and sorrow were in his eyes. She went to him and put her arms around both of them.

"So," he said. His voice was strained. "Do we have a deal? Are you going to ask Adam?"

Kim nodded, unable to form the words. He'd left her no choice.

They went to Adam's shop in the morning. They took the horse and buggy because the car was nearly out of gas. Again, Joe drove the animal in silence, lost in thought.

He had tortured himself all night over what he had done to her. What he had done to himself. He wasn't thinking about Hannah now. He was considering that if he had allowed that apartment to slip away from her through her own obstinacy, then it wouldn't be as easy for her to leave the settlement once this was all over. Maybe, like her brother Adam, she would even stay.

And, he admitted, he wanted her to stay. But he wasn't that kind of man.

He wanted her, in his arms, in his life. He supposed he had been subconsciously aware of that for a while now. And now he had admitted it to himself. But he wanted her to be with him, part of his world, because she had deliberately chosen to. He didn't want her to slide into his life, deluding herself the whole while that it had happened because she'd had no choice. He had his pride, after all.

Kim leaned against the buggy door as the horse's hooves beat a brittle tattoo against the macadam, caught up in her own thoughts. "That was blackmail," she said finally. "What you did last night."

"Yes."

"Don't you have a conscience?" she demanded.

Joe shrugged. "A deal's a deal."

He stopped the buggy on a village side street and got out. She scrambled after him, but stopped when he started toward a small, glass-fronted shop.

"You're just going to leave him here?" she called out.

Joe looked back, surprised. "Who?"

"The horse."

"He never goes anywhere."

"Because every time we've taken him somewhere, you've unhitched him and put him in a paddock."

"Kimberley, you're stalling."

She blanched. "Damned right," she muttered.

"Coward."

"I hate you, Joe."

"Wouldn't that be easy?"

Yes, oh, yes, she thought.

Adam looked up expectantly when the little bell jingled over the door. Then his jaw dropped at the sight of them. It took him a moment to find his voice. "Kimmie?" he asked. "What's up?"

Joe took his hat off and set it on a display case. Kim turned slowly, her arms crossed protectively around her waist, taking everything in. It wasn't just gewgaws and quilts, she saw, though enough of the latter hung from the rafters. Shelves along one wall were laden with preserved fruits and vegetables. There was a table full of carved wooden toys. The other wall was covered with decorative Pennsylvania Dutch plaques, gardening stakes, clocks and wreaths.

"I don't believe this," she murmured, finally turning back to Adam.

He scrubbed a hand over his beard. He looked a little embarrassed. "A man's got to do what a man's got to do," he mumbled. "Got to make a living."

Kim remembered Joe's expression of masculine victory in Dinah's room last night. "You guys need to let off some of this excess testosterone," she muttered.

Joe heard her. His eyes flared. "There's a thought."

Instantly, without warning, everything inside her heated. Kim tried to come up with a witty response, and realized she was tongue-tied.

"So what's going on?" Adam asked again, saving her. "To what do I owe this honor?"

Kim looked his way again. *Ask him.* She opened her mouth and closed it once more. She simply couldn't do it.

But Joe had picked up the baby.

"Kimberley has something she needs to ask you," Joe

prompted. His words felt like an elbow in the ribs. Kim forced herself to nod.

"I...uh, lost my job," she heard herself say. "I've been away too long. My apartment...I'm afraid I'm going to lose that, too. I have no money left. So there goes my health insurance, as well." She looked deliberately over her brother's head at a sampler on the wall as she waited for his response.

"How much do you need?" Adam asked.

"I..." At last she looked at him. "You don't have to do this," she whispered.

"I know that. And I probably won't have the chance."

"I...I don't understand." She gazed at Joe questioningly. He shrugged.

"Not once Jake finds out you need help."

She stared at him. "Jake doesn't know. I've only just asked you."

"Kimmie, I could give you a thousand dollars right now, and I'd do it, except something just occurred to me. You'd be doing Jake a huge favor if you asked him, instead."

She felt a spurt of anger. "Are we back to that again? He fixed my car. He found Grete Guenther. He talked her into giving blood. And it's pure craziness that he ever owed me anything in the first place!"

"He doesn't see it that way. And I've finally figured out that there's no reasoning with him. Believe me, I've tried. You saw how he was that first night you came here. Kimmie, help me out on this. He's torn himself up for a lot of years because he never helped you...back then. And because he never helped Mom."

Color flooded her cheeks "So what? You're going to make me ask him before either of you will help me? Would you like me to jump through a few hoops while I'm at it?" She turned away, more hurt than she would have believed possible. She could have told Joe this wouldn't work. She should have known better. When had a Wallace ever *not* put strings and conditions on giving?

Then she heard a little bell ring, and she looked back. Adam had opened the cash register.

"Here," he said, gathering up a handful of bills, holding them out to her. "For God's sake, Kimmie, it was just a thought. I was just trying to figure out a way to help both of you."

Kim swallowed carefully. Her head hurt. "But—"

"You could give him something, Kimmie. You could both benefit."

*Without strings or conditions.* She heard her own thoughts of a moment before. Except she had never been any good at giving anything to anybody.

"I can give him this," she repeated slowly, staring at the money still in Adam's hand. Then she squared her shoulders. "Fine. Point me in the direction of the nearest pay phone."

"Take a right at the next corner."

She took a step for the door, stopped, then looked back at both Adam and Joe. Her voice was wire thin. "I don't have any change."

Adam went into the register again. This time he put the bills back and pulled out change. Kim went and took it, stared at him a moment longer, then she walked back to the door. Something wriggly and panicked was moving in her stomach. Her heart was pounding.

The little bell above the door jangled wildly with her departure. Joe stared after her, thinking of what this was costing her, and the courage it required. He loved her, he realized. He really loved her. But he still didn't know how he was going to hold on to her. He looked back at Adam to find that the other man had been studying his face.

"Hurt her and you're a dead man," Adam said quietly. "Mariah would kill me for saying this. She hasn't quite forgiven me yet for meddling with Jake and Katya." Admittedly, that had almost turned out to be a disaster. "But Kim's my sister. Blood gets even thicker than friendship, Joe."

Joe gave him a strange smile. "Me? Hurt her? What I'm terribly afraid of is that it's going to be the other way around."

# Chapter 17

Joe went outside and waited for her in the buggy. When she came back around the corner, her color was high. The breeze tossed her long hair. Her hands were balled into fists and thrust deep into her jacket pockets—he could tell by the way they bulged.

What a picture she makes, he thought. Then, as she drew closer, he saw that her eyes were unnaturally bright. He said nothing as she opened the buggy door and slid onto the seat beside him. He decided it would be best to determine which way the wind blew first. He picked up the reins, clucked to the horse, and they began moving.

"Why do you do that when he can't hear you?" she demanded suddenly.

Joe scowled slightly. "Do what?"

"You always make that sound to the horse, but he's on the other side of all this glass."

He looked at her, cocking a brow. "There's a change of subject if I ever heard one."

Kim flushed.

"It's habit," he explained. "So what happened? Did you get through to Jake?"

She nodded. She was having trouble swallowing. "He was so...glad," she said finally. "So glad to do something for me. I don't know who just gave who more."

"He's going to send money?"

"Sure."

"Then what will you do?" he asked carefully. "Will you keep the apartment?"

"I don't know. It seems a waste to keep paying for it if I'm not going back there for a while." She pressed her hands to her temples. "But I don't want to fly back there right now to get my stuff out, Joe."

That was something, he thought.

"I don't want to leave Susannah for even a day. Not if..." She trailed off. "And traveling is so hard on her."

"Is there anyone there you can call to take care of things for you?" he asked.

She gave a quick shake of her head.

"*No* one?"

"I'm not big on friends, Joe. Susannah and I kept to ourselves."

"Then why don't you pay the rent for one more month and...just wait and see how things go?" Every instinct of his fought against suggesting it. Yes, he thought, he wanted her to let the place go. He wanted her to decide, to see, that things were good here, and so much more than what she had had at home.

"I suppose," he thought she said uncertainly. Then once again she changed the subject. Joe let out his breath.

"Want to celebrate?" she blurted. "You know, now that we've both upheld our parts of the bargain?"

"What did you have in mind?"

"I don't know. Another trip to the barn, maybe?"

His heart slammed. Instantly and without reserve. Now he understood why she'd seemed a little pensive earlier.

Her heart fluttered with something almost like hope. Maybe it was a mistake. Maybe she was getting in far too deep, as he had said. She already knew his feelings about what had happened on Friday.

But...she was riding a high. She felt relieved, certainly, about the money. But it was more than that. The pleasure, the relief at doing something for her, had been so real in her brother's voice. Right or wrong, whether she agreed with him or not, it had...touched her. She felt giddy, daring, almost reborn. And she wanted to keep feeling this way for a while longer.

The ride to the farm wasn't long. Joe turned into the drive on the opposite side of the road from the house and went around to the back of the horse barn. But then he drew the reins in and just sat for a moment, trying hard not to be a fool. Trying to be sane, smart, sure. He needed to say certain things, and he wasn't sure how to go about it.

"What you said last night..." he began. And that simply, he felt her stiffen beside him.

"We both said a lot last night," Kim interrupted.

"About California."

"It's a big state. Stretches along a good part of the Pacific coastline."

"About someone there."

She inched a little closer to the door. She hadn't meant to admit that. To anyone. Ever. He did things to her, brought things out of her, that she would never have believed possible.

"Never mind," she said. "This was a bad idea." She started to get out of the buggy. He stopped her.

"I need to know, Kimberley."

She looked back at him, anger in her eyes now. "Why?"

"I want to go into that barn," he said honestly. "God help me, I want it as much as I ever wanted anything. But I need to know how much it matters to you first. You can't just throw the suggestion out all light and casual like that, Kimberley. It means something bigger than that."

"Don't do this to me, Joe." A pleading tone crept into her voice. It struck her then that if making love with him had changed things, then speaking about her feelings could well be the point of no return.

"If it's all a lark to you," he continued, "just something here, something now, then I'm probably better off not doing it. Not getting in any deeper."

"You said it was too late!" she burst out, though she hadn't meant to say that, either. "Last night you said we were already in deep."

"*I* am," he admitted quietly.

Everything inside her began to shake. "What is it that you want me to say?" she demanded. "What are you asking me?"

He honestly didn't know. He just needed...something. Some comfort. Something to hold on to. He needed to hear her say that she didn't roll on hay bales as a matter of course. Was it just male jealousy? Possibly, he thought. He was accepting more and more often lately that he wasn't above other men.

"I was engaged," she said suddenly.

The confession jolted him from his own miserable thoughts. She wouldn't look at him, he realized. She found something inordinately fascinating about the barn door.

"To be married?" By some stroke of pure luck, he managed to keep his voice mild. But something clenched hard and painfully inside him. Something jealous and male. Something possessive when he had no right or reason to possess her, because she was so steadfastly holding her heart back from him. And God help him, but he was the man he was. And he felt that her body was only half of the bargain.

"Uh...how long did that state of affairs last?" he finally asked cautiously.

"Four months."

"Who broke it off?"

"He did."

That surprised him. "Why?"

"He said I was frigid, among other things."

Joe felt his jaw hang. "Sexually?"

"What other way is there?" she snarled.

"Emotionally," he told her.

"Well, I guess that goes hand in hand with it." She pressed her hands to her face. Her cheeks were burning. "Satisfied? He was it. The only one. I spent the first several years after I left Texas just...surviving. I spent the last part knowing better than to try again. Accepting what I am."

"Well, you're not frigid," Joe said.

*Not with you.* Not with an honest and simple Amish farmer who led with his heart and said what he meant, she thought wildly. A man who—unless she badly missed her guess—was trying to get her to say *I'm falling in love with you.*

Was she? No, she thought, no. She didn't know how. Especially since Bobby had let her down, she'd been incapable of it. But Bobby hadn't really let her down. At least, he hadn't had much to say about it. God had just gone waving wands again.

Joe got out of the buggy. Kim sat frozen, afraid to move now. If she had an ounce of sense in her head she would go straight to the house. She would just stay away from him. That was safest.

He opened her buggy door. "Are you coming?"

"Yes. No."

He waited.

"You do something to me," she admitted, her voice breaking.

"That's a start."

"Stop it, Joe! Just *stop* it! Asking me to trust you…I can't do that overnight. Maybe I can't do it at all."

Yes, he thought, that would indeed be a major milestone.

"Especially now," she continued desperately. "With Susannah… You're asking too much."

"All I'm asking is that you accept help and comfort where it's offered."

"That's not true," she said fiercely. "If that was true, you wouldn't have asked me about Mark!"

So now the fiancé had a name. Fine. He would live with that, too.

"Just checking to see how sheer the drop is," he explained. "Before I jump."

Then, for all intents and purposes, he jumped. The hell with it, he thought. He'd lived his whole life cautiously, thoughtfully. Maybe it was time to take what was offered to him, and consequences could be damned.

He caught her around the waist and lifted her from the buggy. And he kept finding proof of things he'd suspected from the start. His big hands nearly did fit around her waist. Before she could argue further, he put her on her feet, her back against the barn wall.

"This was your suggestion, as I remember," he said, just before he captured her mouth.

She couldn't think when he kissed her. She couldn't be practical, couldn't be smart. The slow, sweeping penetration of his tongue, his *finesse,* she thought crazily, made her bones turn to warm sand.

She managed to plant her hands against his chest and push him back a little. "You," she gasped.

"What about me?" His mouth went to her neck, sliding to a spot beneath her ear. She shuddered.

"Turnabout is fair play, Joe," she managed to say. "Maybe I need to know, too."

He drew back to look into her eyes. "Do you?" he asked. That, he thought, would be a very good sign.

She couldn't quite answer. She gave a little nod.

"Sarah," he said. He'd actually said her name, and she hadn't dashed down from heaven to wail her betrayal. There had been no bolt of lightning. He caught Kim's mouth again. She thumped him in the chest.

"*Just* Sarah?" she demanded. She should have expected it, but it shook her.

He lifted one shoulder, spoke against her mouth, pausing to nibble. "I met her when I was a teenager. I married her right away."

"*Just* Sarah?" she cried again. "Then us?"

Us, he thought. He liked the sound of that. It was a word she'd used so rarely. "Kimberley," he said patiently.

"What?"

"Please shut up."

It was overwhelming. Terrifying. What kind of man *was* he? An honest one. A good one. A man who led with his heart, but his head was never too far behind.

She shut up, because if she really considered the magnitude of what he had just said, along with all those other things—*I never did this with Sarah*—she knew, beyond a doubt, that she would run screaming for the nearest highway out of town. And at the moment, there was the matter of his mouth. It made her want to stay.

He had captured her hands—maybe so she wouldn't push him away again—and he held her arms pinned to her sides. He leaned into her and kept up with the slow, relentless meeting of their lips. It seemed easier to simply accept, she decided. To enjoy. To savor.

Something weak went through her body, a slow loosening.

Just when she reached the point where she doubted she could stand much longer, he scooped her up in his arms and carried her inside. He kicked the door closed behind them.

"Performed like a true Neanderthal," she muttered.

He smiled.

She would have felt safer with the explosive heat there had been the first time he'd kissed her. She could have dealt with the need they'd shared last time here in the barn. But she didn't know how to deal with this tenderness. He crossed to the hay bales. He was kissing her again. It was so dark in here, she thought. She wondered how he could see where he was going. Especially if he hadn't consistently carried women into this barn before.

*Don't think about that.*

He didn't lay her down on the bales so much as they sank onto them together. Cleaving and entwined. Her legs encircled him without her conscious thought. There was no deliberate decision this time to get rid of those suspenders, that shirt. She sought his heat, his skin, with blind intent, and made a small, whimpering sound when she found it.

Only one, he thought. Of course there had been Susannah's father, too. But what he shared with her was special. Mark had thought she was frigid. So, obviously, that man had never found the depths below her surface.

He had. He had reached that part of her. She didn't know it yet, but she was his.

He left her, untangled himself from her, to undress her this time. This time he wanted to see, to appreciate. He understood that it was a way of claiming, just as it had been to watch her eyes as she went over the edge the last time. Then he had needed to know that he had done that to her, for her, with her. This time he wanted to take a moment with all the physical barriers gone. He would leave her nothing to hide behind.

He eased her jacket off her shoulders with exquisite care. She reached for him.

"Touch me," she pleaded.

"I will."

"Now."

"Later."

"I hate your patience."

"I love your determination."

Her heart stuttered, shied back. But she made no protest when he pulled her sweater over her head. She just watched him warily. Her eyes narrowed a bit, but she lifted her hips to let him slide her jeans down her hips.

They got tangled over her boots. He got them off and the jeans, too, then he slid his hands back up her body. Slowly. Wonderingly. This time he fully appreciated that the scrap of silk at her hips matched perfectly with the pale peach lace that hid her breasts. He found that fascinating. He thought that he could live without her appliances, but he certainly liked her lingerie.

He finally leaned over her again, but this time, instead of taking her nipple through the lace, he pulled the lace down. He felt a shudder go through her. Even as he suckled, his hand slid under the silk at her hips. Down one side, to the other, sliding that away, too.

Her bones seemed to have melted. Something was wrong here; something was different. She felt it, but couldn't do a thing about it. He was stripping off so much more than her clothing. She knew it, and knew that with that mind of his, he must be fully aware of it. He was doing it deliberately, maybe making a point again, taking some sort of stand. She needed to stop it, but didn't come to the decision in time.

He caught the front clasp of her bra and snapped it free with practiced expertise he couldn't possibly possess. He smoothed the fabric aside. His mouth moved from one nipple to the other, nuzzling, his tongue smooth then rough, his teeth gentle.

Her back arching, she came up off the hay. Needing, no longer caring that she was the only one who was undressed. By the time his hand cupped black curls, by the time his work-roughened fingers found the center of her, it no longer mattered. She would have given him anything, any edge, all her soul.

His mouth was moving, roaming. She was unaware of tossing her head from side to side. She didn't hear herself begging.

It filled him, made him strong, confident, determined. His tongue traced her ribs, dipped into her navel, found places he had never entirely examined on a woman's body before. There were little hollows inside each of her hipbones. They tasted like secrets and shadows. Still, he slid lower, until his name came from her throat again on a torn breath.

*Leave me something,* she thought. But his tongue dipped into her and that was when she went wild. Her nails raked across his shoulders. She could have been trying to stop him or urge him on. Not even she was sure. She knew only that the sound coming from her throat was something close to a sob when he finally eased away from her and removed his own clothing.

Then he was back, without warning, without hesitation, driving into her hard. It was stunning, shattering, and she felt herself unraveling almost immediately. But then he went still, keeping her on the edge. Her arms were flung out to the side. He caught each of her hands and held them tightly, watching her.

For a long time he just stayed that way, sheathed inside her, until his blood pounded and it was almost unbearable not to move again. He'd make damned sure there was nothing like this back in California, he thought, that no one could need her or reach her the way he could.

He finally started moving inside her, slowly then faster, gently then harder. And as he had the last time, he lowered himself to her and kissed her again because it was imperative. He let go of her hands to brace himself on his elbows, and she wrapped herself around him.

For a moment, just a moment, she was his, body and soul.

"Why did you do that to me?" she asked a long time later, when she could speak again. They'd eased up to sit against the highest bales in the back of the pile, shoulder to shoulder.

He didn't pretend to misunderstand. "Grunting and beating my hands against my chest seemed a bit much."

She laughed too easily, then sobered. "Joe, if we're going to keep this up, we need to be more careful. I didn't...I'm not...I don't take those pills."

Joe went still. A moment before, everything inside him had been fire. Now it was ice. A moment before, there had been an odd mingling of peace and triumph. Now his heart roared. He chose his next words carefully. "I thought they were a fairly common thing in the *anner Satt Leit* world."

She felt his terror. It stoked her anger. Or maybe it was just asier to be angry than to know she had brought this fear back o him again with her words. "You thought *anner Satt Leit* vomen all ran around mating like jackrabbits," she corrected arshly.

"No, I thought—"

"I already told you I don't do this as a matter of course!" he interrupted.

He caught her hand. He twined his fingers with hers just as he was thinking of running, of getting away from him. She ad already started to scramble to her feet. He pulled her back.

"Don't run from me," he said quietly, but his voice was nything but calm. "I don't know your world, Kimberley. Not ery well. You'll have to forgive me a few preconceived no-ions. They have nothing to do with you personally."

She hated it when he was so reasonable. When he made her nger and panic seem senseless and immature. Which they vere, she thought, closing her eyes. She could feel herself be-inning to tremble.

"Anyway," he continued, "I suppose worrying about it now s a little like closing the barn door after the horse is gone."

"Not entirely," she contradicted, her throat suddenly dry. "The way things are going, there could still be a few ponies eft."

He gave her hand a quick squeeze. "Whatever you're com-fortable with, then."

That was when she understood.

He wouldn't do anything about birth control because it was—must be—against his religion. Sarah must have taken the pills in defiance of the *ordnung*. Sarah had done it because to con-ceive would mean risking her life. She, on the other hand, came from mainstream America and could be expected to do it as a matter of course.

"Damn you!" She jerked her hand away from him.

"What?" Joe sat up fast, confused.

"You must have thought I was manna from heaven, landing in front of your house that way. A woman you could have without torturing yourself over her. You could have me without fear of the consequences, without having to tangle with all those sticky issues you haven't managed to come to terms with yet!"

His face bleached of color. This time she did get to her feet and he let her go. "Do you honestly think that little of yourself?" he demanded.

She knew from his voice that he was angry now, too. "I was convenient."

"And I'm not ignorant!" he roared.

His voice echoed around the barn. Kim stared at him, hugging herself, fighting tears...again. When had she become so prone to cry? But it hurt, she thought. It hurt a lot. It hurt when she had long considered herself above feeling pain over what people might want from her, or why they might want it.

"You," Joe said more quietly, "have a few preconceived notions of your own." But his voice still vibrated with anger.

"I—" she began.

"Do you think we're all hicks? 'Jackrabbits'?" He used her word. "Mating without care? Without caution?"

"I never—"

"Your pills are only one way, one method. We have a few of our own."

"But Sarah—"

"Sarah needed something foolproof," he said harshly. "And apparently there's no such thing."

Kim paled, feeling like a fool. Of course that would be true. "I'm sorry."

"I didn't need you and your pills! I just needed to feel again. Period!"

She had to turn away from the look in his eyes. "Well, at least the kid would be German and Irish, right?" she said thinly, shakily, just trying to lighten the tension she'd caused. Then she froze as she heard her own words.

Joe stared at her back as she went stone still. His heart had just begun quieting, and now it exploded again. The rage that erupted in his blood was like nothing he had ever felt before.

"Is that why you're not taking those pills?" His voice nearly vibrated. "Have *you* been using *me?* Is that what all this has been?" Was that why she had so steadfastly refused to give him anything more than her body?

Kim spun round again, horrified. "No! No! I never thought about it until just this second!"

She was shouting, she realized distantly. Because what she was suddenly thinking was so horrible, so...well, twisted, she thought helplessly. Conceive one child to save the life of another? Why not? Unless she was mistaken, it had been done before. But not without a media frenzy. Not without a countrywide debate about the morality of it. Without people arguing about whether it was a perfect solution or an unconscionable wrong.

Joe finally got up off the hay bales. She couldn't quite read his expression in the murky darkness of the barn, couldn't tell if that deep anger was still there, the rage that had made his voice go so dangerous for one moment.

"But if it's already happened—" she began.

"That would be convenient, wouldn't it?" he interrupted.

He was still angry, she thought.

"Why do I feel I'm just being bounced along here, out of control?" she whispered. "Like...like something, some big giant hand, is...is pushing me places I wouldn't ordinarily think of going?"

His face softened. He closed the distance between them, catching her shoulders, pulling her close to his chest. "It's called God's will, Kimberley."

She thought of Susannah's illness, of his wife's passing. "Is that supposed to be comforting?"

"There are those who would think so."

"This is not something we should even be discussing," she said frantically.

He wondered which part of their conversation she was referring to. As he was learning to do with her, he waited.

"I can't marry you, so it's impossible."

He wasn't sure how he felt about that. His heart cringed with instinctive hurt, but his lungs gasped for a breath of relief. He honestly had not thought in any such terms. He wanted her. He wanted her to stay. He'd found something with her he couldn't easily let go of. If she conceived from what they had been doing, somewhere he would find the strength and the courage to deal with that. It was the way of his life.

"We're not at all alike," she continued.

"No," he said hoarsely, absently.

"We're like apples and oranges. We're from two completely different worlds."

"That's true. But it's nothing that has to be dealt with right now."

He was wrong, she thought. This time he was wrong. Because this almost perfect, almost heinous idea to save Susannah involved hearts, his and hers. It involved four people, including Susannah and the yet-to-be baby, an Irish-German half sibling who could save her. And if conceiving one child to save the life of another trembled on the brink of being morally unconscionable, what could be said about doing it without giving that child the best life possible, with two parents and all the love a family could hold?

Families didn't guarantee love, she reminded herself frantically. She realized she felt vaguely nauseous, and pulled away from him. She dragged on her jeans, her sweater. She couldn't find her coat. What had he done with her coat? The hell with it, she decided. "I need…to go," she mumbled. "I need to think." She took a single jerky step toward the door. And it opened just as she reached for it.

"Pa?"

Kim jumped back, startled. Joe was right behind her. She bumped into his chest and his strong hands found her waist to steady her. He always steadied her, she realized. And somehow, in that moment, she knew that if she asked him to help her conceive to save Susannah, he would do that, too.

But now, right now, he had a few problems of his own.

"Nathaniel?" he said in disbelief. "What are you doing here?"

Kim couldn't see the boy's eyes. The sun behind him was glaring, far too bright—she could only make out his silhouette. He looked like some kind of avenging angel.

"I don't guess that's the question, is it?" Nathaniel answered, looking at his father's bare chest. "What are *you* doing?" His voice cracked as he turned away again. "Never mind. I guess I'm old enough to figure it out."

He slammed the door closed again as he left, pitching them back into darkness. Joe reached up very slowly to pull a long blade of hay out of Kimberley's tangled hair.

## *Chapter 18*

Kim sat at the kitchen table with her head in her hands. She felt overwhelmed, incapable of even sorting through things to decide what she should worry about first. How had this gotten so complicated, so out of control?

Women all over America had casual sex all the time. She'd tried it once, *once*—Mark and Bobby didn't count because she'd been engaged to both in some fashion. And everything had crashed in around her ears. The next thing she knew, words like *conceive* and *marry* were ringing in her head. While her daughter's life was hanging in the balance. While Joe's son was staring at them as if they were the spawn of Satan himself.

Kim groaned.

Then again, she'd brought this upon herself, she decided. Of all the men in the world she might have gotten intimate with, she had had the really poor sense to choose a devout Amish man with strong beliefs and morals.

The only sane place left in the world was in his arms.

It seemed safest to say that that was why she always went there so readily. She wasn't capable at the moment of wondering why she found sanity there, though a mocking, inner voice kept asking her.

"Kim?"

Her head snapped up. Dinah had come into the kitchen, a reasonably quiet Hannah cuddled against her shoulder.

"Is something wrong?" the girl asked.

"No." *Everything. He wants me to stay. He makes me feel things. I need him. I'm scared.*

"Nathaniel's home."

"Yes," Kim muttered. "I know."

"There's that wedding at the Eitners' on Thursday. He caught a ride down with some folks who'll be going."

Well, she thought, that explained the last little unplanned development—Nathaniel's accusing silhouette in the barn door.

Kim pushed shakily to her feet. She had to make supper. No, she thought, lunch, glancing at her watch. It was only one o'clock. Then she corrected herself. Not lunch, *dinner.* Joe called it "dinner." They didn't even use the same name for their meals. She felt dizzy.

"Where are you going?" Dinah asked, startled, when she swerved for the door.

"Out."

That was all she needed, she decided. To get away, by herself, for just a few moments. To get her legs beneath her again. To be alone so she could feel like herself again. Susannah was well cared for at Mariah's school, and she'd be there for a little while yet. So Kim would drive down to the phone booth and call the hospital.

She grabbed her keys off the kitchen counter and fled. She'd driven aimlessly all the way into Lancaster and back again on a tank of gas bought with Joe's money before she accepted that she couldn't outrun the truth.

This wasn't just about making babies and saving Susannah. Somehow or other, she'd fallen in love with him.

Joe caught up with his son in the dairy barn. Nathaniel was throwing hay out like a madman. The pitchfork flashed in the thin light that came down from a vent in the ceiling.

"We need to talk," Joe said quietly.

"No. None of my business." Hay flew even more wildly, then Nathaniel went on anyway. "Guess this explains why you were so all fired in a hurry to get me off the farm."

That hurt. "This has nothing to do with you."

"The hell it doesn't."

*"Nathaniel."*

"Well, it doesn't. And don't stand there chastising me for swearing when you were just...you were just..."

He couldn't say it, Joe realized.

Nathaniel veered for another tack. "You didn't want anyone around here who might be old enough to figure out what you were up to," he accused.

Joe took a shaky breath. "I sent you away because it was best for you," he replied evenly. "I sent you away for your own happiness."

"You sent me away because you're running around like a bull in a field full of fertile cows!" Nathaniel shouted, throwing the fork aside.

Joe's blood drained. All the old guilt came clawing up, savage little talons digging and gouging. And then he understood something. And there was peace.

"Nathaniel—"

"I see what I see, Pa!"

"You don't see what you *think* you see."

"She had hay in her hair and you didn't have a shirt on!"

"That's true enough."

The quiet admission took some of the wind out of Nathaniel's sails.

"But as for the whole field of cows," Joe continued, "that's where you've made your mistake. That's simply wrong." Joe broke off, thinking. "If that were true," he added carefully, "this would have happened long before it did."

The anger was completely gone from his tone now. There was only bone-deep relief. And wonder. And exhaustion. Because guilt was a powerful foe to do battle with, and he had been doing battle with it for what felt like a lifetime.

"Aunt Frida has been sending moon eyes my way since the harvest," he went on. She was Sarah's youngest sister, widowed herself some two years now. He'd never felt a stirring in her direction. "Elizabeth Byler was coming around every Friday evening before Kimberley arrived," he continued. And until this very moment, it had never even occurred to him why. "And Elisheva Miller. Gretchen Fisher." *So many.* Now he realized, only now did it strike him, how very many women had flocked to his home, to the door of an eligible, newly available man, just as soon as propriety allowed it. He had not wanted a one of them. He breathed, really breathed, for the first time in months, an invisible pressure lifting off his chest.

"So you saved it for one who wore tight jeans," Nathaniel said angrily.

Joe cocked a brow. "You liked them, too," he noted. "Have I raised such a pious, judgmental fool? What's happened to you, Nathaniel? You're more critical now than before you went to Berks."

That stopped his son cold.

"What I was doing in that other barn was nothing more than what young men do the whole settlement over," Joe said, "when they find the woman..." *they want to marry.* He trailed off, his heart chugging hard, then he pushed on. "I might be older, Nathaniel, but I'm not dead, and I have the same rights."

Nathaniel's face became mottled.

"Your mother is gone," Joe continued. "I can't bring her back. I would give up everything else if I could." And he thought he might, for his children.

Nathaniel picked up the pitchfork again. "Do you love her?" he asked as he began to work again frantically.

Funny, Joe thought, how he could think it so easily, yet saying it made his throat swell hard and painfully. In that moment, he understood Kimberley's fear, all her careful defenses. "Yes," he finally managed to answer.

Nathaniel stopped again to stare at him. "Inside of a couple of *weeks?*"

"A month, give or take," Joe corrected. "And, well, I have that propensity."

"What do you mean?" Nathaniel demanded.

"I fell in love with Sarah after five minutes. All things considered, I'm taking this one slow."

Nathaniel continued to stare at him.

"I've always been a man who knows what he wants, Nathaniel," he said. "And in most cases, I go after it and manage to get it. I wanted your mother from the moment I saw her. I determined to have her five minutes later when I introduced myself to her and she spoke my name. And our time together was good, special, a gift the likes of which I never expect to receive again. But in Kimberley, God has given me something entirely different. Perhaps I have the right to happiness twice, to two different kinds, though I can't imagine why I should be so lucky, so blessed."

Nathaniel raked a hand through his hair. He struggled with the words, fought to push them out, and they didn't end up being a question. "You're going to marry her."

And there it was again, that leap of his heart, his breath scrambling for escape. "Maybe."

"That's not good enough," Nathaniel charged. "It's one thing if you're going to marry somebody. That's *rumspringa.* If you're not—"

"I'm an adult, Nathaniel," Joe said. "If I choose to sin, then I will pay the consequences. Or I'll fix it. Grant me the right to make my own choices and pay my own dues."

It occurred to both of them then that there were those who would say he certainly didn't have to explain this to his son, or seek Nathaniel's approval.

Nathaniel looked away. "Some folks came down for the Eitner wedding. I caught a ride with them," he explained, not quite absently.

Joe nodded, waiting.

"Are you two going?"

"We've been invited, though I'm not sure Kimberley will get within nine feet of a roast casserole."

Nathaniel looked at him. "She's not like us, Pa."

"No," he admitted.

"So how are you going to fix *that?* What are you going to do?"

Joe reached to open the barn door again. "This settlement has topped greater reluctance than hers."

But he wasn't sure about that, he realized with an unsettled feeling. The truth was that he just wasn't sure.

* * *

When she came back to the settlement, Kim didn't go inside the quaint wooden phone booth right away. She sat with her back against it, her legs drawn up, her heels digging into the dead garden.

*What am I going to do?*

But she knew. For starters, she was going to ask Dr. Coyle about the idea that had flown into her head this afternoon. Just to *know.* If it was impossible, then she could stop tormenting herself over it.

She got up and went into the booth. She still had six of Adam's quarters left, and some money of Joe's, as well. Through some miracle, the quarters hadn't fallen out of her pocket when Joe had been tossing her clothing all over the barn.

*Don't think about that.*

Eventually she would have to think about it, she knew. About the things that had been said and the look in his eyes and what she felt. But not yet. Not now. She dropped the quarters into the phone and punched out the number for Children's Hospital. She'd do the easiest thing first.

"Dr. Reginald Coyle," she told the hotel operator. "Pediatric Oncology."

A moment later, the man came on the line.

"It's Kimberley...Mancuso." Her head spun. So much had happened lately. So much had come undone. The name she had made her own all those years ago now felt alien and clumsy on her tongue. "I know I'm calling a little early," she continued, "but—"

"No," Dr. Coyle interrupted. "It's fine."

She heard it in his voice. She gave a little cry and backed into the wall behind her, desperately needing a place to sit down. There was none. "You finished," she said, strangled. "They finished the samples."

"Yes."

"And there's nothing."

"I'm sorry. No."

She made a howling sound of despair that she wasn't even aware of holding in her throat.

"We'll keep working with the donor lists, of course."

"There's nothing there!" she cried. "What are the odds of there being anything there?"

"Ten percent, as I've told you."

"I won't give my baby a one in ten chance of surviving!"

He didn't respond to that. They both knew there was nothing else he could say, nothing more she could do.

All in all, she realized, it made what she was about to ask a lot easier. She gulped air. "Can you take marrow from an infant, from a...a newborn?"

"Marrow? No."

She swore violently and punched a hand against the wall hard enough to splinter a plank. She didn't feel the pain as shards of wood pierced her palm. That was that, then.

"Putting an infant under general anesthesia," he continued, "for any other reason than saving its own life is something no reputable doctor in the country would consider. However, if we're talking about a *newborn,* then the same stem cells found in marrow are rife in the umbilical cord and placenta, as well. I...uh, wasn't aware that you were pregnant."

A moment before, her heart had felt as though it had stopped. Now it pumped once, heavily, with a boom that echoed in her chest. It picked up momentum and exploded. "I'm not pregnant," she whispered.

"Ah. Then it's a moot point."

"Maybe. Maybe not. I'll...call you back," she croaked. She hung up and moved blindly for the car.

Joe was in the kitchen when she got back. He was helping Dinah put together sandwiches with some egg salad that Kim had apparently made earlier, though she couldn't remember having done it. Dinah was holding Hannah with her one free arm.

Joe looked over his shoulder at her and felt everything sluice out of him. Her face was bone white. Her eyes were immense, deep, an almost black shade of purple. They were dilated, he realized. She was in shock.

"What happened?" He dropped the knife with a clatter. It hit the edge of the counter and spun onto the floor. "What's wrong?"

Her eyes were fast on the sandwiches. "I forgot to make lunch. Uh, dinner," she said inanely. Her teeth began chattering. "Sorry."

He touched her. Just her arms, holding each one as though it would keep her from shattering. "It doesn't matter."

She finally tore her eyes off the food and looked at him with a weak smile. "Of course it does. I'm falling down on the job." She pulled away from him, dragged a chair out from the table and sat unsteadily. "It's been...quite a day."

He didn't answer that. He hunkered down beside her chair, and he knew. "You called the hospital."

She nodded vaguely.

"They've finished the samples?"

She nodded again.

His heart was booming. "No matches?"

"No. Not a one." She looked around blankly. "Where is she? Where's Suze? Did she come home from school?"

"Not yet," Dinah said, inching closer.

Kim looked up at her and realized the girl's eyes were shining.

"I'm...so sorry," Dinah said. "I wouldn't have wanted...anything like this...to happen to her, to either of you. I...I really like her."

Joe stood again and drew the girl close, baby and all. Dinah turned her face into his chest and sobbed.

Bridges, Kim thought. There was some healing between these two, as well. Something constricted in her chest. Joe's eyes hadn't left her own.

"Well, as you said earlier, there are other ways," he said.

Her head swam and tears burned her eyes because it was an offer, a promise, a hand reaching out to her through impossible darkness. Of course, she thought, that hand would be his. And she knew he would say nothing more about it. He would simply put it out there—another impossible gift—and let her decide.

She was still staring at him, unable to think of a response, when the back door burst open.

"Watch it!" Joe shouted, a little more angrily than usual, looking toward the hall. "You're going to knock it right off its hinges, and I'm not the one who's going to be fixing it this time!''

But it wasn't Matt or Bo, the usual culprits when the door banged and clattered. Adam came into the kitchen. He opened his mouth, closed it, then tried again. One word came out, an odd bleating.

''Help.''

Kim was on her feet in an instant. And if her own very horrible problems were forgotten for a moment, completely forgotten with one look at her brother's terrified face, then she didn't even realize it. She caught his arm and tried to guide him to a chair.

Adam shook off her grip. ''Can't sit down,'' he said.

''What's wrong?'' she demanded.

''Got to find the sisters.''

''What sisters?'' Joe asked. ''*Sarah's* sisters? Why?''

''She's having the baby. Mariah's having the baby. She wants to do it at home, and I don't know what to do.''

# *Chapter 19*

That was when it hit Kim. *German and Irish. German an Irish.* The words bounced and clamored in her head. Maria was German. Adam was Irish. This wasn't left to her and Jo after all.

She felt her breath leave her on a gasp. It was as thoug her blood were draining. Adam didn't share any HLA matche with Susannah. It was just another long shot. But his unbor child would be German *and* Irish, just as Susannah hersel was.

Kim stared at her brother. The rest of the room had becom smeared, out of focus. She had thought once, a lifetime ago of her brother's unborn child as a possible donor. It seeme so long ago now. It had been in a time when she had bee selfishly clawing for answers. Before everything had changed When had so much changed? When had she subconsciousl but completely put this baby right out of her mind?

She had never asked that Bo be tested, either, regardless o the odds, though he had been when the Children's Hospita technicians had come to draw blood from the settlement. B hadn't matched. And Bo was Adam's child. But Bo wasn' Mariah's biological child.

"Adam," she said hoarsely. "I need...your help." And suddenly, asking, needing and reaching out, was the easiest thing in the world.

His eyes jumped to her. "Here? Now? Anything. But later, Kimmie. *Later.*"

She ignored that and plowed on. "Susannah needs the, uh, umbilical cord, the placenta. This baby might be a match. Bo isn't. No one else in the whole settlement is. I just got all the results." She took a deep breath. "Please."

He stared at her, frowning dazedly. "The umbilical cord?" he echoed.

Kim nodded, watching him. Necessities, practicalities, being needed, seemed to clear Adam's head a bit.

"I was there when Bo was born," he answered slowly. "Using the umbilical cord doesn't involve any physical risk to anyone."

"No," she whispered. Then she realized something else. "I just don't know if I would have asked if it did."

"Yes," Adam repeated.

Then to her shock, he lifted her off her feet.

"Yes!" he said again, spinning her around.

"Have you lost your mind?" she squealed.

"She'll do this! Mariah will go to the hospital for you, for Susannah!" He dropped her suddenly. Kim staggered a little.

"She wanted one of the women to come help her," he continued. "But now, for this, she'll go to a hospital. This is it. This is the answer. Thank God." He grabbed Kim again and kissed her hard. Then he charged for the door. "Bring your car around to my place!" he shouted back over his shoulder.

Kim stared after him. Her heart was thundering now. Two birds with one stone, she thought. Just like the favor she had asked Jake. Adam didn't want Mariah to have their baby at home. She needed to test the baby's blood. Somehow she knew, in a place so deep in her heart that she couldn't fathom it, that this as-yet-unborn child was going to be a match.

She swayed a little. Joe caught her.

"Let's go," he said.

"I used your money for gas earlier," she said inanely.

"Good thing. Then we won't have to stop."

They were at the front door before he thought to call back to Dinah. Kim was inordinately glad that he did, because she had ceased thinking in rational terms again. When had so much changed? When had she started leaning on him so completely, depending on him to pick up for her where her own strength left off? And his strength was always unswerving, always so steady.

"Dinah, don't tell anyone," he cautioned. "Maybe Nathaniel, but none of the others. Whatever you do, don't tell Susannah until we're sure if this is going to work out. No sense in getting her hopes up for nothing. She should be here any minute now, if Mariah is home from school."

They went outside, and Kim remembered that the one thing Joe couldn't do for her was drive.

Somehow, she did it. She drove to Adam's first, collected him and Mariah and brought Bo back to stay with Dinah. She guided the Mazda back to Route 30. Somehow, she stopped at all the red lights on the way into Lancaster. She collided with no other cars, no pedestrians, no buggies.

Maybe there was a God watching out for her after all.

She prayed. *If You'll just do this for me, I'll never say a bad word about You again.* Then she grew uncomfortable. *I'm sorry. I'm sorry for always doubting. But, hey, You've got to admit that You haven't always been hanging around with a helping hand.* If He was here now, it wouldn't matter. Her prayers turned to desperation, full and heartfelt and coming all the way up from her soul. *Please let this work, please, please, please.*

She came close to taking out an ambulance when she turned into the emergency lot at the hospital. But it backed up suddenly, and she narrowly missed its bumper. Mariah was puffing and groaning and gasping in the back seat.

"How many minutes apart?" Joe asked from the front passenger seat with that incredible, practical calm.

"Can't tell," Adam answered, his voice strained. "You guys took away my watch when you decided it was a worldly possession."

Kim had hers on, but it didn't have a second hand. "Three minutes," she answered, "give or take. Judging from the sounds she's making back there."

Adam's voice went a little accusing. Kim saw him look at is wife in the rearview mirror. "You felt this coming on this orning, didn't you? And you went to school! You didn't ention it because you thought you could just slide this baby ut while I wasn't looking!"

Kim remembered her own labor. "Men," she muttered. "It ould be so easy."

Joe remembered Sarah's labor. "God willing, that would be e case."

"Not due...for another week," Mariah explained, gasp-uffing.

"You're too smart to think that would matter!" Adam outed.

"Adam. We're here now. It all...worked out. Get e...inside."

So they did, somehow they did, all of them together, until n orderly came out of nowhere, pushing a wheelchair like a oman chariot. He popped Mariah into it. Adam chased off fter them, and Kim and Joe stood in the lobby, watching them o.

Rebekkah Elizabeth Wallace was born at ten after nine that ight. Kim was staring numbly at the television set in the aiting room when Adam came through the swinging doors t the end of the hall. Joe sat beside her. Neither of them oticed him immediately. They had been bickering on and off bout the benefits of having advertisements, near-naked people nd gunfights broadcast into one's home.

Adam cleared his throat. They both looked up sharply.

"She's a girl," he said, his voice raw.

Joe grinned slowly. "Congratulations."

Kim couldn't find her voice. Her skin shrank on her body ntil it felt very tight, then it broke out in gooseflesh. Birth, he thought. A new life in the midst of all this craziness. It nade her feel like crying. Again.

"Can I see her?" she asked finally, carefully.

Adam nodded. "She'll be in the nursery in another five ninutes or so."

"All ten fingers?" Joe asked.

And Kim noticed that this time he didn't quite grimace.

"All ten toes?"

Adam's eyes widened. "Of course. I think so. Dear Go can they be born without them?"

Joe got to his feet and clapped him on the shoulder. "N to worry. I've just been through this a time or five. You lear to ask."

Then Adam swayed.

Kim jumped for him. "Dear God," she gasped, "he's goin to pass out!"

But he didn't. They got him to a chair in time. They s there, the three of them, shell-shocked, shoulder to shoulde Kim in the middle. She looked side to side, and thought the resembled the veterans of a very long, very difficult war. Th was when a familiar face appeared in the waiting area. Ki stared at the woman for a long moment, trying to place her.

"I'm Kathy O'Malley," the woman said. "From Children' Hospital."

One of the technicians, Kim realized, who had come to dra the blood from the settlement.

"Well," Kathy O'Malley said. "I'll be transporting th cord and the placenta back to Children's now. We'll run th necessary tests immediately. You can call at about midnigh or so. We may have something by then."

"Yes," Kim managed to say. "All right."

"Can't you do that here?" Adam roused enough to deman

"If there's a match," Kathy O'Malley explained, "then makes more sense to have everything there, ready to go."

"It's a long shot," Kim whispered, trying to tell hersel that.

"Long shots are what make miracles," Kathy O'Malle said. "Otherwise they'd just be run-of-the-mill occurrences right?" She moved off down the hall again.

Kim and Joe waited to peer at Rebekkah through the win dows of the nursery before they headed home. The baby wa long and scrawny and red. She had a lot of very dark hai She was beautiful.

"That part is Mariah's legacy," Adam said hoarsely, touching a finger to the glass where her dark hair was reflected.

Kim cleared her throat. "Maybe not. Jake and I are dark. So were…our parents."

"But I'm not. Bo's not."

"Your first wife was blond," Joe remarked. At Kim's startled look, he added, "Long story. I met her briefly."

"I guess I was thinking…" Adam trailed off. "When I didn't match Susannah at all, I've been telling myself that maybe…you know…"

Kim stared at him. "What? That you were adopted?"

He gave a short laugh. "Hardly. That would be too normal for our family. Maybe Mom conceived me with someone else before…" His face hardened. "I mean, I'm the eldest. Kimmie, every one of our closets was *crammed* with skeletons. What's one more?"

"Oh, no, you don't," came another voice from behind them.

They all jerked away from the nursery window at the same time. Jake and Katya walked toward them.

"We decided to come back, to check things out. Besides, we knew Mariah was getting close," Jake told them. "Dinah told us you were here." He thrust a finger into Adam's chest. "And I heard you. If you think you're going to dump all those crazy Wallace genes on Kimmie and me, you're out of your mind. You can't weasel out of them that easily."

"I guess we'll know by midnight," Kim said. Actually, the possibility had occurred to her, too, if only because she had thought more about genetics lately than she ever had before in her life.

She felt them all looking at her and she cleared her throat. "I just meant…I don't suppose Rebekkah can be a good match unless Adam is…you know, a full sibling," she explained, "unless there's *some* Wallace scooting around in his system somewhere."

"If Adam isn't a full sibling," Jake commented, stepping up to look through the glass at the baby, "then there's still the same ten percent chance as the donor registries. Probably a little higher because of the ethnic match." Suddenly, he frowned. "Do babies always come out looking that…uh mushed up and wrinkled?"

"Watch yourself," Adam warned. "That's my daughter."

"Just wondering. I have a staked interest."

"Usually," Katya said. "Think of what that poor little thing had to go through to get here."

Jake paled. "I'd rather not." He stepped back from the window fast. "Anyway, given that you're as screwed up as the rest of us, bro, then this little one should probably be a match. She's German, she's Irish and she's kin."

Kim looked at both her brothers. "That's what scares me."

"What?" they asked in unison.

"Neither of you is all that screwed up anymore."

They went back to the farm, then returned to the phone booth at twelve-thirty. Joe wanted to go at midnight. Before they had left, Adam had urged them to wait until one. The half hour seemed a good compromise.

Kim stepped into the booth on wobbly legs and picked up the phone with cold hands. They were all waiting for her in the car—Jake and Katya, Joe and Nathaniel. She felt their eyes boring through the wood, touching her. She put the phone down again and stepped outside.

Joe got out of the car immediately. "Did you call?"

"No."

A million emotions crossed his face. "Why?"

"I don't…I can't do this alone."

He thought about that, then nodded. "Want me to do it?"

Kim trembled harder. "Yes, please."

He went into the phone booth. She waited outside. One by one the others got out of the car to flank her, even Nathaniel. She wasn't sure which hand of hers was in whose. She jumped when the booth door creaked open again behind them.

Jake was the first to speak. "Well?" he demanded.

Kim's eyes sought Joe's. She could tell nothing from his face. "Tell me," she whispered.

He nodded. He *nodded.*

"Five antigens. Dr. Coyle wanted six, but under the circumstances, he'll take it. Rebekkah is a match."

## *Chapter 20*

The week passed in a blur—whirlwind images of hospital walls in soothing, muted tones, too much coffee to contemplate, hushed, serious voices...and Joe. Always, there was Joe.

Kim thought once or twice about asking him how the farm could function without him, even in this time after the harvest. But Nathaniel was still there, she remembered, and the truth was that she was afraid of his answer. She was very afraid that he would nod, say it couldn't, that he had to go back now.

Her mother had always told her that it was pure tomfoolery to look a gift horse in the mouth. And her mother ought to have known, Kim thought, huddling in a hard chair in yet another waiting room. Few enough gift horses had ever found their way to the Wallace door.

Of course, Joe would go eventually. She'd have to stand on her own two feet again...eventually. But not yet. Not now.

She roused a little at the scent of more coffee. She looked vacantly at her watch before she reached to take the paper cup from Joe's hand. Somewhere beyond these sterile walls, the sun was rising. It was nearly six o'clock.

"Thanks," she murmured.

"How are you holding up?" He dropped into the chair beside her. He couldn't hide the little groan of relief that escape his throat at finally sitting down, hard plastic or not.

Kim smiled wanly. "I'm holding. Where's...well, every one?"

She hadn't been back to the farm, but she knew that it wa once again in the grip of full chaos, with Jake and Katya an all their kids. Joe had mentioned that one or two of the sister had poked their noses back into the kitchen in her absence And all those people, even people she only barely remembere from the blood drive, had visited the hospital at one time o another, to offer moral support or merely hold Susannah' hand.

"I chased everyone home," Joe answered. "You know, never knew how effective I could be by just shouting."

"Don't make it a habit."

He lifted a brow at her. He waited. He needed to hear he say that she'd had enough shouting for a lifetime, and sh wanted to spend the rest of her life with him in peace. Sh didn't do it. He let out a rough breath. "Any word yet?"

Kim sipped coffee and shook her head. "No. Then again what could they possibly tell us this soon?"

They'd done Susannah's irradiation over the course of th past six days. They'd done it by something they called "frac tionated schedules." By now, Kim had more medical termi nology zinging around in her brain than she'd ever thought i could hold. But what she'd understood was that the fraction ated chemotherapy and irradiation somehow minimized th risk of side effects. Dr. Coyle, expert that he was, preferred i over single-dose therapy. And that was good enough for Kim

They'd begun the peripheral blood stem cell transfusion vi intravenous catheter last night. It was called the "rescue pro cess." Rebekkah's stem cells would travel through Susannah's bloodstream to the marrow that had been destroyed. The en graftment, the blood cell production from the transplante stem cells, wouldn't take place for another two to four weeks It would take years for Susannah's immune system to recove completely. But they were years in which she would more tha likely be alive.

Susannah would spend at least the next two months in th hospital. Oh, God, the bills, Kim thought, sinking a little lowe in her chair. The insurance company—the company she still had thanks to Jake—hadn't yet started bleating about their ceiling, but she knew that would come. And somehow, she would pay the difference. Because the most serious side effect of the irradiation and the transfusion was something called "immunosuppression." Susannah's body would be rendered even more incapable of defending itself against infection and germs for a while. She could not leave the protective isolation of her hospital room.

She was already one sick little cookie, Kim thought, cringing. When she had seen her last night, just before they'd started the transfusion, she'd been wan, lethargic, sick to her stomach from the conditioning therapy. But as Dr. Coyle had said, one couldn't rebuild until one had first torn down.

Those words haunted her. They echoed in her head, over and over again. Was that what had happened to her? Her defenses—all those perfect defenses she had left Dr. Parra's office with a lifetime ago—had been assaulted and torn asunder this past month. By Adam. By Jake. But most of all, above all, by Joe. She glanced over at him. He was staring unseeingly at the television again. A shiver worked its way slowly, with exquisite care, over her skin.

She thought she loved him. But after all they had both been through recently, how could she know? It seemed to her this was something she wanted to be very sure of. She *needed* to be sure. Without her defenses, she was vulnerable, raw, terrified to move or make any decisions. She was like Susannah, needing to stay in a sterile environment for a little while, she'd decided, with no chances taken.

"I've been thinking," they both said at the same time.

Kim flushed. Joe gave a weak grin. Then they both spoke in unison again. "You first."

Kim laughed nervously. Silence fell, heavy and weighted. She finally cleared her throat. "I'm going to have to get another job," she said. "I can't spend the next two months without any income. And the best place for a cocktail waitress to collect good tips is in a city the size of this one."

He felt her words as though each of them had points, as though they were so much deadly, shattering glass, cutting into him, drawing blood. "I see," he said carefully.

"I want to get an apartment here. In Philly. To be close to Susannah."

It made all the sense in the world, and none at all. The two-hour drive had not been insurmountable so far, and he'd been making it with one friend or another for days now. Even so, if he thought it was just a simple relocation of her home base for practicality's sake, he could live with that. But he knew it wasn't. He knew it with every instinct, each time her eyes tried to slide and hide from his own. She was going to go back behind her walls again. She'd grab some mortar and a trowel and she would start busily putting the bricks back until everything was safe and secure once more. Until she was alone.

Joe felt his heart explode like thunder—angry, frustrated thunder. "I see," he said again, his words clipped this time.

She looked at him. "It only makes sense."

"Do you want me to argue with you?" And God, what an effort it took for him to keep his voice flat.

*Yes.* "No."

"So there's not much for me to say."

"Except whatever you were going to say in the first place."

"Doesn't matter now."

It probably didn't. So why did that hurt so much?

"I appreciate everything—" she began. And that was all it took.

*"Don't,"* he snarled, turning to her. "Don't do it, Kimberley. Don't thank me. Don't act as though it was a minor inconvenience on my part to have you and your child in my home. To be a part of your life."

"You weren't—"

"*I was.* And now you're trying to push me back, as if I never got close enough to feel your terror!"

"I'm not doing that," she insisted.

"You're trying to look the other way and pretend that it didn't happen."

"I'm trying to rebuild!" She heard herself and paled, because she realized she was thinking of Dr. Coyle's analogy again.

Joe hadn't meant to touch her. He didn't dare. The rage and helplessness were so big and alive inside him—a gnarly animal fighting to get free. He had vowed never to hurt her. He had never laid a hand on anyone in anger. But he had never wanted something so desperately, only to be told that he couldn't have it, case closed.

He couldn't let her leave him.

He was on his feet in an instant. He found his hands on her arms, just below her shoulders. He lifted her from her chair. He heard her cry out, but the sound seemed to come from a very long way away. It was somewhere on the other side of the roaring of his blood.

"Haven't you learned anything?" he demanded furiously.

Kim stared at him, her throat working. "Don't do this to me," she begged. "I never promised you anything, Joe."

"You came here hating the world," he argued, his voice grating. "You hated yourself for being a bunch of things you're not. You came here hating your family, and anything that ever had anything to do with any of them. I've watched you reach out without getting your hand slapped away. I've watched you get steady and sure and bloom. I've watched you come apart beneath me and give. And now you're going to stand here and tell me that you're going to throw all that away and run again?"

"I didn't say I was going back to California. I'll be right here in the city." Why couldn't that be enough for him? It was what she needed, she thought again desperately. A protective environment, a safe place, where too much was not asked of her for a while. But he wasn't going to give it with his blessing. And she needed his blessing, too. She needed it badly.

"Some distances aren't measured in miles!" he shouted.

"Then what do you want me to do?" she cried.

"Marry me!" And then he heard himself and cursed himself. Because he hadn't meant to do it like this, so angrily, so desperately. He certainly hadn't meant to ask her in a way that was almost certain to send her running. But he was all emotion now, and it was volatile.

Her jaw fell. Not fast, not hard, but slowly, a little more each time her heart boomed. "You're crazy," she whispered. "We've already talked about this."

She snapped her mouth shut and began shaking her head.

"No. No, we didn't. We talked of why it was crazy. Why it's impossible."

"We never got to finish before Nathaniel came in and interrupted us."

"We finished."

"I didn't."

"You weren't even thinking about that when we talked in the barn, not until I mentioned birth control." The panic, she thought, oh, God, the sheer panic. It was driving with a fury through her blood. She wanted...and she feared. And unlike with her father's doughnuts, this time she just couldn't figure out which was stronger.

"We were talking about an eventuality," she said wretchedly, trying to explain. "If we...I mean, if I...had to go that...that other route to save Susannah."

"So the idea has grown on me," he stated.

"Is that supposed to be *romantic?*"

"I don't traipse around with flowers in my hand, Kimberley. But that doesn't negate what I feel for you."

"Then say it, Joe!" she shouted recklessly. "Say whatever it is you came here to say and get it over with!"

"I love you."

Everything washed out of her. She'd provoked him out of temper, and with that she was lost, overwhelmed. Her anger, her panic, even the sweet, sweet hope and relief she was holding on to on Susannah's behalf sluiced out of her.

Kim felt her knees give. Joe let go of her and she sank back down into her chair. "Don't say that," she croaked out of habit.

He ignored her. Of course he would ignore her. She might as well tell the wind not to blow. He could be like a pit bull when he got something in his head, she thought, when he thought he had a point to make.

"I spent four months hating myself as much as you hated yourself when you got here," he said more quietly. "I believed in some measure that I had killed Sarah. That my baser instincts killed Sarah. And I blamed Hannah, because she was the living proof. I wanted you the first time I saw you, and I hated myself for that, too. Until you wanted me back. Until you gave so fiercely, so ferociously, you rocked my world and everything I thought I knew about myself. Because it was *only you.* It wasn't every other woman who came sniffing around my door after Sarah died, because they weren't strong enough, didn't understand loss enough, couldn't heal *with* me. That's what we did, Kimberley. We leaned on each other and we healed together. I cradled the baby, and you asked Adam. I needed, and you gave. You needed, I gave.''

''So we're friends,'' she said. ''Maybe we'll—'' It was all she got out before she found herself out of the chair again. He'd hauled her back to her feet.

''I have never known anyone more stubborn in my entire life!'' he said angrily.

Kim managed a weak attempt at a smile. ''It's a Wallace family trait.''

He stared into her eyes for a moment, then he crushed his mouth to her own. His tongue swept, and this time he didn't come up for breath. This time his kiss was relentless, pummeling, bruising and angry. When he finally stopped, they were both breathing hard.

''That's not friends,'' he said. ''Don't lie to yourself, and damn it, don't lie to me.''

She groaned. She wanted to find that place in his arms again where everything was safe. Except she couldn't have it anymore, because he'd gone and put conditions on it. She backed up. Her legs hit the chair behind her and she bounced off, scooting around him, putting space between them.

Her eyes were on fire, he thought. At least he had reached her.

''I can't do it,'' she cried, taking them both by surprise. ''I can't cook on that damned woodstove for the rest of my life, Joe. I won't eat roast. I can't slide into your cozy, quaint world. I like Chinese food! Don't you get it? What's the point in my going back? If I go back to your house, and this last month stretches into two, three, four and we keep sneaking out to the barn, where is it going to go?'' That was what terrified her, she realized. It was what terrified her most of all. *Tear down. Rebuild.* ''I'll tell you where. I'd need you so desperately by then that there'd be no getting out. I'd start listening to the rhythm of the seasons. I'd start wearing ugly dresses. If you want me so much, then let me keep being *me.*

I don't even recognize myself anymore as it is. I'd lose *everything,* just as Susannah's lost all her marrow. And you'll just keep on trundling out there every morning to your stupid cows without even missing a step.''

He stared at her, stunned. ''Susannah's marrow was killing her,'' he said evenly. ''It was not a good thing.''

His point rang between them as clearly as if he had shouted it: *Your old world was killing something inside you, too.*

''It was all I ever had,'' she whispered. ''I can't give it up.''

''Even if what's built in its place is better?''

''It's too much of a risk.'' Her eyes flared. ''And don't give me that look. You're not willing to risk, either.''

''Of course I am.''

''No,'' she said, trembling. She spun away from him. '''Marry me','' she mimicked him. '''I love you.' I haven't heard you mention anything about throwing some clothes in a suitcase and running back to California with me.'' She waited. Oh, God, she thought, she was waiting for him to say he'd do it. Was she out of her mind?

''I can't do that,'' he answered.

Her breath left her with a painful burst of loss. ''Of course not.''

''You don't understand.''

She looked at him bitterly. ''Sure I do. *I* can tear things down, but you want no part of it.''

It was true enough to make him lose color. ''Kimberley, I *can't.* I'm a deacon. And that's for the rest of my life.''

''Katya left here!'' She shouted it. And as soon as the words were out of her mouth, she realized that that was what she had been holding on to all along. She'd been clinging to the idea that it *was* possible for these people to turn their backs on their odd life-styles, to walk away. That the man and the way he lived could be separated. She didn't necessarily have to love one to love the other. She knew he didn't totally believe in that *meidung* thing. He'd sent his elder son to a more lenient *gemeide.*

''You said you didn't always agree with things here!'' she cried desperately, hating herself for the plea in her voice.

He thought he nodded, but he wasn't sure. His muscles felt

as hard and unyielding as oak now. "I...don't," he rasped. "Not always. But I took a vow. I promised these people something. That I would always be here. I wouldn't have done it *after* Sarah died. She was my reason for staying in Lancaster. Maybe I would have gone back to Berks. But I can't now. It didn't happen that way."

She made a strangled sound and refused to look at him. "So that's that, then."

He tried again to explain. "I'm not Katya. The settlement couldn't give her anything back."

"So go back to your settlement, then!" she shouted, suddenly furious. "Stop asking me to uproot my whole life, everything I am, when you're not willing to give a goddamned thing!"

He couldn't think, Joe realized. He couldn't see reason. Nor could she. His blood roared. He wanted to shake her. And in that moment he hated the people who needed him. He had to leave while something was still standing. Before he raged like the bull Nathaniel had accused him of being and destroyed things that couldn't be set right again.

"I need to get back to the farm," he said neutrally.

She dragged a hand under her eyes. Damn it, she was crying again. She didn't answer.

"I'll try to get over to the phone tonight, to call and see how Susannah is doing," he continued.

Kim nodded. He wouldn't. Or, at least, she hoped he wouldn't.

It would be better this way, she thought. Of course it would. She was totally, one hundred percent right about this. They couldn't keep pretending there was a future between them. There wasn't. Not unless she tore down the last of her own walls and began again.

She would wait a few days, hang out here at the hospital as she had been doing, she decided. Then she would quietly ask Jake or Adam to bring whatever clothes and possessions she and Susannah had left in Joe's home.

She finally turned to watch him go, leaving her walls intact. The problem was, the place he left her in felt very, very cold.

* * *

She was dozing, her head down on a table in the cafeteria, when she felt a hand on her shoulder. Kim snapped awake, her heart leaping, hope flaring.

It wasn't Joe.

"What are you doing here?" she muttered, sitting back in the chair, rubbing her hands over her face. Unwilling to admit that she was disappointed. She glanced at her watch. It was already dinnertime. Somehow, the whole day had gone by. She had no recollection of it, she realized.

"Taking over the vigil," Jake answered.

"It's going to be a long vigil. Weeks' worth, until we know anything. Suze doesn't need someone staring down at her at all times."

"Then come home," he replied.

She didn't have a home anymore. That simply, that easily, Kim began sobbing.

She put her head back down, trying to hide it. But she wasn't quick enough, and she couldn't be quiet enough about it anyway. It felt as though everything from the very bottom of her soul was heaving up.

Maybe it was. It was the parts of herself that were left to her, she realized, those parts she didn't want to relinquish. It was the little girl who had hidden so very quietly behind a rocking chair while her father raged, praying that he wouldn't find her. But God hadn't heard her, and Edward had caught her. There'd been no one to help her. She'd taken his fists, and there'd been no one to save her.

So she'd learned, and she'd gotten strong. Strong enough to take every blow that came her way, often without flinching or crying out. Strong enough to try to send Jake away that day when he would have intervened. She'd been strong enough to save her unborn child by running. Strong enough to survive once she'd gone. She'd done it, on her own, and she'd learned the hard way that she could rely on herself. As long as she had that, she had everything. It was much, much too late to start leaning on others, to trust them and depend upon them for her strength and sanity. That was far too dangerous to contemplate.

But Jake had moved. He'd sat first in the chair on the other side of the table, across from her, but she heard the chair scrape back and then he was in the seat beside her. He pulled her head to his shoulder, letting her weep. And she did. For a long time. She did until she felt him move, until she blinked and looked up, and she realized that he'd put his feet up on the chair across from him. He had settled in for the long haul. And she knew then he'd sit like that for as long as it took.

"Don't you see how God worked it all out?" he asked finally, his voice musing. "It's neat, when you think about it. This intricately meshed puzzle."

"You don't believe in God." She sniffed.

"Sure I do."

"You never did."

"I just didn't think He liked me much."

"Maybe He doesn't."

"Well, then, He wouldn't have sent me Katie." He thought about that for a moment. "Actually, He dragged me *to* Katie." She felt his shoulder lift in a shrug.

"Same difference."

"You're always telling her and Adam not to spout religion," she said. "I've heard you a time or two."

"Appearances. I have an image to maintain."

Kim couldn't believe she laughed. Admittedly, it was a soggy sound.

She needed to move, to put space between them again. But she was so very tired. She let her head drop back to his shoulder.

"I mean, here I was looking for you through ChildSearch," Jake continued, "and God zaps you with this thunderbolt and drops you into Joe Lapp's yard. And all along, there's your answer in Mariah's womb. But none of us realized it. Not even me, and I'm undeniably brilliant at seeking and finding answers. None of us even thought about it, when it was right there in front of our noses and Mariah was the size of one of Joe's cows."

She had thought about it, Kim remembered uncomfortably. At first. But then she'd forgotten again. Somehow. "Get to the point, Jake." She finally dragged herself upright.

"Well, it's just that if we had found the solution too soon, none of the rest of this would have had the opportunity to happen."

Her eyes narrowed. "Did Joe send you?" she asked suspiciously.

"Nope."

"Then what's this all about?" Kim demanded.

"I guess I have one last thing to give you after all."

"What?"

"A kick in the pants."

She jerked back even farther. "No, thanks."

"You're not seeing the big picture here, Kimmie," he said patiently.

"So I guess you're going to focus it," she snapped.

"Sure. Be glad to."

"That wasn't a request."

"You're going to hear it anyway." He paused to take a swig from his coffee, then he passed the paper cup to her. Kim sipped, watching him warily.

"Time, Kimmie. *Time* was needed. While you were chasing down all the blood samples in the settlement and getting them analyzed, while I was working on the Internet and whatnot we all got to know one another again. And you got to know Joe. And Joe got to know you. And now everybody's one big happy family."

"That's reaching," she told him.

"Granted, it's simplified. But the bottom line is still the same."

She was too tired to argue with him. Everything inside her sagged. "That's just it, Jake. I need more time. And he won't give it to me."

"Sure he will."

"No, he—"

"He just doesn't want to risk losing you while it's ticking by."

"He *did* talk to you."

"Nope. Not a word."

"Then how do you know?"

He leaned forward suddenly and caught her chin in his hand. "Because," he said slowly, "I see myself in your eyes."

Kim paled.

"I was there, Kimmie. Been there, done that, as they say

This can work two ways. You can try to run, as I did. But I'm here to tell you that there's nowhere to go. And you'll risk losing the best thing you've ever found if you keep tearing off, trying to get away from it. Or...you can just stay put. I'm not saying you shouldn't take your time. Katya and I did. We just came to terms first. We both knew what we wanted the end results to be.

"I'm just saying that you ought to give some thought to taking that time *with* Joe," he continued, then he stood abruptly. "Tell you what, you two have given me a couple of my finest hours."

Kim scowled at him. "Who? Me and Joe?"

"No. You and Adam. That was right up there with the speech I gave him a year ago or so."

Kim closed her eyes again, her head swimming. "It's not that easy, Jake."

"Sure it is."

"No. If I stay there at the farm, if we...keep up as we have been, there won't be any way out again. Don't you see? It would be like leading him on." It would be like leading her own heart on. "It would make it too difficult to break away later."

Jake thought about that a moment. "If nothing else, let's consider practicalities. What choice do you have? You can't sleep in the waiting room here until you get a job and save enough to rent an apartment."

She panicked again. "I can't go back there, Jake! He wants to *marry* me."

He grabbed her hand and hauled her to her feet. "Yeah, well, the rest of us Wallaces went down kicking and screaming. Why should you be any different?"

"This isn't a joke."

"Life's a joke, Kimmie. At least there's a good bit of humor in it, if you choose to see it. Now, are you coming home or not? I hate to break this to you, sweetheart, but you need a shower and a bed. You look like hell. Put these decisions on hold and get a grip first before you deal with them."

Kim nodded. She was exhausted, she admitted. She'd do it for one night, she told herself. She'd go back there for one night. She could get her stuff out herself. She would not be coward.

"I need to kiss Susannah good-night," she murmured.

"Then go do it. I already saw her before I tracked you dov dozing in your Danish." He picked the pastry up and toss it in the trash with his empty coffee cup. "I'll wait in t car."

He was a good ten feet on his way before he stopped a turned around. "And just for the record, it doesn't hurt wh you land. At least not much."

Then he was gone again, swinging through the doors at t end of the corridor, his black hair too long, his stride t arrogant, his departing grin the devil's own. And in that pr cise moment, she remembered. She remembered that grin.

Kim pressed her hands to her cheeks. She remembered Ja dragging her down the hall so fast she thought her arm wou come out of its socket. She remembered being airborne, l erally *airborne,* as he picked her up and hurled her at Ada And Adam had caught her, then his big hand had clamp down on the crown of her head, shoving her unceremonious under the covers. Jake had jumped in beside them and bo boys had drawn their knees up so an extra small lump und the covers wouldn't be noticed.

And that time Edward hadn't found her. That time, at lea that one time, Edward had left again. And Jake had lifted t covers to peer in at her under there. Grinning. Grinning ju the way he had now.

"You're safe, darlin'," he'd said.

Kim got as far as Susannah's room before she put her ba to the wall and slid down it. She hugged her up-drawn kne and rested her cheek upon them. But she didn't cry this tim Jake was right. Hitting bottom didn't hurt that much after a

Especially when she wasn't alone there. Especially whe she was with company she'd had before.

# Chapter 21

Joe threw himself into his work. Or he tried to. Unfortunately, there was precious little to do, since Nathaniel was home again.

It was a long day. By supper, it dawned on him that Kimberley probably wasn't going to come back. Period. She would quietly and surreptitiously retrieve her belongings. There would be no last, awkward scene, no painful goodbyes, no words of appreciation he couldn't bear to hear. No, that wouldn't be her style. She would disappear from his life as she had come into it—without ceremony or fanfare or advance notice.

By nightfall, he was so tired his eyes felt grainy. He realized he had spent almost as much time at the hospital as she had lately, and he'd kept his herds going besides. Yet he knew he wasn't going to be able to sleep. When the house quieted—and it took a while with so many people under the roof again—he looked at the sofa for a long time, then he turned away from it and went outside.

This time he did not stop in the backyard. He crossed the creek. Instead of turning in the direction of the tree line and the boulder he had shared with Kimberley on that day he had talked her into staying, he went the other way. His feet kept moving steadily, his hands thrust deeply into his pockets.

The headstones at the far fence line of his property were all white, of identical size and shape. They were set out in precise, neat lines. Aside from the names and the dates, the brief words of prayer and the tributes etched upon each one were pretty much the same. That, too, was the Amish way.

Sarah's family had shared this section of land with the Stoltzfuses and the Bylers for generations. And the generations stretched back to the Amish arrival in America. Joe had not been here since Sarah had been laid to rest.

Continuity, he thought, stepping past the small graves of the children he and Sarah had lost before birth. Continuity had always soothed him, like the steady and predictable turn of the seasons, everything happening the same way it always had. He had found comfort, too, in much of the *ordnung,* in the given rules of behavior that lent structure and predictability to his life.

What had he done to deserve this upheaval? But he knew. Of course he knew. He had believed himself above it.

He stopped at Sarah's headstone and eased down to sit on the large, gnarled root of a nearby elm. Moonlight slanted across her name.

"I suppose you've been watching all this," he said finally.

There was no response. It didn't deter him.

"And you let me blunder through on my own," he continued. "I'd forgotten how to do that, Sarah. You were always there to set me straight. Oh, you did it quietly. Somewhere along the line I convinced myself that you didn't do it at all. That everything about us was my way. But you had your say, didn't you? Like with that appalled little look you would give me with your eyes. Or that barely there shake of your head."

He broke off, smiling slightly, then his expression turned pained. "Or sometimes your eyes were red, and I knew you had been crying.

"Mostly I just plowed right on through anyway, didn't I? Not all the time, but much of it. And when I did that, you always stayed beside me, even when you didn't approve. Like when I decided the old *gemeide* had to look for the missing children, that I couldn't live with myself otherwise. You were terrified by what that would mean to us, to our family, but you went along with me on it just the same."

He put his head down, scrubbed his face with his hands. "I did take it for granted, Sarah. That much is true. And I guess that's what's been bothering me most of all. That's what I was always thinking whenever I looked at Hannah. I wanted, you knew it was dangerous, but you went along. It was so much more than sex. It was your sense of giving.

"Maybe that was why I was drawn to Kimberley at first. Because she wouldn't let me re-create my sins. She wouldn't just give and give and give and let me keep taking. But now that she's not giving, I'm angry at her for that. Now that she's not doing as you would have done, since she's not throwing all her own needs and desires aside to follow my wishes, I feel betrayed. And angry." Yes, he thought, he was angry.

He tossed his hat aside. "I'm trying to make this black-and-white, aren't I? Just as I tried to make your death a black-and-white issue. All my fault. All my doing. But there were just so many gray areas. There always are. Ah, but I'm a hard-headed German. I want to see things as all one way or another.

"I told Nathaniel that Kimberley was a completely different sort of gift. I spouted words without listening to myself, Sarah. Without hearing myself. Then I turned right around and made demands that she couldn't possibly meet." He made a strangled sound. "I'm going to have to do the unconscionable, Sarah. I'm going to have to walk away from this *gemeide* and all I've vowed to them. I see no other way to make this right. I can't be hardheaded and stand on principle as though it's absolute. Because nothing is absolute. If nothing else, I've learned that much."

He fell quiet for a long time. His heart was beating fast now.

"Does that betray you?" he asked finally. "I don't think so. Because you can't be here. And knowing you, you wouldn't want me to keep blundering through alone. You'd want a mama for your babies. You'd rather see someone else do it than have them muddle through life with just me. You'd trust my decision, even if it pained you."

"There's always middle ground."

Kimberley's voice came out of nowhere. For one horrible,

near paralyzing moment, he actually thought Sarah had spoken back to him. But Sarah's voice had never been husky, with an edge of steel.

Joe jerked upright, leaping off the tree root, and turned fast and hard. Somehow, in the time he had been here, the moon had moved, sliding farther along in the sky. The beam of light that had been slanted across Sarah's headstone was now illuminating Kimberley's face. Then she stepped toward him, beneath the tree, and she was caught in shadows again.

"Doesn't it strike you as a little...off, to be talking to your wife about me?" she murmured.

How long had she been standing there? he wondered. How long had she been listening? She had come home. No, he corrected, she had come back. There was a difference. Her home was in California, in a world that was alien to him. One he was going to have to bend enough to learn about, if she'd have him.

"There are those who might say you shouldn't have eavesdropped," he replied hoarsely.

"Well, you were right. I'm no saint," she answered. "Not like your Sarah. That's quelling, too, Joe. It's really scary. Because she gave everything, and I have a hell of a time giving anything. But I do know one thing. I can't let you do all the giving. I can't let you do this, Joe. Because unless I badly miss my guess, you wouldn't be able to live with yourself if you broke the vows you've made to these people. You'd end up hating me for asking it of you. Because you're not that kind of a man. You can't back away from a promise, Joe. That would turn you inside out. It would make you someone other than the man I've...needed."

He couldn't deny that, so he chose another avenue. "I would never have wanted you if you were like Sarah."

She would have thought that horribly cruel if she had not heard what he had just said to Sarah's ghost. She just nodded.

She was trembling, Kim realized. Partly it was the cold, the unrelenting cold of this place now that it was nearly winter. But mostly it was because of the things she had yet to say.

She was terrified. But there was, quite simply, no way to retreat now. She'd realized that on the long, silent drive back with Jake. Everything had been torn down, just as Susannah's system had been, whether she liked it or not. If some new life wasn't infused, she would die.

"You were right, you know," she continued. "We've come a long way together these past weeks. Middle ground," she said again, musingly. "God knocked one leg out from under me when Susannah was diagnosed—I sort of had to incline to one side. And there you were, inching into that middle ground, too, for reasons of your own. I guess we sort of held each other up."

"Yeah," he said finally, hoarsely.

"So if either one of us moves now, the other one is going to fall flat."

"It's occurred to me," he said in his best reasonable tone.

"I was afraid to stay in your house any longer than I absolutely had to because I was afraid of all this...all this comfort and family and...and you. That it would all close around me and I wouldn't be able to get out again. All along, I've told myself that I could—would—go again. But by the same token, when I had every right and reason to go, when I lost my job, I found reasons to stay." She took a deep breath. "I've done a little soul-searching of my own, Joe. And what I've realized is that once Susannah's transplant is completed, I'm left with only one logical reason to stay here. Because I want to. And that scares the devil out of me. That was what I couldn't admit back in the hospital. To you *or* to myself."

"We'd be crazy if we weren't afraid," he said roughly. "I'm afraid to leave this *gemeide,* my faith. But I'd do it."

"I know you would." And that was true. "No, Joe. No. That's not the answer. We both have to lean. As you said, that's what's brought us this far."

"What are you saying?"

She took a deep, shaky breath. "I'll try."

He was afraid to breathe.

"Maybe it won't work. We'd have to be open to that eventuality, too. I mean, I can't stand here and promise you that I'll start wearing plain dresses and actually put that chicken stuff in my mouth. But I'll...I'll marry you. If we can do a civil ceremony like Adam and Mariah did. If you can live with that." If it was asking a lot, she thought, then it took all the courage in the world for her. "I can't live without you, Joe. I just need a little more time to get used to your world."

"My people would consider it living in sin."

She couldn't read his face. She couldn't tell from his tone if he was serious or not. What in the name of God was she going to do if he said no?

He came toward her, and took her hand. "I love you, Kimberley. I can't live without you. And if that means we have to squeeze a few conflicting customs together, so be it."

It was that easy for him, she thought.

That shaking feeling started inside her again. And when he made the offer, she knew she no longer needed it. "I love you, too. I don't need time to know that. Let me try."

And the amazing thing was, the words came out like a prayer, with no trouble at all.

# *Epilogue*

Susannah came home from the hospital on the first day of March. There were twelve inches of snow on the ground, and more was falling hard.

The engraftment had taken. Susannah was in complete remission. So far, Kim thought, so good. She knew, intellectually, that it would be another five years before they would know if she'd need another transfusion, or if she was one of those who would be blessed with a lifetime of good health. But there was hope.

Suze's eyes glowed with it these days. Kim's heart hurt with it. Because even if she did need another transfusion, there was nothing prohibiting another engraftment later, another swipe at the sky for another handful of stars. Rebekkah matched with five antigens. And the Wallace clan showed no sign of slowing down on the procreation front, Kim thought. Where there were children, kin, family, there was hope.

She glanced over her shoulder at her daughter as she worked in Joe's kitchen. Susannah was sitting at the table, playing a card game with most of Joe's kids, and Jake and Katya's. Nathaniel was home again for the weekend. The house was a zoo. Everyone had come together for Susannah's homecoming. Only Adam and Mariah, Bo and Rebekkah were missing and they would be around shortly for supper, after the baby woke up from her nap.

The silly grin Kim had been wearing all morning grew wider. Then she turned back to the tub on the counter in front of her, and she gave a small shudder.

"Ugh."

"Another one?" Joe asked, coming to lean against the counter beside her, his arms crossed over his chest.

"That leg just kicked." She aimed her knife at one of the birds. He leaned to look at it more closely.

"It was your imagination."

"Tell me that when it's up and running out the door again."

He laughed and took the knife from her hand. "I'll finish."

"But I—"

"I know. You already have feathers stuck all over your skin. That's what I'm counting on."

Her heart kicked. Her grin widened even further. "Yeah?"

"Yeah." He leaned close to her ear. "Meet me in the barn in ten minutes. We can pick them off each other. This house is too crazy for any privacy."

"There's an offer I can't refuse." Besides, she thought, the barn was their place. She'd developed an odd sort of…fondness for it.

All the same, she stopped in the bathroom and washed up before she went across the road. She wondered if anyone thought it odd that Joe so steadfastly refused to put those bales of hay up in the loft. And she laughed.

He was as good as his word. Not more than five minutes later, the door creaked open and he stepped inside.

There was never any time to waste. Even as they came together, Joe elbowed open the door of the last stall and pulled her inside. No one had ever asked why he had suddenly taken to storing bales in there, either, or why there was now a quilt and a lantern sitting on a new shelf built on the wall.

Before the door swung fully closed behind them, Kim's coat hit the sawdust on the floor. Before she'd pushed his suspenders away and dragged his shirt free of his pants, he had her sweater over her head. But always he kissed the same, as though they had all the time until eternity, slowly, relentlessly, covering her mouth, easing away. Everything inside her was going warm and liquid again.

"No feathers," he complained when he got down to skin, his mouth sliding down, down, between her breasts.

"Keep going. You might find a few if you work real hard at it."

"I'll give it my best," he assured her.

He would. He always did.

They didn't fall onto the bales together until they were naked. The hay was old and dry now, scratchy and unyielding. Joe grabbed the quilt off the shelf and spread it out.

As he rolled and took her on top of him, he watched the cold air pebble her skin. He slid his hands over her, warming her with the friction. Her head dropped back, her hair spilling behind her shoulders. He watched her breasts as her nipples hardened, and he thought he was the luckiest man in the world.

She moved to take him inside her, but he wouldn't let her. She snapped her head forward to look at him again. And, as always, his eyes were steady, watching her, as though to take in every move she made.

She was thinking about that when his strong fingers found home, sliding inside, then teasing and circling. A hungry sound ripped from her throat, somehow both high-pitched and throaty. He sat forward suddenly, and his lips covered her nipple, sucking hard.

The pleasure shattered something inside her. If she had had any defenses left against him, they would have been gone then. Though he had touched her like this a hundred times, somehow he left more of his healing love with her each time he did it.

She cried out and drove her hands into his hair to hold him in place. He tumbled her back onto the hay and moved to her other breast, his mouth just as demanding, the touch of his tongue in gentle counterpoint. Then he was inside her.

He never gave her time to give. He was an assault on her senses that sent her spinning out of control whenever he touched her. Still he kept kissing her, until she could no longer think. He moved inside her with slow, delicious rhythm, the same way he kissed. Her body rose to meet his and they tangled together, rolling again, the hay bristling beneath the quilt.

She was hurtling now with no time for breath. Sensation built in her.

He watched her eyes, seeing it, knowing just when to thrust deeper, harder.

So she clung. And she cried out with pleasure, with need, with the pure impact of his giving, until the tension spiraled and shattered and shuddered inside her.

He followed her over the edge, and dropped his head onto her shoulder as his breath steadied. He pulled hay out of her hair, though his hand still shook with release.

She laughed huskily. "Do you honestly think no one knows about this?"

His mouth quirked. "The Amish are masters at looking the other way. And as I've always said, they consider me a heathen here anyway."

"Tolerant," she said. Their civil marriage hadn't helped. A few people had left the *gemeide,* unable to accept it from one of their deacons. But the bishop, Sarah's father, surprisingly gave his full support. He said times were changing, and they had to learn to bend with the wind. The key was not to break from one's faith.

"We're nonresisting," Joe corrected. "That's different. If something is going to bother you, don't acknowledge it."

"No one's mentioned that I ought to make an honest man out of you?"

"I'm as honest as the day is long."

"We'll have to make adjustments soon, though."

He sat up, pulling her with him. "There's no rush, Kimberley."

"You're not hearing me."

He looked at her. Really looked at her. Then he knew she'd decided it was time.

There were those chickens, for one thing. She'd *offered* to make roast today. He'd told himself it was for Susannah's homecoming, but Susannah still steadfastly refused to eat the stuff, also.

And Kimberley had gone to services last Sunday. She'd stayed far in the back, with a fierce look of concentration on her face. She hadn't been permitted to take part in either the hymns or the prayers, because she hadn't yet been baptized. But she'd been there.

"We need to find new middle ground, Joe," she continued.

"Uh, okay." He got a grip on himself. "Not that I'm unhappy with this ground," he assured her quickly. Then he chose his words with great care. "What, precisely, are you saying?"

"I'm pregnant." She waited, her breath lodged hard and hot in her chest.

Joe could have sworn the hay moved beneath him. Or maybe it was the earth. *This* he had not foreseen.

"How did I miss it?" he asked slowly, tenderly. "I know these things."

"You were carefully looking the other way, good Amish man that you are."

"Uh...possibly."

"Are you afraid?" Her voice changed, and it took on a little fear of its own. He was, she thought, probably as shaken as she'd ever seen him.

"You're not Sarah," he said, his voice haggard.

"No, Joe. I'm not."

"You never had a problem with Susannah." He said it as though trying to convince himself.

"Not a one, except fainting that time. I trust you won't make me work two eight-hour shifts without a break." She tried to smile. She failed when he looked so horrified at the thought. "Maybe it's God's will," she suggested. "You've always been big on that, Joe. I'm about three months along." It had happened one of those first two times they were together. She had known for a while now. She had just wanted to wait to...be sure. Of the pregnancy. And of the faith she would embrace.

He met her eyes. "Do *you* believe that? About God's will?"

She felt a quick shiver. "You've got to admit that things have a way of happening here in this settlement that boggles the mind."

"Like that giant hand pushing you along," he said cautiously.

"I mean, maybe He didn't abandon us—the Wallaces, I mean. One way or another, He got all three of us here to the

settlement when it didn't appear that we were going to accom
plish anything on our own.'' She had finally learned the fu
story—of Adam's first wife leaving Bo here, *here,* of all th
places in the world she might have put him for safekeepin
And how the same man who had been responsible for th
twist of fate had then begun to slowly and systematically ab
duct the settlement's children until Adam had called Jake he
to find them.

''I was the hardest sell,'' she murmured. ''Maybe I require
drastic measures. If Jake had found me through ChildSearc
when he was looking, I probably would have slammed th
door in his face. I'm willing to concede that the only thin
that could have brought me here was *me* needing *him.* An
this place does seem to have a sort of…well, a unique wa
about it. I'll even go so far as to say maybe it's not somethin
in the water.''

Joe laughed quietly.

''Will you marry me, Joe? Make an honest woman of me
As long as I don't have to eat roast at the wedding.''

No, he thought, she didn't follow him unquestioningl
She'd never be meek or quiet. But they had come through th
fire together, and their bond was perhaps one of the stronge
ever forged.

''The way I've got it figured,'' she continued, ''is that yo
and Susannah and this baby inside me are the most importa
things in the world. I just want to draw you all around me an
keep you close and be secure.''

''It's called *Gelasseneit.*''

''What?'' she asked suspiciously.

''Peace and happiness and contentment with your world.'

The barn door opened. Adam's voice boomed over th
stalls.

''The least you guys can do is wait until cover of darkne
and use your own bedroom!'' Adam shouted.

''He and Mariah got caught in a buggy by the cops,'' Jo
said in an undertone against Kim's ear.

Kim's eyes widened. ''Can you actually make love in
buggy? How does the horse feel about it?''

Joe's grin was wicked. ''Now, why do you think we trai
them so well?''

She laughed, muffling the sound against his chest.

"Anyhow," he continued, "from the way I hear it, Adam almost managed it. As for Jake, he more or less just shut the bedroom door with Katya in the bedroom and thumbed his nose at all of us, Adam in particular."

"Sounds like him."

"In the meantime," Adam interjected again, "when you're through whispering, Mariah wants to borrow some of those disposable diapers. We can't find them. She wants to know where Kimmie put them."

The door closed again. Joe rummaged around in the hay and handed her her bra. "Time to go back."

"Speaking of diapers," she began, "the rules don't change with our second wedding."

"You don't wash diapers, you don't eat roast, and if I don't rig up some kind of generator-run clothes dryer soon, I'm a dead man."

She grinned. "You're so *smart*."

He studied the matching piece of lace and satin he held. "Open-minded," he corrected. "Flexible. These can stay, too." He held up the panties. "All in the interest of middle ground, of course."

"Of course."

She folded the quilt and put it back on the shelf, giving it a fond little pat. "Guess we won't be needing this anymore."

Joe laughed suddenly. "God only knows who I should pass it on to. It didn't turn out to be so safe with me after all."

Kim frowned. "What are you talking about?"

Joe ran a finger over the edge of the quilt. "Have you ever noticed the pattern?"

"No, I can't say I was paying much attention to it when we used it," she said dryly.

"Wedding rings." He lifted a corner of it to show her.

"So?"

"So it's centuries old, and it's magic."

She raised one brow skeptically. "Right."

"It's true. There's this Amish custom called bundling. Essentially it's when two people sleep together—just sleep together—during *rumspringa,* that time when we're all running around getting to know each other before getting married."

"Getting to know each other in an intimate sense," sh said.

"*Just* sleeping," Joe repeated.

"That leaves us out." She watched him closely, but his fac didn't change.

"Who's to say those other folks who used it were just sleep ing also? I mean, it's *said* they were...until Adam and Maria used it, and so did Jake and Katya. And I'm reasonably sur neither Adam nor Jake had *any* inclinations toward gettin married at the time. But everyone who...bundles with it, s to speak, seems to end up that way."

"You're absolutely serious."

"It's true."

"Well, the Wallaces certainly can't prove it wrong Magic," she said. "Like some sort of a spell? Is that wha happened to us, Joe?"

He kissed her again. "That's the legend. We've got to pas it on now, you know."

"Uh...we might want to give some thought to that."

"It's been given a great deal of thought before." Jo laughed aloud. "It started out in Mariah's possession—it wa her family's. She gave it to Katya, because Katya was tech nically married to Frank then, at least in our Amish faith though she was separated from him. That meant she couldn marry anyone else, so Mariah thought it would be safe wit her."

"Surprise," Kim murmured.

"Exactly. Then Katya handed it on to me—while Sarah wa still alive."

Kim's skin pulled into gooseflesh. "The attic?" she sug gested. "Mothballs? Maybe that's what we should do with it."

"I'd almost hate to end its reign."

"But—"

"Wherever it's been, things have worked out for the bes In the long run." His voice changed. "Kimberley, the qui had nothing to do with Sarah's passing. It just saved me onc she was gone."

Her eyes misted. "Or it saved me."

"Maybe it saved both of us."

They went back to the house, hand in hand. When they g

through the front door, they found Matt chasing Bo down the staircase by way of the banister. Susannah and Dinah were in the living room, showing Mariah how to work the little tabs on the diapers—they'd found the package. Jake and Adam were arguing about something in the kitchen, but Jake, at least, was grinning. The back door slammed nearly off its hinges as Levi and Sam came inside, and Joe took Hannah from Gracie so she could play with Delilah and Rachel.

*Gelasseneit?* Kim thought. It had a nice ring to it, but she thought she'd just call this place "home."

* * * * *

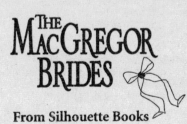

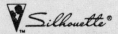

# SHARON SALA

**Continues the twelve-book series—36 HOURS— in October 1997 with Book Four**

# FOR HER EYES ONLY

The storm was over. The mayor was dead. Jessica Hanson had an aching head…and sinister visions of murder. And only one man was willing to take her seriously—Detective Stone Richardson. He knew that unlocking Jessica's secrets would put him in danger, but the rugged cop had never expected to fall for her, too. Danger he could handle. But love…?

For Stone and Jessica and *all* the residents of Grand Springs, Colorado, the storm-induced blackout was just the beginning of 36 Hours that changed *everything!* You won't want to miss a single book.

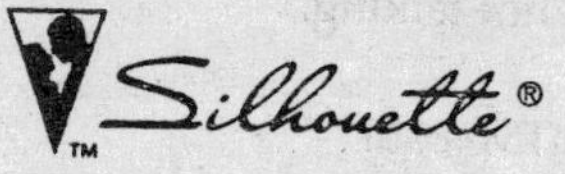